A FACE IN THE SHADOW

By Tiffany Colter

Writing Career Coach Press (a division of Writing Career Coach, 14665 Fike Rd., Riga, MI 49276) functions only as book publisher. As such, the ultimate design, content, editorial accuracy, and views expressed or implied in this work are those of the author.

ISBN-10: 1938283066
ISBN-13: 978-1-938283-06-2

Table of Contents

Getting Ready to Write

Welcome to a new way to learn writing. This is actually a book like none you've ever seen before. This book is designed to teach you how to write by critiquing another person's writing. This is the BEST way I've ever used to learn how to write.

Why is that? Because you'll recognize flaws in another person's writing that you're totally blinded to in your own. I learned this when I started judging writing contests. I began to see annoying traits in the writers who were ALMOST ready to be published. There was always something a little…underdeveloped. It is like soup that is missing something. It just doesn't quite grab you.

Normally, I found the issue was a pet phrase or a clichéd character. It got to the point that I could spot these things almost before they happened. I could FEEL the writer building up to some great REVEAL that I'd spotted 30 pages ago.

It wasn't until after serving as a judge for 20 entries of unpubbed writers and a dozen pubbed writers contests that I stepped out to being paid to edit. These were people who were one step below the entries many times. These were RAW manuscripts. I could see the great stories hidden beneath the stone of slow pacing or bad dialog. I chipped away at these and studied ways to help my clients write better. After months of doing this I finally had time to get back to my books.

What I saw STUNNED me and birthed the idea for this book.

My writing was just as bad, or worse, than the writing I'd been judging. How could I have such HORRIFIC craft? Was it always so hideous?

No, I was just able to recognize the errors now. It wasn't that it was junk, it just wasn't as good as I'd thought. I'd learned how to quickly spot errors. And now I knew how to fix them.

And that is the learning I now want to give to you.

In this book you'll have lots of space to edit my writing. Please, get a pencil. Scratch out sentences. Rewrite scenes. Move words around. That is the purpose of this. I want you to feel at liberty to edit this and learn from it.

This writing isn't horrible. It just isn't quite there. I want you to work to find what makes great writing by editing good writing.

What makes this book unique is that it was not written for a person to learn from. This book was twice a requested full by royalty publishers. This book was viewed by 3 different agents (requested manuscripts). This book was almost there, but not quite.

That is where your writing might be stuck. Now you can try to figure out why.

What are the fundamentals of great writing?

First, you have to grab the reader. You can do that with a car chase scene or with something else dramatic, but underlying all of that is introducing a question. That question may carry the reader for a page, a chapter, or for the entire book, but without that question or sense of something to be discovered, you'll lose the reader.

You also need to create someone that the reader will want to know. That means that they need to be flawed but still sympathetic. I need to care about them, but not feel they're so perfect as to be unlikable or hard to relate to.

Throughout the course of this book you'll be learning and applying the principles of good writing by editing another person's writing.

Let's do our first lesson.

What are the traits of someone you like and respect?

Without using those actual words, demonstrate those traits by writing a very small scene or piece of dialog. [This is called showing]

Now, create a small scenario where you [or the character you created] have to violate this most fundamental trait. Make sure we feel the conflict.

That is called prewriting. It gets your brain juices flowing. For more lessons on how to do that you can go to my website or buy my Writing Ideas Workbook.

One

Logan stalked the red-head with his sunglass hidden eyes.

It was time to begin his pursuit.

He meandered at a safe distance from his target. He knew her path and routine. She never

deviated. She'd go to her dorm now but in an hour she'd come back down the same walk and

into a private study room at the library. Always the same one. In the basement past the bound

periodicals and around the corner. She valued her privacy, and so did he.

The air was sticky without a whisper of breeze. A small bead of sweat tickled his cheek

as it ran down. He wiped it away then slowed his pace a bit.

Up ahead his lady advanced with quick strides never making eye contact with anyone.

Hopefully she'd resist just a little.

He wiped away another bead of sweat. The blond wig was hot. The human hair had been

expensive but if any fibers remained the cops couldn't tie them to him. He went to the left and in

the library's entryway. She turned right up the path to the dorms.

Soon.

The blast of cold air both refreshed and chilled him. He walked past the information desk and check-out counters. Very few students visited the college's library during the summer months. Three librarians continued their conversation without looking at him. The air smelled of rotting pages and mildew. Air didn't flow and sounds didn't carry here.

He went to the basement and stepped through the first set of doors. A few metal shelves lined the walls covered with periodicals that only college professors and their unfortunate students ever read. In the far corner, tucked away from view were the private study rooms. These were rooms designed for a group of students to talk without disturbing other library patrons. They were designed to muffle sounds. In the summer there was little need but she still used them. A creature of habit.

The basement was cold and slightly damp. The yellowed florescent lights created shadows in the far corner of shelves. He turned away from the periodicals and entered the microfiche room to wait. The basement was silent except for a low hum. The air conditioner must be close by. He checked his watch and waited. Five minutes until she'd arrive. The dim yellow screen of the microfiche screamed the headline "The Fratboy Killer claims second victim."

"I'd hardly call myself a fratboy." He dropped a nickel in the slot and clicked print. No fratboy would take the time to do all the planning he did. Behind him the door to the periodical

room closed with a muffled bump followed a few moments later by the click of the study room

door. He collected the articles, returned the microfiche to the drawer and wiped everything

down.

      "So predictable."

      No one was in the basement, no cameras on the walls. He walked to the far end and

looked through the glass. On the other side she lifted a pile of books out of her bag and began to

arrange them on the table. His heart thudded and he imagined for a moment how good this would

be.

      No, he would resist. He needed to be slow, woo her. He had to maintain control.

      Alpha Mu Epsilon required it.

      It would make the time with his red-haired angel so much better. He smoothed down his

shirt and picked off a small piece of black lint. He was handsome. Women were usually willing

to exchange small talk with him which worked to his advantage.

      This woman was lovely. Long strands of hair hung down from her clip. She aroused in

him the urge to steal her away and keep her. Maybe he could…

He stepped back for a moment. No. He'd planned this. Stick to the plan. When emotions took over was when mistakes were made. Bundy's fall came when he didn't prepare, he let one get away. Sloppiness was his downfall.

He took a deep breath and opened the door. She turned quickly.

"I'm sorry this room is occupied." Her eyes directed him back out of the room.

"You are a vision from a renaissance master." He'd rehearsed the greeting all week. Letting women know how attractive they were was important in the art of Romance. Women had to be lured gently at first. Let them know they are beautiful and special. Slowly they open their hearts.

"Excuse me?" Her voice faltered for a moment. Fear was good. Enough fear to keep her quiet.

He stepped in the room and closed the door behind him, never taking his eyes off of his prize. Her body straightened in response.

"I'll scream."

"That wouldn't be wise." He lifted his shirt enough to let her see the knife clipped to his belt.

"What do you want?" Her fingers felt around the table but there was nothing on that table strong enough to keep him from his purpose.

"Alpha."

"What is alpha?" Tears slid down her face. Her eyes were slightly red. It ruined her creamy white skin.

"You're trying to destroy the moment."

He grabbed her and spun her around so she wasn't facing him. Remember the image of her beautiful. He had to lock that image in his head. Anger squeezed him and he shoved her to the floor. She fell forward and her hair splayed out and formed a halo.

Desire consumed him afresh and he pounced on top of her and reached around to cover her mouth with his hand.

"If you're quiet" he whispered "This will go much better for you."

She nodded her head and he took what he'd come for. She remained nearly silent and he was only mildly distracted by the tears that ran across the back of his hand. Without standing up he reached around to his backpack and pulled out the noose. A few moments later it was over.

He rolled her over and pushed her hair away from her face. Two startling blue eyes frozen in time. A master's statue. He slid the rope over her head and and adjusted her hair. He'd preserved her forever.

Inside the bag his hand groped around until his fingers felt the bouquet of roses. The petals were cool and soft against his skin. He pushed back the tissue paper and looked for the one he had for her.

There were thirteen roses most red, a few pink, two yellow and a single white rose. Superstition was the religion of the ignorant. He pulled out the white rose and tied a black ribbon around the stem. It moved back and forth wafting its scent. Flowers knew what it was to give, to share.

Women were very much like roses. They were things of beauty growing from something vile. The best remained pure and grew straight. And when they were most beautiful, just as the bloom began to open it was time to pick them.

And like roses once the flower was removed all that was left was an ugly, rotten stem that needed to be cut off and burned. He laid the rose across her chest with the bloom barely touching her cheek.

"This is yours, precious"

He opened her hand and placed a small golden charm in her palm then pushed her hand

closed.

She was his.

Alpha Mu Epsilon.

Let's do our first lesson.

What are the traits of someone you like and respect?

Without using those actual words, demonstrate those traits by writing a very small scene or piece of dialog. [This is called showing]

Now, create a small scenario where you [or the character you created] has to violate this most fundamental trait. Make sure we feel the conflict.

That is called prewriting. It gets your brain juices flowing. For more lessons on how to do that you can go to my website or buy my Writing Ideas Workbook.

Two

Rachel stared at the final flecks of coco powder and mocha swirling in the bottom of her oversized mug. A few feet away people lined up for their fancy coffees and overpriced muffins, register drawers opened and slammed closed.

"Grande Mocha Up." Someone yelled over the hollow squeal of baristas steaming milk for countless lattes less than ten feet away. Rachel rubbed her forehead as the clanging sliced through her brain.

"If I didn't have month end reports to go over after lunch I'd go home." Rachel said to her mom without looking up. She tried to put her elbow on the table but two mugs and a small plate were almost more than the table could handle.

"You not feelin' well?"

"Headache."

"I got some Tylenol." The way her mom said it sounded more like Tylenaw, something Rachel first noticed when she returned from Michigan. Up there everyone pronounced A's through their nose.

"I'll be fine, thanks. What were you saying about Adam?"

"Oh, Yvonne is just being her stubborn self is all. Honestly, I don't know what your brother sees in that woman some days."

"Takes two mom."

"Well she knew when the two of them got married he was deaf."

Her mom continued on paying no attention to Rachel's comment. "I tell ya Rachel, don't know how much worse this old world can get." Her mom sipped her coffee and held up her finger so Rachel wouldn't interrupt her monologue. "I watch the T.V. and praise God I raised the two of you before all of this mess. I'd hate to be starting off in these days." She broke off a bite of blueberry muffin and held it between her fingers as she spoke.

Clearly the conversation on Adam had finished. Rachel followed her mom down this next rabbit trail. "Every generation has their dangers."

"And you wanna tell me things are getting better." Mom's Kentucky drawl did nothing to take the edge off her tone.

"No, just that it is part of the cosmos."

"The cosmos?" Her mom lifted an eyebrow and squared her shoulders. Why had she chosen that word to use with her mom?

"May be true in the big scheme but here in Woodhaven…well I just don't know."

"Excuse me." A woman hit Rachel in the head with her purse. Coffee splattered out of her cup and landed on her cell phone. Always when she had a headache.

"What is up with all these people today?" Rachel blotted the coffee off the camera lens of her phone.

"Dunno," her mom wiped the table with a second napkin then continued. "There's someone killing young ladies, here. Did you hear 'bout this Fratboy killer?"

Rachel set the large ceramic cup to the side and leaned forward on the table. "I've been following it on the internet. Real sicko."

"I worry 'bout you workin' s' late with this goin' on."

"I took self-defense training."

Her mom waved away the answer. "You screamin' fire'll do nothing against a gun."

"Then it's a good thing this guy isn't shooting people isn't it." The squeezing pain in her head made it come out sharper than she'd intended. She paused and forced her words out a bit gentler. "Woodhaven is twenty minutes away, mom."

"You think killers don't have cars?"

"I imagine they do that's why I'm careful if I have to leave after dark."

"Yes but you work such long hours. You should-."

"I know mom. As soon as we have these new reps trained I won't have to do their job and mine."

"And Shannon can't do any of it?"

"She works new clients and leads I work personnel and bookkeeping."

"You should be making enough that you could hire a security guy for the parking lot at the very least."

Rachel dug in her purse. There must be some headache medicine in her bag someplace. How many times would they walk around the same mountain at these afternoon coffee breaks? She found her pill case in the side pocket and swallowed down two pills. "Do they have any leads yet?"

"I get it. Stay out of running your business." Mom leaned back and folded her arms.

"Yep."

"Well none they're tellin' anybody. The paper said they call him the Fratboy killer 'cause he leaves some fraternity charm on all the girls along with a white rose."

"I'd heard about the charm. Alpha something something. Is it for sure a fraternity?"

"I don't follow all that Greek stuff. I'm sure they're just guessin' anyways. D'you hear about the latest young lady?"

"When?"

"Day or two ago."

"No." Someone came over and took Rachel's tray. Her mom lowered her voice and leaned forward.

"She makes number four in the last year. Broke my heart when I saw the picture." Her mom put her hand over her chest. "She was a beautiful young lady in her early 20s, with such pretty red-brown hair. It was on the front page."

"I don't get the paper. I read my news on-line."

"Right-right." Her mom wiped at the air then continued. "Said she was an education major but I thought she could be a model easy. Paper said he's speeding up. They're coming closer and closer together. They found her in the basement of the library."

"And nobody saw anything." How could someone rape and murder a woman without anyone noticing a thing. A shiver ran up her spine. "I don't know what possess some people."

"Well that's exactly it." Her mom poked her finger on the table as she spoke. "These people are possessed by pure evil." Rachel nodded her head in agreement. Mom looked past Rachel for a moment, her eyes glassy. "Why don't you come over this weekend and visit for a bit?" The pleasant southern belle voice was back after a momentary northern lapse.

"Mom-."

"I know but the people there just adore you."

"Maybe another time."

"If that's how you want it."

"Mom, I'm fine."

"I know, Rach, I worry. It's a mom's prerogative."

"It would be nice to have one afternoon together without bringing this up?" Her mom's shoulders fell. So she'd disappointed her mom again. What else was new?

"You're right. Let's not ruin our lunch speakin' bout such unpleasant things."

Three

"Mrs. Nylski I'm going to throw these roses out for you."

"Thank you Logan. You were such a dear to bring them over in the first place. Made the house smell so sweet."

"When I saw them I had to get them for my favorite lady."

He pulled the dozen mixed roses out of the vase on the small end table and threw them into her trash can. Mrs. Nylski pushed her walker slowly into the front room of her small condominium. The woman was nearly ninety. She'd deserved much better than this teeny place her stingy son had arranged for her.

Logan washed the vase out and put it back in the cupboard. The red haired angel had been all he'd hoped for. Once she was subdued he'd given her the rose, her rose. She was now beautifully frozen in time. Her body would never be tattered by the ravages of time. A perfect pure rose.

"Logan, could you bring me a glass of water when you come out."

"Certainly, Mrs. Nylski."

Alpha Mu Epsilon.

She had to be lovely when they found her. For them to understand why he loved her, had to have her.

Logan filled a glass of water for Mrs. Nylski and took it in the other room.

"You need anything else before I go?"

"Did you feed Sammy?" She stroked her ten year old toy poodle with a skinny wrinkled hand. Purple lines crisscrossed thin bones that moved with her fingers.

"Food is in his bowl along with fresh water." The dog closed his eyes and drifted off on the old woman's lap.

"Thank you, I'm sure I'll be fine now."

"I'll see you again tomorrow Mrs. Nylski."

"Thank you, Logan."

Setting Up Your Opening

What questions did these opening chapters set up? Who are the main characters? What do you know about them? What is your opinion of them? Make some notes below.

How does the setting integrate with the characters and the plot? Do they work together or could this story just as easily have taken place someplace else? Why? Is that good or bad?

Four

"Bye, I'll see you guys later. I need to go home and soak in a tub." Jenny waved to her

sorority sisters. Wednesday night aerobics had been tougher than usual this week.

"Are you sure you don't want us to follow you home?" April asked.

"No, I'll be fine. The police drive up and down the street all the time." Jen worked to

control the waver in her voice.

"I don't feel right leaving you alone. The other girl had the same rose."

Bile rose in her throat. "It may still be a prank."

"I don't think the sisters would hold on to a prank this long. It's been three roses. Every

sister knows the cops are involved."

"You don't need to keep saying that. I know how many roses there have been." Her face

burned hot. The parking lot lights would be too dim to show what must have been a glowing red

face. "Plus only our sorority sisters know the cops are watching me. It could be the ones we

T.P.ed."

They stopped next to Jen's car. April set her bag down by her feet. "I doubt it. They

wouldn't focus in on one person so long."

"April, it's a prank. Every rose has been found on a dead body."

"It's a pretty sick prank."

"And when I find out who it is I'm never going to speak to them again." Jen eyed her

sisters for any twitch of guilt. None of them would be cruel enough to put her through this.

"Then why won't you stay with one of us until things are safer?"

"I don't want to be around campus." She leaned her back against the car. The metal

against her back made her feel less vulnerable. "I appreciate the offer. I'll call Logan on the way

home." She unlocked the door and tossed her bag in the back seat to display confidence she

didn't have. "I'll be fine. Logan isn't far if I need him."

"Okay." April hugged her tight before turning to the sorority house with the others.

Jenny jumped in her car and scanned the parking lot. Once she cleared the buildings on

the edge of campus she saw the remaining slivers of red sunlight low in the horizon and partially

covered by clouds.

A knot tightened in her stomach. She'd pretended not to hear about the lady killed a

couple weeks ago. Education major who lived on this campus. Jen's hands began to shake and

uncontrollable tears gushed down her cheeks. Some sicko was playing with her. Waiting and maybe watching. There was nothing she could do, the police could do. She could drop out of college and fly back to Minnesota. Erase any memory from the campus.

But that would mean leaving Logan. The cool chill of fear melted in the center of her chest. She dialed Logan's number on her cell phone. After one ring he picked up.

"Hi Jen."

"Hey. How's your evening going?"

"Fine. Work was a little crazy but I got everything done. I spent a couple of hours at Mrs. Nylski's helping her with lawn work. She pays too much for those grounds keepers to let her place go like that."

"When will I get to meet her? She sounds like such a sweet lady."

"Soon. How are you tonight?"

"Scared."

"I'll come over if it will make you feel better." He has added a sultry flow to his voice.

"I'm sure you would, with one thing on your mind."

"Who? Me? Never."

She smiled. "I need to hear a friendly voice. Can I talk to you while I drive?"

"Sure. I'm on my way over anyway. I was waiting for you to call."

"Logan I can't have you guarding me 24/7." She said it but even as the words came out

she hoped he'd insist.

"You could if you'd just say yes."

"Logan." Her voice trailed off for a moment.

"I told you before I won't pressure you. I want you to know that I mean it. I can't

imagine my life without you."

"I know."

"Think about it then."

"I will." She swerved to miss a car that stopped suddenly. "I still have three more

semesters until my degree."

"Yes but as soon as you change your mind all I need is a yes from you. The offer remains

on the table." They could have the wedding after graduation. But she would only do this once.

Why rush it? Long engagements were so tacky.

"I know. Maybe when classes are-."

"Don't worry about when, Jen. I want you to be my wife. I will do what I have to if it means you'll be mine."

"Thank you." She turned in to the parking lot of her apartment. As usual the guy in the red sports car parked sideways. She groaned and parked in the next row. It was the furthest spot from her door. "I'm home now. I'll let you go and we can talk more tomorrow."

"I love you Jen."

"Love you too Logan." She flipped her phone shut and got out of the car. The sun was gone and a few crickets chirped in the grass a couple of yards away. It reminded her of summers in the country. Here the sound of traffic usually blotted out the crickets and footsteps-

The sound surprised her. Footsteps in a heavy, steady rhythm. It was a jogger. Just in case she snatched her bag from the backseat and put it over her shoulder. Don't act alarmed. Get to the door. Stay calm. The traffic was unusually calm tonight. That was why she could hear the footsteps echo closer. She reached down and scooped up her books.

"Ouch." She pulled her hand back from the seat of her car. A white rose, this one full of thorns, sat on the seat under her books.

The footsteps were closer now. She slammed the door and turned to the apartment. The echo from her car door ricocheted between the apartment buildings but was replaced again by the sound of her feet pounding on the blacktop. Her duffle bounced against her thigh. The keys

rattled in her shaky fingers as she stumbled up the grassy hill and on to the sidewalk.

In the darkness of the stoop every key looked the same. They rattled as she tried to find

the one to the outside security doors. The footsteps sped up.

"C'mon." One key crossed over another and into the ring. She was trapped now between

the security door and the footsteps. A whimper escaped her lips when she pulled the key free and

began one by one to stick it in the door. Finally one slid in the hole and she turned the handle and

ripped her key back out of the lock.

The footsteps were closer. They padded with an even *thump-thump, thump-thump.*

The door swung open and she threw the bag inside. It swung back and knocked the keys

out of her hand and in the grass behind her. She groped around in the dark grass. Why didn't

they ever mow this stuff? Her hand landed on beer bottle lids and what felt like pebbles or

broken glass.

"Hey, hold the door." A deep voice demanded only a few feet away.

Her fingers wrapped around the keys. She stood.

"Hold the door." She spun toward the voice. A man silhouetted by the streetlight was less than twenty feet away. In an instant she was in the building. She slammed the door shut behind her, grabbed the bag and sprinted up the steps two at a time. Her heart thumped hard in her chest and the muscles in her legs groaned. Adrenaline pushed her to the third floor. She stumbled down the hall to her door and jammed the key in the lock. Below the security door squeaked open.

"Thanks for holding the door." A voice screamed followed by an explicative. His voice resonated through the halls and his footsteps fell hard down the hallway on the floor below hers.

She closed her door, slid the chain in its holder and double checked the deadbolt.

Footsteps thudded up to the third floor then someone pounded on the door down the hall. She jumped and backed away from her door.

"Does a dark haired lady live with you?" The man said to her neighbor.

Muffled voices followed. A door closing. Then knocking on another door. There were only eight doors on each floor.

Jen walked in the kitchen and pulled a knife from the butchers block on her counter.

Muffled pounds. Three.

Footsteps. Muffled pounds. Four.

"Bang…bang…bang." He knocked with such force the chain on her door rattled. Jen

stifled a scream and gripped the knife tighter.

Five

"Rachel, your mom is on line three." Shannon yelled from the receptionist desk.

"Thanks. Did you find the papers yet?" She yelled back.

"No, I have no clue where I put them." Shannon walked in the office. "I'll look more tomorrow. We have plenty of other work to do before then. Aren't you going to pick up line three?"

"Do I hafta?" She laughed.

"At least she only called twice today." Shannon scooped up the sales analysis they'd been discussing.

"Yes but I know she's going to bug me again about visiting."

"Your fault for saying 'in a couple of weeks.'"

Rachel pushed the button for line three. "Hi Mom."

"Hi. How's your day?"

"Busy. I had meetings all afternoon."

"Lots a new clients or are you servicing the ones you got?"

"Little of both."

"Things keeping you pretty busy."

"Uh-huh, it is." She looked over the charts and graphs on her desk. "Probably got another hour of work to do."

"When do you ever sleep?"

Rachel looked up at the clock. "Mom, it's almost eight. Why did you call me at the office?"

"I tried your cell first but you didn't answer." Rachel reached in her purse and pulled out her cell phone.

"Oh, sorry. I had it on vibrate earlier. I must have forgotten to put it back on ring." Five missed calls? She scrolled down through them. Mom, mom, mom, their new sales man, mom.

"Why weren't your phones forwarded?"

"We just left them go since we were here."

Rachel caught a glimpse of something out of the corner of her eye. Shannon held up a legal pad with two stick figures inside of a heart.

"No." Rachel mouthed without speaking.

"The reason I'm calling is the house on the corner went up on the market today. I saw the realtor when he was putting the sign in the yard.”

“Did it?” Rachel drew a box with a triangle roof on her notebook and held it up for

Shannon.

“A house?” Shannon said.

“Yes.” She whispered back.

“What?”

“Nothing mom. I was answering Shannon’s question.”

“I was saying. It’s such a great deal. Little bit of a fixer-upper but being s’ close dad

could help you with the bigger jobs like drywall and plumbing. I can help you with decorating,

wallpaper, paint and those kinds of things.”

“That’s fine mom but I’m really not looking for a house right now.”

“I need a house.” Shannon yelled over.

“Mom, Shannon said she needs a house.”

“There ya go. Shannon can be your roommate.”

“No, I’m too neat for Shannon.” Rachel cleared three files from her desk. “I like my

apartment. And your house is half an hour away from my work.”

"I know but you drive twenty minutes as it is. Nevermind, just trying to help out a bit."

"I appreciate it mom but I'm in a lease-"

"And I was thinking with interest rates going back up. Might be a good time to get in a place."

"I know but-"

"What is ten minutes more when you're traveling twenty already? And it's such a nice little place. Three bedrooms, two baths, a fenced double lot and a basement. Basement is nice sized and could be finished off."

"Okay, I'll come look at it." Why was she even trying to win this fight?

"Sucker." Shannon sang over from her desk. Rachel swatted at her.

"Come up Friday night for dinner. You can look at the house and go to church with us."

"Friday? I think I have plans."

"With who? Tell Shannon she can come along. We always have a wonderful time when she visits. There's a nice young businessman who started attending our church. Maybe she'd like to meet him."

"Oh really? A guy Shannon's type started going to your church. I'll have to tell her."

Shannon waved both of her arms in an X motion in front of her. Rachel nodded her head back at

Shannon. "All right mom we'll come up but we have to get these monthlies looked over if I'm

ever going to get out of here tonight."

"That'll be just fine. I'll talk to you in a couple a days. Mean time I'll give the realtor a

call and figure a time to see the place."

"Okay mom, bye."

Six

Jenny stood a few feet from the door.

"Open up." The man boomed from the other side. She held the knife, blade pointed toward the door and tiptoed toward the living room. She slid her trembling hand behind the curtain to check the window latch. She didn't want to risk seeing another shadow peering at her from the darkness. She felt the slide inside of its latch but lifted just a bit on the handle to be sure it was locked. She slid her hand back out and clipped the curtains closed with a clothes pin.

"Thanks for holding the door." The door rattled hard. Then he yelled an explicative again and stomped down the steps.

Slow, deep breaths. Calm down now, everything is fine. "God has not given me a spirit of fear…He has not given me a spirit of fear…God has not given me a spirit of fear." She whispered and pulled back the edge of the curtain covering her sliding glass door. The broom handle was still wedged in the track. She let the curtain fall back. The apartment plunged in to darkness other that the faint glow of street lights that slipped around her blinds.

She stepped backwards softly from the window.

"Hello beautiful." The sultry voice behind her was less than five feet away. Her breath caught in her throat and with it her ability to scream. The last drops of adrenaline pulsed through

her veins. She spun around, heart racing.

"Aren't you going to answer me?" The voice said again. She grabbed her chest in relief,

flipped open her cell phone and without a hello gushed in the phone.

"I could kill you for that stupid ring tone!"

"Why?" Logan's voice, the one on the ring tone, was like melted chocolate.

"Because it scared the life out of me." He started laughing. She still held her chest but the

burning heat of fear was fading. She set the knife down on her end table and sat on the couch.

"What happened?" His voice suddenly commanding without a hint of laughter remaining.

"I found a flower in my car after I hung up with you then-." She glanced again to the

clothespin holding the curtain shut.

"I'll be over in five minutes."

"But it'll take you at least fifteen or twenty to get all the way -."

"I'm just around the corner from you. I didn't like the way things ended on the phone. I

got a little something for you."

"Logan, someone followed me in to the building."

"Was it him?"

"I don't know but he's really angry. He pounded up and down the hall looking for me and-."

"I'll call when I'm in the parking lot. Buzz me up. I dare him to say a word when I'm around."

"Thank you." She didn't hide the relief in her voice.

"I'll talk to you soon."

She went down the short hall to her bedroom and flipped on the light. Quickly she pulled off the yoga suit she had worn home from the gym and slid on jeans and her cream colored shirt.

"I need to change that ring tone." She said then set the phone on vibrate and clipped it to her hip. Why did Logan like this outfit on her so much. White wasn't a slimming color, but he always insisted she looked beautiful in cream colors.

She straightened the blankets on her bed and draped her new chenille throw at an angle across it. The room was neat and tidy like Logan wanted it. He loved structure and order-

"He'll be here any time."

Her eyes lingered on the side of her bed that was empty night after night. She imagined

Logan there beside her, protecting her when she slept. She had never met a man who knew how to make a woman feel beautiful and special like he did. Even his constant need for structure was adorable with him.

"I want to marry him."

It was a light bulb flashing on in her brain. The stupid fears of being saddled in another bad relationship had nearly stolen the man who completed her. She spun to the oval mirror hanging above her dresser. Quickly she put on her makeup and brushed through her hair. She would tell him yes today. She beamed at her reflection. Logan, he will plop down on the couch shocked.

"No, he's going to throw his arms around me and kiss me."

She scurried back down the hall to the living room and fixed the pillows on her couch. Her cell vibrated against her hip.

"Come on up." She said then flipped the phone shut and buzzed the security door release. Wonder if he has the ring with him? He probably didn't. She had already turned him down once tonight.

"Jen it's me." He called gently through the door as he tapped. She pulled the door open, threw her arms around him and kissed him passionately. He pulled her close and returned the

kiss. He wrapped his arms around her and squeezed her tight against him. She pushed against his

chest for air but he grabbed the back of her head and forced her tighter.

"Lo…gan." She gasped. He loosened his hold a little and allowed her to breath.

"What in the world was that?" She said smoothing down her shirt.

"Sorry, I was glad to see you."

She studied him for a moment then took him by the hand and led him to the living room.

"I'm glad to see you too I want-."

He spun her around with a jerk. His eyes grabbed hers and his fingers pressed hard in to

her arm.

"Logan, you're hurting…me." She wiggled but he squeezed harder…and smiled.

"Isn't it okay for me to kiss you, Jen? Are you going to say no to that too?"

"Of course I want to-. Logan, you're hurting me." She grunted and pried at his fingers

that were digging in her arm. The last time he looked at her like this was the night he had taken

her purity. She had surrendered to him, but only because he'd made it clear it could have

happened with or without her permission. Once she relented to him he was gentle and loving but-

"So he left you another rose?" He released his grip with a jerk. She stepped back and rubbed her arm.

"I don't want to talk about that…Logan I've been thinking about us getting married and-."

"So have I." He stepped toward her. His eyes narrowed. Jen took a corresponding step back. "I've wondered why our relationship was moving forward until some strange man started leaving you flowers."

"That had nothing to do with it. I-."

"Oh no? You gave yourself to me, Jen. I thought that meant we were going to be together forever."

"And I-." Jen bumped up against the couch and fell down.

"You what, Jen? You want me to come night after night and be your savior and expect nothing in return? You expect me to-."

"Logan, I want to m-."

"Jen, you hurt me. I can't let some other man come between us."

"But there is no -."

"I had to know." He grabbed his head with both hands. See, Jen, Just like God put the Tree in the Garden with Adam and Eve to give them a choice, I gave you a choice."

"What?"

"Every day Adam and Eve looked at that Tree and they made a decision if they would love and obey God or if they would obey their flesh. The tree was there so they could decide who they loved. I needed to know who you loved, Jen."

"I love-."

"No, Jen. You don't. See you can't force love. You have to choose it. I needed to know if you loved me more than anyone else."

"I do-."

"No you don't." His voice was a low growl and his eyes were two white slits on his red face.

"Yes." She squeaked out. He straightened. The red faded and his natural color returned.

"See Jen. That's all I needed to hear." He was calm and charming.

"What?" She scooted up on to her elbows but still felt vulnerable on the couch.

"Yes. All I needed to hear from you was yes. I've loved you Jen." His voice rose again and he moved his arms wildly. She sat up and planted her feet on the ground.

"Logan?" Who was this man standing in her apartment. His eyes were intense and narrow. His voice commanding.

"What's the matter, Jen?" He took a step toward her.

"I just-. I don't know why you're acting like this. I thought that…after I told you…what I wanted to tell you…that maybe…you'd…uh…spend the night." Her voice betrayed the fear pulsating through her veins.

"Good." He tiled his head down a bit and gawked at her. He curled the right side of his mouth up.

"I brought you a little something, Beautiful." He stepped back toward the front door and picked something up from the floor in the hallway. "A little something special for my girl." He picked up the white rose with a black ribbon tied around it.

"That's not funny." She whispered.

"No, I agree. It's not funny that you love a man that would hurt you more than a man who tried to love you."

"But-."

"I brought you this too." He held up the small silver charm.

"No." She scampered to her feet but Logan blocked the exit.

"Jenny, don't run." He taunted. She stood on one side of the table, Logan on the other. He

kept the rose to his nose and smiled at her.

The door. She remembered the patio door behind her. He didn't have a weapon. Without

breaking eye contact she backed herself to the sliding glass door. Logan tossed the rose on the

couch and stepped toward her. Closer. She waited…He stepped closer and lifted the Greek

charm. Closer.

"No!" She screamed at the same instant she kicked him with all the force her tired legs

could muster. She spun around, jumped behind the curtain and unlocked the sliding glass door

then jerked-." It barely budged.

"C'mon." She grimaced. It opened only a smidge. The bar-.

"Jenny." Logan yelled.

She knelt down and flipped the bar out of the door track.

Thud

Something thudded against the glass over her head. She stood up quickly and grabbed the door handle of the sliding door. She would rip it open, run out on the balcony, then jump.

Fingers wrapped around her throat. She released the door handle and reached up to pry them loose.

Air. She needed.

"How dare you." Logan jerked her in the apartment and shoved her down. "You are mine, Jenny. Alpha Mu Epsilon."

It made no sense. His words were like echoes in her mind, incoherent really. Her head was in a vice grip as she fought for air. He had her on the ground. He was sitting on her and holding her throat with his right hand. Her tired limbs were pinned down. The darkness enveloped her with only a glimmer of light slicing down Logan's calm expression.

He held the charm in front of her. Jenny kicked her legs around but couldn't push free.

She needed to breathe. He leaned down in her face. His breath was hot against her ear.

"Alpha Mu Epsilon."

Building Characters
What do you think of these characters? Why?

Some writers seek to turn the setting in to a character too. Is this setting a character? Why or why not?

Seven

He hated this part of relationships. The exhilaration of firsts had ended. The first glance,
the first date, the first time their hands had gently brushed each other. He held her hand in his
and stroked her icy fingers. Neither person said a word. He studied the beauty of her well-
manicured nails. She was leaning back in the tub. Eyes fixed on Logan.

"I'm really sorry things didn't work out better." He let go of her hand and it dropped back
in her lap. She had no words left to say.

He really was sorry. The smell of bleach and ammonia burned his eyes. He lifted her
perfume and inhaled deeply. The vanilla bean scent flooded his nostrils and cleansed his
conscience for a moment. He sprayed it on her and for a moment he remembered their first date.
He had been sure Jen was the One.

No, she lied. She failed the test.

"Do you mind if I use your cell phone?"

She didn't answer.

"Of course you don't." It was polite to ask anyway. He slid on his black leather gloves
before he pulled her cell phone out of her purse and dialed the number.

"9-1-1 What's your emergency?"

"I'd like to report a murder." He made his voice deep, much deeper than his true voice. It didn't sound fake. That was an amateur mistake. He kept his voice calm and measured. The deed was done. Losing control of ones emotions is what led to people getting caught. No reason to get excited.

The first one had been exciting but each time they got easier, more routine. He lightly kissed his gloved fingers and pressed them against her bottom lip.

"The address is 7815 Wi-." He flipped the cell closed. The police would have to look for a while to find the place. When they did everyone would likely assume that loudmouth on the second floor who was searching door-to-door for her had done it.

A stroke of luck really.

He gently laid a white rose on Jen's chest next to the Alpha Mu Epsilon charm. The metal rings on her shower curtain scraped as he pulled the curtain almost closed. He turned on the hot water and watched it cascade from her forehead down the length of her body.

The evidence would wash away along with his painful memories. When the room started to steam up he pushed in the lock and closed the bathroom door. Emotions roiled inside him with alternating waves of regret and rage. Why couldn't she have been faithful? Been worthy? He screamed out a word usually reserved for foul-mouthed bar-hoppers or other such riffraff then went in to the kitchen and dropped her cell phone in the bucket of bleach he'd used to clean up the blood in the bathroom.

He had invested almost a year in this relationship and now she was gone. Certainly there was a woman out there who would appreciate all he had to offer.

Eight

Rachel pulled up the entrance ramp to the interstate.

"You have got to be kidding me." All three lanes in each direction were creeping along.

She slowly nosed to the left only merging in when someone let her in. She waved a thank you

and flipped on the radio

And we'll have your next traffic update in ten minutes on WJ-

She clicked it back off. August sunlight was stronger than her air conditioning. She

clicked the fan to four and held her hand over the vent.

"Great, one more thing to fix."

She turned the fan as high as it would go and pointed the vents to her and dialed her

mom's number.

"Mom, it's me."

"Hey, darlin' I was settin' the table. You on your way?"

"Yes but I'm stuck in some nasty traffic. We're moving about twenty under right now."

"Get here when you can. I've got dinner waitin'."

"Hopefully I'll be there in about ½ an hour. I had a last minute project dropped on my desk."

"We're meeting Drew at 7:30."

"Who?"

"Drew, the realtor." She had to be kidding. Rachel looked over at the clock. It was 5:37.

"He's coming over?"

"No, we're meetin' him down the way. Owners just knocked $15,000 off the price."

"You told him I'm not really in the market to-?"

"Rach, other line's beepin'. We'll talk when you get here."

She flipped her phone shut and set it in her lap. Up ahead traffic was starting to move. The State street exit always slowed things down on Friday. Should have remembered that.

Shannon had managed to back out at the last minute. Some lame excuse about a last minute date. A few minutes later she passed the State street exit and accelerated to a little over the speed limit. She moved toward the center lane on the highway to avoid the rush hour racecars that plowed through this two mile stretch of highway.

It would be nice if her mom bugged Adam half as much as she did Rachel. Rachel pushed down on the accelerator and zipped past a VW bug. The man inside was hunched over the wheel and looked way too tall for such a small car.

"What kind of guy drives a bug anyway?"

Maybe once her parents stopped treating her like a child and acknowledge that she had done something with her life. Her older brother Adam was the golden child married to a beautiful woman who could have modeled. Mom would add 'if it hadn't caused a brother to fall to the sin of lust.'

Rachel loved Adam, didn't like him too much though. He was too judgmental, too much like their parents and -.

A streak of red flashed past on her left. A dodge squealed in to her lane. She slammed her brakes to avoid running in to him.

"*This* is why I stay in the office until 6:30." Her voice echoed in the near silent car. She was not in the mood for this traffic, a visit with her family or the guilt picking at her. Two CD's were in her glove compartment. She reached over and took the first one her fingers wrapped around. No time to mess with the thoughts in her head. Accept who your family is and don't try to change them. Let them be who they are, and limit contact. It had worked in the eight years since graduation.

She turned up the volume and let the music take her thoughts away from the cacophony

in her mind.

Applying Character Lessons to your Story

What do you learn about the character by examining their relationship with others?

How can you work that in to your stories?

Nine

"It's okay. Momma will be back soon." Logan spoke quietly to Mrs. Nylski's dog,

Sammy. The dog was nearly senile according to the vet. The man wanted to murder the poor dog

but Logan had insisted the dog be allowed to live out his days. It sickened him that people were

so willing to kill a dog at the first sign of sickness.

"Dogs deserve better don't they boy." He carefully lifted the dog to his shoulder and

rubbed him with his cheek.

"Oh now Sammy that boy's gonna spoil you." Mrs. Nylski said as she came back in the

living room. "A man like you with so much love to give should have a family rather than passing

your days with an old lady."

Logan stood and gently set the dog on the couch so he could help Mrs. Nylski in to her

chair. "I made you something for dinner. It's in the oven so it stays warm."

"A young man who cook-."

"Careful-." Logan helped lower her the last few inches then brought Sammy to sit on her

lap.

"Thank you, dear." She stroked Sammy while Logan positioned her walker so she could get back up when she needed to. "Why don't you stay on and have supper with me this evening."

"If you don't mind."

"Of course not. You don't have a meeting with a young lady friend, do you?"

"No." Jen's smile popped in his head but he pushed it away. The pain of her betrayal still fresh. "I start my new job at the senior center next week."

"Really?"

"Yes." He picked up a bit of trash and tossed it in the waste basket. "I'm going to work two days a week there."

"The one in Woodhaven?"

"That's the one. If you'd like I could drive you over on days I work and you could spend the days with them."

She smiled, her dentures loose in her mouth, then looked back down at the dog on her lap. "I don't know. Sammy would get lonely."

"Take'em along." Logan scratched the little dog's ears.

"I'll set the table and we can eat now."

Ten

Rachel maneuvered her Taurus off the highway while cars continued to rush by. You'd

think it was the Autobahn the way people zipped through the stretch of highway. She turned

right off the ramp and left at the first light. Construction signs flashed ahead and traffic was

beginning to back up. Whe cranked her wheel to the right on to Maple instead of driving all the

way down to Fairmont. She could take it a mile or two then take a connecting street over to

Fairmont. The staccato ping of her cell phone's ring tone pulled her eyes from the road for a

moment. She reached down for her earpiece. Shannon Cell was on her phone display along with

a picture of Shannon's car.

"Hey former best friend."

"Ha-Ha. You at your mom's place yet?"

"No, you on your hot date yet?"

"Canceled."

"I'll bet." Rachel slowed down and scanned the signs. She didn't remember Fairmont

being this far down.

"Have you seen…" Rachel's car lunged forward and her phone flew off the seat ripping the cord out.

"Oh, no." Rachel looked in the rearview mirror at the shocked driver behind her then

groped around on the floor until her fingers wrapped around her phone. She opened it. "You still

there Shannon?"

"Yeah, I'm here. What happened?"

"I think someone just hit me." Rachel eased her car off to the right. The curb was almost

completely blocked with cars so she double parked. "I'll call you back."

"Are you okay?"

"Yeah, I'm fine. I'll call you later. Bye." She closed the phone and opened the door. A

young man jumped out of his pick-up and nearly ran to her.

"Are you alright?"

"I'm fine." She walked to the back of her car and rubbed the scuff above the wheel well.

"I got your tail light too." His voice was young, a bit high pitched for a man his age. She

walked around to the back. A four inch long section was broken out of the tail light. Enough

damage to be annoying, and less than her deductible.

"It doesn't look like there's too much damage. Let's exchange information." She walked quickly back to the car and pulled out the small black wallet that held all of her information in

the glove compartment. "This should be all the information you need." She scribbled on the

notebook page without looking up. "And here is my card with my phone number." She handed

him the card.

"Could I use a piece of your paper, uh" He looked down at her card. "Rachel?"

She tore off a sheet of paper and gave it to him. "What's your name?"

"Jeremy Wright." He leaned on the hood of his black pick-up truck and wrote his

information. "Sorry again. I was changing lanes and not paying attention to what I was doing.

Here's my information." He gave her the piece of paper. "If you don't mind I'd like to pay for

this myself without putting it through insurance."

"Why?" A request like that came from people who were shady and not going to pay for

the repair. That was Rachel's experience.

He pursed his lips as if holding back a smile. "And my card." He gave her his business

card. She scanned it and laughed.

"You're an insurance agent?"

"Well, I'm not actually an agent. I work for the company's public relations department."

"I must say I am very impressed with you as a representative of the agency." She leaned back against her car and eyed him a moment. What was she doing? Her mom already had her prince charming waiting with a house. She straightened back up and smoothed down her clothes. "If you won't mind paying all the repairs, and for a loaner if I need it, I won't reveal your secret."

"Of course." He looked down at her card again. "You don't live in Woodhaven?"

"No, I'm visiting my parents." She rubbed the dent. It should be an easy repair. "I should thank you for making me a little late."

"Really?"

"My parents are a little-." She searched for the right words. "Eager to get me back in the neighborhood…preferably with a husband for me and grandchildren for them."

"Okay, welcome to the neighborhood."

"I wouldn't go that far yet." She walked to her driver side door and put her hand on the handle. The traffic had thinned down considerably.

"Call me as soon as you get the bill." He said, waved and walked to his truck.

Eleven

"The house is just down the block would you like to walk?" Rachel's mom asked as she

slid in to her walking shoes.

"Sure." Rachel put her keys back in her purse and looked down at her stiletto ankle boots.

"Oh heavens you can't walk in those." Her mom looked down at Rachel's feet.

"They'll be fine…how far down is the house?"

"Ten minutes or so."

"I'll be fine." She held the door for her mom and followed her up the street. After fifteen

minutes of walking they turned down a cul-de-sac.

"There it is." Her mom pointed to a two story white house in desperate need of paint

surrounded by an old chain link fence. The grass needed mowed but there were flowers in

mulched beds lining the walk up to the house. The fence squeaked as she opened it.

"Go on up." Her mom urged her.

Already this house was a 'no'.

"You must be Rachel." The realtor came out the front door and down the steps to where

she stood with her mom. He wore a grey suit, looked to be fine wool. She had seen similar outfits on some of the business owners she worked with. The clothes only momentarily distracted her

from his painfully good looks. "I'm Drew. I've heard a great deal about you."

Rachel shook his outstretched hand. His grip was firm. A confident man. She looked over

at her mom. "So then my mom has told you I'm not really actively looking for a house."

"No she hadn't mentioned that…" he looked past her to her mom. "But I appreciate the

opportunity to show you around just the same." He opened the back door for the women then

followed behind.

"The stove and refrigerator are negotiable but the sellers are taking the microwave with

them to their new house." Drew said. He stepped to the corner of the small kitchen as he spoke.

Rachel scanned the dripping faucet and scuffed countertop. To the left of the refrigerator

a cupboard door was partially open. She opened it the rest of the way with her finger. The dim

light in the center of the kitchen didn't reach to the back of the shelf but she saw enough. Ripped

and bubbling greenish-orange swirl contact paper lined the shelves in the cupboards. She pulled

out a drawer…contact paper there too.

"You know, Rachel-," Her mom pushed the drawer closed and walked her closer to the

center of the small kitchen "Drew was telling me they recently redid the bathroom."

"Good." Rachel looked under the sink. No water spots but she caught a whiff of something pungent. It threatened to steal the dinner she had eaten at her mom's house. "What is that smell?"

"Oh…uh…they forgot to clean out the freezer when they moved." Drew pushed on the freezer door as he walked past Rachel to a small door. There is also a nice pantry here." He pulled the door open. "It is large enough to hold cleaning supplies and possibly canned goods on these shelves.

Rachel nodded and looked again at the Fridge. No wonder appliances were negotiable. Why not have someone pay you to throw out your old stuff.

She leaned over to her mom. "Kitchen needs a lot of work."

"You don't cook much. Let's not judge until we look at the rest of the house." Rachel followed her mom to the living room.

"And the carpet could be replaced." Drew said as he ran in behind her.

"I told you it is a lovely fixer-upper." Her mom said.

Were they even looking at the same house? How could her mom have chosen this place for her? Nothing here whispered modern, trendy or even clean for that matter.

"What I'm really looking for-." Rachel said surveying the great room that made the front of the house "is something newer. Maybe built in the last five to ten years if possible in this price range plus or minus fifteen thousand." She walked over to the windows overlooking the front yard. "And no chain link fence. Wood fence is fine, no fence is better."

She looked back. Drew was writing something down and her mom looked at her with pursed lips and arms crossed.

Find something positive to say about the place. She looked from Drew back to her mom. "But I love the landscaping. If there are perennials I'd be thrilled."

"I did the landscaping." Drew said without looking up from his notebook.

"You did?" Her mom's charm returned. "Drew, you did an excellent job."

"I agree, it's this house's best feature." Rachel laughed….alone.

Drew continued, "My grandparents owned a green house when I was younger. I remember how my grandpa was convinced that you could learn all you needed to know about a person by their favorite flower."

"You don't say." Her mom had folded her arms again but this time to support her fingers on her chin.

"Really-." Drew looked up at Rachel. "He even said the color of the particular flower was important to knowing who that person was inside."

Rachel looked back out the front window. "So what do these flowers tell me about you?" She motioned over her shoulder to the flower beds lining the sidewalk.

Drew handed her his business card with a note on the back. "That I take my job very seriously." She looked down at the note. It said "Dinner sometime?" She slid his card in her wallet then gave him hers. "Call me with more details."

Her mom stepped forward. "You want to go look upstairs."

"No, I don't think this is the place I'm looking for right now."

"But you didn't give it a chance."

"Fine."

Her mom grabbed her by the arm and took her up the stairs. "Look at the master bedroom, Rachel. It's so huge."

"Yes, it's good size."

"And look at the bathroom they redid."

"It's nice but I don't like yellow."

Her mom waved away her concern and walked through the room and down the hall.

"There are two other bedrooms" She called over her shoulder. "They are much smaller but one could be a guest room and the other an office if you'd like.

"I try to leave work at work." She said following behind her mom.

"Those upstairs bathrooms have all new plumbing too." Drew yelled up the steps.

"Thanks." Rachel yelled down. "Mom, it's nice but not really what I'm looking for."

"Then why did I go through all this bother?"

"Mom, I didn't ask you to find me a house."

"Well you have no time with all the workin' you do. You don't date, you don't do anything 'cept work and go home."

Rachel walked down the steps and over to Drew. "Thank you for showing me the house. I'll look forward to your call on Monday."

"Feel free to email and tell me exactly what you're looking for. My address is on the card."

"Thank you, I will." She turned to the steps and called up. "Mom, the realtor is going to email me some other properties we can look at. He said he'd get with me Monday."

"Make sure they're close to Woodhaven, Drew."

False Friends: Using POV to feed wrong information

Remember, our perception of the scene must be influenced by the point of view character. That means sometimes the way we see things will be wrong. That is how life is. That is how you can make your stories more realistic. What is the perception we are feeling through this character?

Twelve

"Shannon you would not believe this realtor at my mom's this weekend."

"That good or that bad?"

"Come on down to my office." Shannon walked around cardboard filing boxes and an oversized coat rack. "When are you going to have someone take those to storage?"

"I'll get to it. I've been busy."

Shannon was always too busy to store the files. That was why she walked around boxes from two or three years ago and drove around town to meet with clients rather than put the boxes away and meet them in her office.

"Well, tell me all about him." Shannon crossed one leg under the other and sat down in the chair across from Rachel.

"We walk in to this awful house. It stuck like rotten food and mold."

"Lovely."

"No joke. But I felt really bad for the guy. He didn't seem to think the house was anything worth buying either."

"Did he say that?"

"No. Well I guess he did put in the flowers out front to dress the place up."

"He put in flowers?"

"Yes. Anyway, he was really nice but you know how sometimes you can tell someone is checking you out?" Rachel pulled out Drew's card and pecked his homepage in her browser. His photo might be up on his website.

"Yes-." Shannon's voice was urgent. She scooted the chair closer to Rachel's desk.

"Okay, I'm talking about what kind of house I'd really like to see and he's writing on this note pad. Then real quick he gives me this card." She gave the business card to Shannon.

"Smooth."

"That's what I thought." She put the card in her wallet. ""See what happens when you lie about having a date. You miss out on hot guys."

"Oh, so he *is* attractive." Shannon leaned back in her chair.

"Didn't I say that?"

"Not really."

"Yes, very handsome. Athletic, dark eyes and hair and stylish. Looks live one of those GQ kind of guys."

"GQ guys are usually shallow."

"You know, he reminds me of that really hot teaching assistant in our 300 level economics class senior year."

"Is he *that* cute?" Shannon's eyes were wide.

"I think he is." The website popped up. "Aw, his photo isn't loading." she pointed to the little icon that indicated a photo should have been there.

"Keep me posted then." Shannon got up and walked back to her office. Rachel opened her email and started scrolling down deleting spam as she went. Her cell phone vibrated on her hip.

"Hello?"

"Is this Rachel?"

"Yes."

"This is Jeremy Wright. Our cars met last Friday."

"Oh yeah. Hello Jeremy."

"Mail Truck." Her computer announced. Rachel clicked it open.

"I was calling…see if you…body shops…"

"I'm sorry there's a really bad connection. I haven't found a body shop."

"Okay, I'll…better time…names." The line went dead. She closed her phone and scanned the email she'd just opened from Drew. It included a link to view a number of properties. She opened it and five came on the screen. She clicked on each one but the first three were nothing she wanted to look in to. The fourth one looked promising. She picked up the phone and dialed Shannon's extension.

"Shannon I found a house I want to look at. You want to go with me?"

"Of course."

"All right. Email is sent. I told him to call me so we could schedule a time to look at it."

"Try to avoid the weekend or you know your mom will have us stay."

"I went to church with her this past weekend. That should pay me up for at least a month. Looking at her house should give me another month or two for credit."

"Good. I'm free every night but Thursday. Let me know when he emails."

"I will."

"We still going to Panera Bread for lunch?"

"I was planning on it. We need to go at 11:30 if we want to be back in time for our conference call this afternoon.”

“Rachel you have a call on line two.” The receptionist called over the intercom.

“Who is it?”

“Drew, with Goldman Realty.”

“Thank you.”

“Gotta go Shannon.”

“Bye.” She switched over to Drew’s line.

“This is Rachel.”

“Hello Rachel, this is Drew at Goldman Realty.”

“Hello Drew.”

Thirteen

Rachel looked over her Scrabble tiles. All vowels and a Q. "I like the old Scrabble games."

"What's the difference?" Shannon added the score sheet. "I'm only beating you by eighty tonight."

"In the old version the Qu was a single tile."

"Stuck with the Q. Good to know."

"Not if I don't find a word."

"Dumping?"

The phone rang on the wall behind her. Rachel reached back and answered it. A shrill whine like a Fax machine assaulted her ear. "I'll be right back." Rachel said over her shoulder as she went to the TDD machine in the front room.

"Rachel here GA."

"Where are mom and dad? GA."

Shannon came behind her. "Adam?"

"Looks that way." Rachel's older brother was born profoundly deaf and was the golden child in the family because of his abilities, not disabilities.

"What does GA mean?"

"Go ahead."

"They're out. Probably looking for a house or husband for me. GA."

"Laugh…"

"If you want to take a break this could take a bit. He hasn't even said go ahead yet."

Rachel said. Shannon was reading the screen over her shoulder. One of Rachel's peeves.

"You want coffee?"

"Sure."

"I need to come home…GA."

With or without Yvonne? She wanted to ask but how could she ask her big brother if his

marriage was over.

"When do you guys want to come? GA."

"Just me. ASAP. GA."

Rachel flipped open her cell and had her mom on the phone a few rings later.

"Mom. Adam's on the phone. I think things are bad with Yvonne."

Her mom's words were slow. "What exactly did he say?"

"Said he needed to come home. I asked when they were coming-."

"You there? GA." Adam asked again.

Rachel cradled the cell the best she could and typed, "Asking mom. Give me a minute.

GA."

"He said he needed to come home alone ASAP."

"I'll be home as soon as I can."

"Mom, I've got him on the phone. What do you want me to tell him?"

"I'll handle it. Tell him I'll call when I'm home. We're walking out now."

"Mom on way home. She will call you. Anything I can do? GA."

"Yvonne out of love with me. Need time apart. Coming home. Need a roommate? GA."

"Always place for you. GA."

"Thanks. Tell mom to call at my office. GA or Hang up."

"Bye. Hang up."

"His wife left him." Her big brother was on the other side of the country, alone.

"Why?" Shannon walked out and showed as much shock as Rachel. Yvonne wasn't her mom's first choice for Adam, but then no woman ever would be. This would not be a reconcilable disagreement if mom had her way.

"I'm not sure. Do you mind if I go upstairs for a few minutes."

"No, sure go."

Rachel walked up the small staircase to the second level of her mom's split level house. She padded down the carpeted floor and in to her old room. Mom had turned it in to a guest room after Rachel graduated from college but other than a few family members Rachel had been the only guest to use it.

The room was decorated in bright colors and there were pictures of chubby babies dressed up like animals and flowers on the walls. She walked to her old bed and slid her legs under the covers.

"She left him." The words squeezed her heart. They had moved from Ohio to California a few years ago following what Adam thought was God's call. They were two halves of a whole, Yvonne and Adam, despite her mom's opinion of the relationship. Yvonne never once complained about Adam to her. Even when Rachel would get frustrated Yvonne would tell her that she would never stand to hear Adam insulted in her presence.

Adam for his part wouldn't allow Yvonne to be insulted. That, more than a divine call, was the real reason he moved his wife and life to the west coast. Rachel never blamed Adam for the way mom compared the two of them. Adam wasn't in to all that anyway. He stayed true to who he was.

But now they'd split up.

It couldn't have hurt any more if it were her own break up. It might as well be. This was more evidence that the old notion of meeting one person and loving forever was never realistic. It was an economic arrangement where women traded their body for-."

"Rachel?"

"Yeah."

"Wanted to give you fair warning your parents are pulling in."

"Come on in."

Shannon slipped in the room and closed the door. "Should I lock it?"

"No." Rachel patted the bed for Shannon to sit on the end. "Mom won't be up here until she's called Adam and made sure he's okay."

"You don't sound happy about that."

Rachel sat up with her back to the headboard and hugged her pillow. "I'm fine with it. I

don't think it will be a fair fight."

"A fair fight?"

"Mom will try to tell Adam why Yvonne is the worst thing that ever happened to him and

why Adam never did anything wrong. Then Adam and her will squabble…never mind. It will be

a while until she tries to find us."

"Don't forget we need to leave a little before seven to look at the new place Drew found."

"I know…I hope mom isn't mean to Yvonne."

"I don't think she'll call here."

"Would it be a betrayal if I called her?" Rachel scanned through her cell's phone book.

"If she's at their place I've got that number in my phone."

"Do you know why they split?"

"No clue." The screen blinked off on her phone. "Is mom talking to him?"

"How should I know?"

"Listen for typing."

Shannon walked to the door and opened it a few inches. "I hear keys clanking."

"Close the door. I'm going to call." She scrolled down and pushed send.

"Hello?" Yvonne's voice was quiet.

"It's Rachel."

"Hi." Yvonne hesitated a moment. "Your brother isn't here right now."

"I've talked to him." She willed back the tears that threatened to escape her eyes. Yvonne was in pain. She was without her husband and her mom was going to be no help in the situation.

"What can I do?"

"I've asked myself that question a lot lately."

"Adam said you left him."

"It was mutual." There was muffled nose blowing on the other end. "We've been drifting apart since we moved out here. We thought maybe a break would help." Yvonne sniffled. "So I'm staying here and Adam said he'd stay with your parents."

"Is that what you want?"

"Um...well...not really."

"Rachel?" Her mom called through the door. "Rachel your brother's on the phone. Wants to talk to ya."

Rachel held her hand over the cell phone. "I've gotta run. I'm at my parents' house and mom's at the door."

"Oh my, don't let her know you're talking to me."

"I'll think good thoughts."

"Rachel? You comin'?"

"Yeah mom." She closed the phone and Shannon opened the door.

"What took so long?"

"Girl stuff." Rachel exchanged a nervous glance with Shannon.

"Don't forget 'bout your appointment this evenin'."

"I won't."

"Adam's waitin' on ya." Her mom motioned to the steps. Rachel swiped her hand across the wrinkles on her comforter and went down the steps.

Fourteen

This house was far better than the one her mom found for her. The exterior was red brick

with delicate gingerbread work in the peaks along the roof. It was quaint with white accents

around the house and a white painted porch.

"Do you think the swing stays?" Rachel pointed to the porch as she spoke.

"If not I know someone who can make you a nice one." Shannon said then unbuckled her

seatbelt.

They stepped around the car and looked up at the house from the sidewalk. The lawn was

plush green without a single visible dandelion. Small purple and pink flowers lined the walk,

wonder if it was Drew's doing? The yard was large for the neighborhood, even though the

houses in the neighborhood were considerably large.

"What do you think Shannon?"

"Rachel, good to see you again." Drew came around from the back of the house. He

motioned back. "I think you'll really like this home."

Shannon bumped Rachel with her arm. "It's nice so far. This is my business partner

Shannon."

"Nice to meet you." Drew shook her hand and returned to Rachel. "Would you like to see

the inside?"

He stepped back and allowed them to pass. She stepped in the front door. No bizarre

smells greeted her this time. The walls of the house were decorated in tans and browns but

accented with white trim and dark furnishings. The carpet was plush and white.

Drew stepped beside her. "A young couple has lived here for the last four years." They

redecorated a year ago and are moving for a new job. Drew stepped in to the dining room "The

floors are natural hardwood and were redone a year ago as well."

She could see herself in this house. She walked past Drew in to the kitchen. It was small

with lots of cupboards. Pots and pans hung from the ceiling over a tiled island. The afternoon sun

filtered in through the western windows and splashed little rainbows from the decorative window

across the counter.

Shannon's feet clanked across the ceramic tile. "Rachel, you going to ask him out?"

"Wasn't planning on it now. Did you see these cupboards?" Rachel ran her hand over the

blond wood. "I've never seen a place quite like this."

"It's nice but I can't see you living here."

"Why not?"

"A little too Ozzie and Harriet."

"It is not." Rachel laughed and looked under the sink.

"Look at that Rachel. They're neat freaks like you."

Rachel had to laugh at the cleaning supplies in neat rows under the sink. "At least I'm not

the only one on this planet who likes things nice."

"Have they ever used this sink?"

"Oh stop." Rachel stood and gently closed the cupboard doors.

"Go ask him out." Shannon poked Rachel's arm as she spoke.

"I dunno-."

Shannon sighed and walked to the other room.

"Would you ladies like to see the upstairs?"

Rachel nodded and followed Drew up the narrow steps to the second floor. There were

two small bedrooms and a bathroom to the right and the master bedroom to the left. She stood at

the top of the steps and looked in to each room. The master bedroom was cramped and narrow.

The queen sized bed took most of the space.

She walked back down. "Upstairs is kinda small."

"Drew." Shannon called up the steps. "How would you like to ask my friend Rachel out on a date?"

Rachel spun around. "Shannon-."

"Well I thought that-." Drew stammered.

"Drew, I'm sorry. Shannon can be a bit-."

"So what do you think?" Shannon smiled. "Two successful people meeting to discuss life and business? You know my friend is very attracted to you."

Rachel's face burned red. This level of embarrassment was usually reserved for when her mom was with her. Drew looked between the two women and back to Rachel. The mood turned awkward. Shannon still smiled looking between Rachel and Curtis.

Fifteen

"Are you going to be mad at me all weekend?" Shannon asked after ten minutes of

silence.

"Why did you do that?" Rachel's voice was firm but she managed to keep from yelling.

"Neither one of you were going to say anything."

"Do you think maybe there was a reason for that? Sometimes subtly is in order."

"And sometimes you're a chicken." Shannon still acted like what she had done was

funny. Rachel didn't see any humor.

"I felt humiliated back there."

"Why?" Shannon's phone started chirping.

Rachel turned in to her parents' neighborhood. The yards weren't as big here as they

were where she had been. Kids lined the streets here with their bikes and scooters when she was

younger. The park was a five minute walk away and when you were old enough to take your first

trip without mom and dad it marked the beginning of life as a big kid.

The kids she grew up with were starting to come home to visit with their fiancés,

husbands and even some children. One by one they left her to move on to the wife club or the mommy club. Their discussions were of late night feedings and first words. More and more Rachel was isolated to a group of college friends who had pursued careers instead of minivans. They went to homecoming games at the Alma Mater and visited parties in the Greek village.

Now most of them were married too. The few who weren't she had lost touch with a long time ago. When her and Nate had moved in together, against their parents' wishes, she had imagined coming back to the neighborhood and joining the soon-to-be-Mrs group.

A small ache on the edge of consciousness threatened to grab her but she wasn't going to go back there.

Shannon's conversation was wrapping up. Whenever her answers became all uh-huh's she was done.

Rachel wandered on to other thoughts. Was the home today her first step toward car pools and minivans? She was thirty, maybe it should be. Adam's marriage may be on the rocks but they married young. You marry too young or too old and there'll be trouble. Too young and you're immature and selfish. Too old your set in your ways and selfish. She and Nate had been too young.

Sixteen

"Thank you for coming up this weekend." Rachel said to Shannon as they drove to church.

"You're welcome."

"This house was so much better than the other one."

"Have you decided on an offer yet?" Shannon's nail file made a loud scraping sound.

"I have to look over the numbers."

"Of course you do."

Rachel smiled. "I also need to decide if I want to be that close to my parents' house."

"It's only a difference of ten minutes."

"Yes, but ten minutes can be the difference between them popping in for dinner or only coming on weekends."

"Of course you would have thought that through. Did you notice this church is pretty close to that house too?" Shannon shook her head and went back to filing her nails. "Can we sit in the back of the church or do we have to sit way up in the front?"

"Wherever. That's the church up there." Rachel turned left in the parking lot and pulled in to the first parking space she saw. "They're going to think I found religion. This is the second week in a row I've been here."

The back of the church had a long hallway with a drinking fountain and restrooms. Her mom's voice echoed down the hall.

"I think we found your mom." Shannon said.

Rachel turned the corner and stood beside her mom. She was talking to a young man with sparkling blue eyes and bright hair.

"Oh, honey. I didn't see you there." She took Rachel's arm and brought her forward a step. "Rachel, this is Curtis. He is the man who helped us with our mortgage."

"Nice to meet you." He leaned forward and extended his hand. Rachel shook it. "And this is Shannon." Rachel stepped back so they could shank hands.

"Mortgages?" She nodded her head as she spoke. He seemed too young to be done with college. "Mom has been busy."

"It's good to have connections is all." Her mom chimed in.

"Your mother tells me you're looking for a house in the area."

"It's more like looking *at* a house in the area. I'm not sure I'm in the market to buy quite yet.”

“It’s a buyer’s market so if you’d like to stop paying rent now would be a good time to do

that.” Curtis shifted his large Bible from one hand to the other then reached in his pocket. “If you

decide to buy I’d be happy to get you the kind of deal I got for your parents.”

“He cut ‘bout a hundred dollars a month off our mortgage.” Her mom patted Rachel’s

arm as she spoke.

“Oh really? That’s a good deal. I’ll keep that in mind.” A couple of ladies walked by and

waved to her mom. Her mom whispered back hello with exaggerated facial expressions.

“I need to get up stairs.” Curtis tapped his watch. “I’m leading the junior high today.”

“So we’ll see you at one?” Her mom said

“One?” Rachel repeated.

“Curtis is joining us for lunch.”

“I’m not imposing am I?” He looked between Rachel and her mom.

“Not at all.” Rachel tried to recover from her faux pas. “It’s fine. I need to be back on the

road by three so I can finish up some preparation for Monday.”

“Yes, we have big clients first thing Monday.” Shannon quickly added.

"Don't tell me you work on Sundays." Curtis gently teased.

"Isn't that what you are doing?"

He nodded his head as if to say touché. "I guess you could call it work. I prefer to look at it as talking." He started walking down the hall. "I'm sorry Lisa. I really do need to get down there."

"Go on. We'll see you this afternoon."

"Rachel, Shannon, it was nice to meet you. Lisa I'll see you this afternoon."

Evaluating Dialog

Dialog is often one of the most difficult things for a writer to master. That is because we need it to sound realistic, but it cannot model actual speech. When a writer is skilled at writing dialog, however, there is a wealth of information that can be conveyed by what is said, how it is said, and the non-verbal communication [tics] that accompany the writing.

Evaluate the dialog in this book and identify what works in the dialog and what doesn't work. Write notes here and in the manuscript itself.

Seventeen

"See what I mean. This Pastor isn't too bad." Rachel whispered to Shannon as they went

back down the long hallway that led to the parking lot.

"I could come here every once in a while if that's the kind of stuff he preaches on. I get

sick of hearing how I'm such a bad person because I don't go to church." Shannon answered.

"I've only been here twice. I'm sure he gets around to that too." She pointed to the

direction of the car. People were all over the parking lot talking. The sun kept the temperature

pleasant and most of the people seemed to be in no rush to leave. "I wrote down that thing the

pastor said about achievement."

They walked between the cars and down to the row they had parked in. The car stood

alone at the far end of the row.

"Which thing?"

Rachel reached in her purse and pulled out a small notebook. "Comfort is the enemy of

achievement."

"You brought a notebook to church?" Shannon shook her head.

"No, I keep a notebook to write things down so I don't have to wait for my Palm Pilot to turn on to jot a note."

"That's right."

"I want to get my suitcase packed up as soon as we get back to mom and dad's house. I need to get back home at a decent time."

"It looks like your mom isn't taking any chances with you finding the man of your dreams."

"That's what I thought. Of course it could be her way of making sure I buy that house too."

"True."

"Or she might have picked him out for you." She winked at Shannon then clicked the remote on her key ring and walked around the back of the car.

"What is that?" Shannon pointed.

Rachel walked to the front of the car. A white rose with a black ribbon tied around it rested on the windshield. She stood frozen a moment. Headlines announcing another murder flipped through her memory.

Slowly she lifted the rose hoping to find a church flier or a welcome note below it.

Nothing.

Her throat tightened around words she wanted to scream. She pulled her eyes from the rose and looked at Shannon then the stream of people milling around the parking lot by the church.

Why her car? Was it because she had parked in the back corner where no one would notice someone walking down the row?

"Maybe he doesn't know who you are?" Shannon offered. Her eyes fixed to the rose.

"He does if he's watching." She looked around for anyone who might be looking at them. She looked at the playground and along the tree line. Should she go to her mom's house? What if he was following her? Goosebumps picked her flesh raised when the cool breeze blew across the droplets of perspiration forming on Rachel's arms and neck.

"Um, maybe we should put it down and call the police?"

Rachel began to take some control of her emotions. "We don't know for sure it's him and if it isn't we're going to get mom's church all riled up for no reason."

"But if it is you need to be protected."

This was nothing more than a coincidence. Some ill-timed gesture of friendship from her mom's church. Someone who maybe wasn't following the Fratboy murders thought it nice to

give a rose. Rachel felt silly for getting worked up over a welcome gift. She opened her door and

tossed the rose in the back seat.

"Aren't you going to do anything?"

"Maybe it is your rose. You were the first time guest."

"But it's your car."

"It's a coincidence." Rachel assured her with her rational mind now fully in control of her

faculties. "The murders were on campus or college girls. I'm neither and the college is on the

other side of town.

Eighteen

Logan stood just far enough away that Rachel couldn't see him. From the first moment they spoke he knew that she was it; she was the one. He held the digital camera to his eye and zoomed it in tight.

She walked to her car and tucked hair behind her ear. Then smiled.

Click.

She walked around to the front of the car. She found it…..now.

Click.

She lifted the rose and held it.

Click.

 She looked around the parking lot and the wind blew a few wisps of hair across her face.

Click.

"A beautiful rose for a beautiful woman." He said. She is perfect.

Part II: Darkness Falls

One

"Don't mention anything about the rose at my mom's house." Rachel was firm. There was going to be enough tension with a guest and the Adam/Yvonne thing looming. "It couldn't be the stalker so there is no reason to bring it up."

"But that stalker is leaving roses for the women when he kills them." Shannon no longer sounded scared. This voice was bossy. Rachel could give it right back to her.

"Yes, and the fact that you know that means other people know it. It may be nothing more than a prank."

"But if it's from him…"

"If it were from him I'd be dead." Rachel yelled just as loud as Shannon had. "He leaves them with the dead bodies of women. When we get to the house I'm going to put it under my seat so Mom doesn't see it."

"Then you aren't going to mention it at all?"

"No." She slowed the car as they reached her parents' street. "Listen, I don't want my mom all worked up over nothing. The stalker goes after college girls. Every single one has been in her late teens or early twenties *and* they were college students. I don't go to the U, I'm not anything like the other girls and unfortunately I passed twenty about a decade ago."

"I won't mention anything to your mom but you should consider telling the cops."

"I'll think about it. Do you really believe I would put my life in danger?"

"No."

Rachel parked the car and hid the rose under the seat.

"It doesn't look like they're here yet." Rachel said as they walked up to the front porch.

She unlocked the door and went in the house. "Adam called."

"How do you know?"

"Caller ID."

Rachel dialed Adam and waited for him to pick up.

"Adam, it's Rachel. GA."

"Sorry forgot Church. Did you go?! GA."

"Yes. When are you coming.? GA."

"Tuesday. GA"

"Is there anything I can do for you? GA."

Rachel stood in front of the machine waiting for him to answer. She thought Yvonne was nice enough. Never really saw the reason her mom didn't like her. Adam was a great-."

"Pray. GA."

"Of course. GA."

"Thank you. Tell mom my flight info." Rachel wrote down the airline, times and flight

number.

"Is Adam on the phone?" Rachel's mom came in the door and straight to the TDD.

Rachel stepped away from the machine and left the paper with the flight on the table next to her

mom. Her mom typed quickly.

"Lisa, don't forget Curtis will be here soon."

"I know."

Dad had tried but Adam was on the phone. Until mom had finished nothing would get

done unless they did it. Rachel padded up the steps to her room.

"Why do you let her do that?" Shannon was smoothing her clothes down in her suitcase.

A quirk she had when she was very angry. What could have happened since they arrived-. "She

comes in and you step aside."

"Adam wanted to talk to mom."

"But you were talking to Adam."

"I'll see him when he gets here." She lifted her suitcase on the bed and started laying her things in it. "It makes mom feel good to mother him."

"You become invisible."

"No I don't." She put her toiletries in a small cloth bag and zipped it shut. "I know how my mom feels about me."

"Everyone does. It's obvious."

"Stop." Rachel spun around and threw her cosmetics in her suitcase. "I will not have you insult my parents in their house."

Shannon held Rachel's stare for a moment then broke it without a word. They finished packing the suitcase in silence.

"Ladies." Her dad yelled up. "Could you help me get things finished up in the kitchen? Curtis will be here in twenty minutes."

"Remember. Happy." Rachel said to Shannon then painted on a smile. Shannon sneered back and yanked the door open.

They placed delicate china plates with pink flowers and gold foil edges around the table followed by two pieces of stemware, salad bowl, bread plate, silver and cloth napkins.

"Dad, what is mom up to?" Rachel said filling a small gravy bowl.

"She told me she wanted to thank him for helping on our mortgage."

"Good, then it has nothing to do with me."

"Of course not." His words were thick with sarcasm.

"Adam'll be here Tuesday." Rachel's mom announced. She lifted the gravy bowl out of Rachel's hands and put it on the table in the dining room.

"Oh, you put out those glasses?"

"You said the-."

"Yes, it's fine. We'll make due." She patted Rachel and went in the kitchen. Rachel turned and saw Curtis walking slowly up the side walk. She pulled open the door and stepped out on the porch.

"Hello again, Curtis."

"Rachel. It's nice to see you." She stepped out on the porch next to him and closed the storm door. The clanging of last minute preparations muffled by the thump when the door closed.

"It's warm in there." She stepped over to the bench in the yard. "I hope you don't mind

sitting out here for a moment."

"No, I us-."

"I'm sorry." She laughed. "Mom was on the phone with Adam and is getting everything

perfect in there. If she saw you before she was ready she'd freak."

"This is fine." He sat on the bench and crossed his leg away from her. "Your mom and

dad are nice people."

"Thank you." Across the sidewalk a sparrow landed and hopped around picking

periodically. In a couple more months no one would spend pleasant afternoons on benches

watching birds. The cold sting of winter would invade and blanket everyone in to an icy prison.

"I love Sparrows."

"Oh really." He turned toward her. "Why is that?"

"Because I only notice them in the summer. And I like summer."

"Guess that's as good a reason as any." He spun his body so he faced her front on. "Lisa

tells me you own a business. What do you do?"

"It's a marketing and sales business. What I personally do is keep on top of the books and make sure Shannon gets everywhere on time.”

“That woman I met at church?”

“Yep, that’s her. We’ve been chums since college. She’s my balance and I’m hers.”

“That’s a great thing to have.” He nodded and quietly looked away. The two of them sat

still but the silence was comfortable. Neither seemed to feel the need to fill the air with worthless

words or idle banter. Well, Rachel didn’t. Curtis closed his eyes and leaned back a bit on the

bench with a gentle grin penciled across his face.

Rachel leaned back and imitated Curtis. The warm sun beat down on her face and was

balanced by the cool breeze that seemed to know exactly when to blow so as to keep them at the

perfect temperature. Someone walking by would surely wonder what they were doing. Rachel

hadn’t felt it wise before to lay with her eyes closed in the front yard on a city block. But then

she was uptight.

The front door opened and Rachel turned to face the porch.

“Your mom’s lookin’ for-.”

“I’m coming.”

“Curtis right?” Shannon walked out and shot Rachel a dirty look before turning to Curtis with a smile. "Lisa's been in there all a flutter wonderin' when you'd be comin' along."

"That was an awful imitation of my mom's accent."

"I know. Too much North in me to pull it off. Your mom's looking for you though."

"Curtis," Rachel turned to him. "You remember Shannon?"

"Of course." He shook her hand. "Rachel and I were out here enjoying the weather."

"I could see that." Rachel registered the disdain in Shannon's voice. Curtis either didn't

notice or didn't care.

"Well Curtis, why you sittin' out here?" Rachel's mom came on to the porch and hugged

Curtis as if greeting family.

"Hi Lisa, quite the welcome you had for me." He motioned to Rachel and Shannon. "You

send out all these nice young ladies."

"You act like you're some old man." Her mom led Curtis in the house leaving Rachel and

Shannon standing alone in the yard.

"I'm sure he was just being polite." Shannon said looking directly at Rachel. Her lips

were pressed in a straight line across her face.

"What?" Rachel felt like a puppy that'd piddled on the new rug. "I needed to get out of there.”

“I’m sure that’s what it was.”

“I didn’t do anything wrong.” For all Shannon’s open-mindedness she had a bear trap tight mind when it came to dating relationships. And a broad definition of one. Once any man expressed any sort of interest in Rachel it was a requirement that the relationship continue until Shannon saw it as unhealthy or no longer worthwhile. Rachel had only defied Shannon’s judgment one time.

“What about Drew?”

“I’m not interested in this guy. He’s mom’s friend. I have to be polite.”

Shannon’s face softened. “I know Rachel. I don’t want to see you hurt again is all. You tend to think life is going to work out like one of your romance novels.”

“Yes, and you remind me frequently that it won’t.” The edge of bite in her voice had been intentional.

“We keep each other in balance. You remind me why I can’t buy everything with plastic and I remind you of what happened when you didn’t trust me.”

This was as close to winning as Rachel was going to get in this argument. Shannon was right. She was always as right on relational issues as Rachel was on financial ones and there was no reason to-."

"Rachel, you goin' to keep our guest waiting all day ta eat? Poor things gonna blow away in here." Her mom called out and closed the door, not waiting for the answer.

"Better get inside." Rachel followed Shannon in the door. Her mom had seated Curtis with an empty chair to his right. Shannon walked straight to the chair and sat down.

"I want Rachel to be able to face our guest." She said by way of explanation.

Rachel made eye contact with no one and only walked to the other side of the rectangular table and sat in the lone chair on that side. Her dad said the blessing and they began passing food around the table. Periodically her mom would interrupt the eating sounds with a question or observation that was quickly answered and then dropped.

"I'm going to get the dessert." Her mom said a moment before moving swiftly to the kitchen to retrieve her signature chocolate cake. That was followed by her dad clearing his throat. Rachel quickly obeyed.

"So Curtis, tell me…er…us about yourself."

"What would you like to know?"

Her dad jumped in. "Tell Rachel about your idea for a business."

Curtis' face lit up. "Your parents have shared with me some of the concerns they had raising a deaf son. Well, I'd love to start-."

Shannon stood. "Excuse me please." She whispered then went up the steps. Curtis paused and watched her go up the steps. When the door closed he continued.

"I'd like to start a business designed specifically to cater to the deaf community and run by deaf individuals."

"That's a rather broad business plan. What specifically do you plan to do?" Rachel wasn't interested in someone talking about 'businesses' that will help her family unless they were really profitable. Too many people these days were big on ideas, small on execution and planning.

He pushed his plate back a bit and started rearranging imaginary blocks on the table as he outlined his general proposal.

"Here, let me gather up…well now, where's Shannon off to?" Her mom said while she stacked the plates in a messy pile. Rachel picked up the gravy bowl. "I got it. You stay out here and listen to Curtis' idea. I'd like to know your take on it."

Shannon returned dragging a suitcase. "What will you do about telecommunication issues?" she asked in the first break. Her tone was gentler than when she went up the steps.

"That is one issue I'm still trying to resolve. Initially I thought a TDD would suffice but when I really started mapping out the business plan I saw that wasn't practical."

Rachel's mom returned with a tray full of white plates and thick black slices of chocolate cake. "Pretty clever don't cha think?" She said as she set a plate in front of Rachel.

"I think it sounds great. Shannon?" Shannon paused, fork in her mouth. She chewed quickly and looked back at Rachel.

"Why didn't you think of it?"

"I'd love for the two of you to help me with marketing when the time comes." Curtis asked then cut in to his cake.

"Of course. You know Adam is going to be here in a couple of days. You should get his input."

"He's been talking to him a bit, in the beginning stages."

Rachel paused. How long had this deal been in the works and why was this the first she heard of it. She quietly chewed on the cake that was no longer a treat but merely a dessert to her.

Okay, that was a bit harsh but she was hurt. She was the only person in the family who'd had both business training and had worked with the deaf for literally her entire life. They hadn't even considered her as a consultant on the project.

The other four continued to banter about and brainstorm. Shannon was suddenly in on the excitement too. Now that she realized Curtis really wasn't a dating prospect but was really a business opportunity Shannon's sour attitude had sweetened considerably.

Rachel excused herself and went up to her room to zip up her suitcase and steal a few moments alone. Still the walls of the 'guest' room showed memories of her childhood. A few stuffed dollies and a sun bleached unicorn sat in a corner shelf. The ribbons were no longer on her wall nor were any trophies. The room had remained, and likely would continue to be, an ode to Rachel's childhood.

As if eternally nine years old, twenty year old photographs adorned the walls and pink ribbons on old ballet shoes served as decorations on a child's dresser. Her dresser.

Graduation with honors wasn't enough, nor was striking out on her own and starting a business. She would always be their little girl, but not in a good way.

Backstory
Information that takes place before the actual events of the book is

called back story. A common issue with writers is they want to insert large amounts of back story in their writing. This is a huge mistake. It distracts from the story, it is almost ALWAYS telling, and it really serves the writer more than the reader or the story.

As you're reading, look for times when it appears there is back story that is distracting because of the way it is shared or because of the amount given in a single place. Mark it here and identify it in your own story.

Two

Rachel picked up a decorating magazine on the end table. She had arrived five minutes

early to Drew's office so she could make an offer on the house her and Shannon had looked at.

She liked the house but wasn't sure that she really wanted to move at the moment.

She hadn't been sure until Shannon talked her in to it on the ride home…

"Make a ridiculous offer and when they turn it down you can have Drew show you

another place." Shannon had insisted.

"But I can call him for a date without needing a house."

"You *can* but you *won't*."

Shannon was, as usual, right. On manners of the heart Shannon was dead on almost every

time. She prided herself in being the conscience of the office. Shannon was the conscience and

Rachel was the calculator.

That was why Shannon had never calculated in what Rachel should do if these people

actually took the offer.

"Rachel? Drew can see you now." the woman behind the desk indicated to a hallway.

Rachel got up and started in the direction she'd pointed. Drew appeared out of a door half way down.

"Oh, good. Rachel. I was coming out to get you."

"They told me you were ready."

Drew nodded and pointed to a long table sitting in the middle of a rather cramped room. The deep burgundy walls added to the sense of claustrophobia Rachel experienced when Drew closed the door behind them.

He opened a manila colored file folder. "Okay, so you want to offer ten thousand less than the asking price on the Healey place?"

"Yes." She said.

He wrote in the numbers and filled out the rest of the form to make an offer on the house he'd shown her last week.

"Do you have financing yet?"

"No but I have someone I can call if we need that."

"That's fine. I will write in that this offer is subject to you getting financing. That protects you from being bound if you aren't able to get a loan."

"Okay."

He checked off some boxes and scratched a few words in to blanks then spun the form around and gave her a pen. "I need you to sign and date it here."

She signed it and gave it back to him. "When will I know if they have accepted my offer?"

"Their agent should notify them of the offer today or tomorrow but they have thirty days to give us a decision." He peeled off the bottom copy and gave it to Rachel. "I wondered if you'd be interested in maybe going out some time?"

Shannon's plan works again.

"Sure, I'd like that."

"I don't often ask clients out but I felt like we made a connection at that first place we looked at."

"What can I say? Guys who have a fondness for giving flowers impress me."

He paused for a moment then the light of recollection popped on his face. "That's right. The flowers I planted along the walkway."

"Yep."

"I didn't know flowerbeds could be a pickup line but in this case I'm glad it worked." He looked down at his calendar. "How does tomorrow night look for you?"

She opened her palm pilot and scrolled down the calendar. "I have an appointment at six-thirty with a client. Does the next night work at all for you?"

"That works. When would you like me to pick you up?"

"My house is a fair distance from Woodhaven. Why don't you call me so we can figure out a place to eat and we can meet there?"

"Does six or seven work better for you?" He asked, as he looked up from his calendar.

"Let's do six-thirty."

"I'll see you then." He stood and shook her hand. Seemed a bit formal given the new level in their relationship but Rachel passed it off. His boss most likely frowned upon their agents dating their clients.

"But don't forget to call and tell me where."

"Right." He laughed and stuck out his hand.

"I have to say this, for once I'm glad my mom felt compelled to stick her nose in my personal life."

He continued packing up the papers she had just signed but stole quick glances a few times. "Did she tell you to go out with me?"

"No, she is the one who decided her daughter was thirty and needed a house so why not

call the cute realtor pictured on the sign." The second the sentence left her mouth she wanted to

grab it and cram it back in before it reached his ears. "I really didn't mean that the way it

sounded." She said in a desperate attempt to not make it sound like this date would be...well,

exactly what it was. A well orchestrated accident.

After a momentary pause he finished packing up his things and looked up at Rachel.

"Thank your mom for me." He said then winked. "I'll talk to you in a couple of days?"

"Yep." She walked through the door he was holding for her and out of the office. The

next thing she needed to check on was the financing. Curtis' number was somewhere in her

planner. She skimmed her address book but didn't see it. No, because it was in the business card

section. She flipped open the first page and lifted out the card, dialed the number, put in her

earpiece. He answered on the second ring.

"Hi Curtis this is Rachel, Jeff and Lisa's daughter."

"Hello Rachel. Good to hear from you. What can I do for you?"

"I made an offer on a house and I was wondering if you could do up a pre-approval for me.”

“Sure no problem. I can take the information over the phone but the easiest way is to

have you fill out the quick form on the website. I can plug that straight over and as soon as I hear

from the bank I can call.”

“How long does that take?”

“Couple of days usually.”

“Thanks. I’m heading back to the office. You should have it in your email by three.”

“I’ll watch for it.”

She hung up the phone. Her stomach tightened. When had she last eaten? Had to have

been at least six hours ago. There was a place not far down the road that her parents liked. She

turned in to Schmucker’s Restaurant parking lot. A neon sign blinked alternating lines of white

‘steam’ off of a red neon pie.

Inside the dining area was only large enough to hold five or six tables. She walked to the

counter and sat on one of the three empty stools. A paper menu with peeling laminate was stuck

between the salt shaker and the napkin dispenser.

“Can I help you?” A large woman in her sixties in a pink plaid dress and white apron stood across the counter.

Rachel scanned up and down the menu. "Do you have BLTs?"

"Sure do."

"I'll take that with a bowl of beef vegetable but could I have half of my BLT in a to go box?"

"Of course. Something to drink?"

"Water's fine."

The woman put the order back and Rachel scanned the diner. It was a snippet of the old Woodhaven. The one before the shopping mall came in on the eastern edge of town. Her parents had decried the subdivisions and retail outlets that soon followed but Rachel was seventeen when Woodhaven started to grow. For her having shopping and movies right there in town was an answer to prayer. That was when she did pray.

The woman came back with her food and Rachel finished up her lunch and left a 100 % tip which brought her bill to ten dollars. The look on the woman's face had been priceless. When she got back out to the car her cell phone was vibrating. Shannon's cell was on the display.

She pushed the call back button but it went straight to voicemail.

"Shannon, it's Rachel. Who's tall, dark and handsome and has a date with me Thursday? Call my cell to find out. Bye"

She hung up the phone but left the earpiece in her ear. For the next few miles she drove along quietly. Where would he decide to go for dinner? It didn't matter much. Mom would approve of this one. If she didn't then Rachel would completely give up on finding someone her parents would approve of.

"I told you it was a good idea to go house hunting." She said, imitating her mom's voice.

"You're right mom. And he's a good kisser too." That would get her riled. The phone started its new age ring. She pushed the button to answer.

"So Rachel, who is this date with? Not some completely hot Real Estate Agent is it?" Shannon gushed.

"Yes, that's exactly who it is."

"Details."

"There are none. I put in an offer on the house and he asked me out. The details don't come until after the date."

"There had better be details after a date with him."

Her phone beeped. She looked down at the screen. "Mom's beeping in. Adam's flight should be in soon. Let me take this call and I'll talk to you when I get to the office."

She clicked over to her mom.

"Hi hon. It's mom." Her mom's voice was at once frantic and mundane. A strange combination but the best one she could think of to describe the hurried speech but bored tone.

"Hi."

Rachel, do you think you could get Adam?"

Rachel looked down at the dashboard clock. "When does he get in?"

"Three-forty I think."

"That only gives me about an hour and a half to get to the office and out to the airport."

"You're not in the office?"

"No, I'm in Woodhaven."

"Why's that?" Her mom's voice changed. It was no longer urgent. Rachel noted it as odd but didn't think on it further.

"I made an offer on the place Shannon and I looked at when we were out this past weekend."

Her mom squealed. "That is wonderful hon. When will we know more?"

We? It was just a manner of speech but her mom's self-inclusion in to every major aspect of Rachel's decision making it grated at her just the same. She pushed away the voice in her head that said *tell her there's no 'we' in this decision* and opted instead to be polite. "He said he'd call me in a few days hopefully."

"Hopefully?"

"I guess they have up to thirty days to get back with me on the offer."

"That long?" Her voice was shrill. Apparently the notion of such a wait was offensive to her mom.

"You know it won't take that long. The house has been on the market for a few months now I think. I already called Curtis about pre-approval on financing."

"OOOhhh." Her mom said, somehow with a southern drawl at the end. "I'm so excited."

"Mom, I'm getting on the highway. Do you need me to get Adam?"

"Is it possible?"

"Yes. Is there something wrong?"

"Well, not really. Your daddy just overdid it outside doing lawn work and I'd feel better tendin' to him."

Every fall for the past three years daddy overdid the lawn work so Rachel knew exactly what her mom was dealing with. Although not old, unless someone thought the mid-fifties old, her daddy was cursed with a bad back that exerted its will every fall when it came time to cut back roses, rake leaves and cover perennials.

"I'll get Adam. You take care of daddy."

"Thank you." She gave Rachel the flight information and Rachel scribbled it all down balancing the notebook on the steering wheel.

"I'll see you tonight then mom." Rachel hung up the phone. She'd spent more time in Woodhaven these last few weeks than she had in the previous six months. As long as all of this didn't get her too far behind in work she wouldn't have a problem with it. She scanned her mental calendar and decided she was fine. There were no meetings on her agenda this week other than with Shannon. That was a stroke of luck given how busy they'd been recently.

When she got to the office she stopped long enough to pick up some work to do at home and to fill out and email the mortgage pre-approval application to Curtis. As promised she pushed the send key a little before three o'clock then she loaded up and went back out the door.

Three

The airport smelled like body odor and diesel. There were two airports Adam could have used. This was the smaller, and dirtier, of the two. Rachel stood between the two luggage belts. A large group of people gathered around them like dessert animals around a puddle. The monitor said that the belt on her right would have Adam's luggage so she split her attention between that belt and the door that people were coming through.

Now that she was here and she'd have the next little bit alone with her brother she allowed herself to get a bit excited. The broken, filtered information her mom had been feeding her about the relationship likely held little resemblance to the reality. Despite her mom's position as leader of the Wednesday Bible study she was known to bend the truth, sometimes substantially, when a situation involved her children.

It was that character trait that has caused their falling out. But that whole situation was in the past now and to dig it up would only cause more problems. Right now she needed to keep her attention on Adam and his problems so she could protect Adam.

Since no one had protected her.

The conveyor belt whirred to life followed shortly after by a gush of people through the door. She saw him and quickly ran in his direction. He looked up and saw her. His smile and

wave were a poor mask for the pain in his face. He had aged years since she saw him six months

ago. His skin was dull and his eyes droopy with dark bags underneath.

"Rachel." He said.

She signed his name by tapping her "A" hand against her temple. Tears burned her eyes.

She couldn't let him see her cry. Not when his pain was so intense. She threw her arms around

his neck and hugged him. Sobs ripped through his body and he hugged her tight.

Her big brother was broken and it was killing Rachel inside. He composed himself and

they walked to the belt to retrieve his luggage.

"You want go restaurant?" she signed in American Sign Language.

"Yes, we go eat before see mom, dad." He signed back.

She picked up his suitcase and carried it to the car. He tapped her shoulder.

"Cold here."

"Yes, long time beautiful sun. Two days ago change cold now, continue maybe through

spring. Don't know."

She lifted the suitcase in the trunk. It was fairly light. Hopefully that meant that despite his one way ticket he was planning on returning to California and Yvonne soon.

They decided to stop at Wendy's on the way to mom's house so they could talk without mom worrying about their delay.

Rachel picked at a salad while Adam shoved a double cheeseburger and fries in his mouth.

"You know mom have food home?" She asked him.

"Yes. Hungry now. Eat again mom, dad house."

Her stomach tightened but she wanted to know what had drug Adam away from the woman he adored in Southern California all the way back to Ohio, in the fall…alone.

Rachel gently touched Adam's hand to get his attention. He looked up. The whites of his eyes were covered with red lines. Rachel's eyes stung with tears again.

"Adam, what happen?"

He looked away for a moment before starting. "We go California things change."

That was why she had told him, begged him really, not to go out to California. Yvonne had confided in her that she didn't think God was calling them out to California. Rachel didn't get in to the God thing but she had a really bad feeling about them going too. Of course Mom had chalked it up to Rachel not wanting her big brother to leave. She hesitated before continuing.

"What change in California?"

"Yvonne stop love me."

Rachel's ears burned, something reserved for extreme anger. "Yvonne never stop love you." She signed so hard that she accidentally banged the edge of her hand on the table which threw it off balance. It tipped and she grabbed for her pop. She caught it but her salad slid off the side of the table and splattered all over the floor.

She dove to the ground and scooped up lettuce on to the plate. One of the Wendy's crew, a chubby boy with bad skin came over and mopped up the dressing. She threw the salad in the trash and tried to regain some composure. She looked hard in Adam's eyes and signed again, this time with more control.

"Yvonne never stop love you. Yvonne adore you." Adam looked away and Rachel touched his arm. He turned and faced her. "Why you think Yvonne no love you?"

"Sometimes know."

And that was all he had to say on the topic. Rachel pressed a little harder but Adam was no different than Mom. When a topic was closed it would not be discussed again until they decided. They gathered their things and went back to the car for the silent drive to their parents'

house.

As she expected when they arrived her mom immediately took Adam off to his old room

where the two of them could talk without the prying eyes or Rachel, or daddy.

"Hope your back gets better, daddy."

"It will." He grunted and pushed on the arms of his recliner as he stood. "You be safe

going home." He kissed her on the forehead.

"I will daddy. Take care of Adam."

"You know I do." He gave her a hug. Daddy's quiet strength was one of the few things

that gave her confidence that Yvonne and Adam's marriage could be saved. Daddy had a way

with Mom, just as she had a way with him. Their marriage was stronger than anyone else she

knew which made her mom's attitude towards Adam's marriage more confusing.

"I'll see you soon, daddy."

She went out to her car and drove home.

Four

Logan sat quietly watching the wind blow through the leaves of the large Oak tree in his

back yard. From his kitchen table he imagined a world where people would love each other.

Where they could be loyal. Aunt Tulla had taught him all about love and loyalty. She had been

his guardian for all the life he could remember. She took him to church on Sundays and made

sure he went to school.

She had an Oak tree too.

When he was a naughty boy she'd make him sleep under that Oak tree with boxer, her

half-blind German shepherd.

Boxer was a good boy. He was loyal.

Aunt Tulla had tried to teach Logan about Alpha Mu Epsilon.

Under the Oak Tree.

In Logan's back yard a dry leaf succumbed to the power of the wind and fluttered down

to the grass. It let go of the tree and fell. When it held down the winds could whip it around and

smash it in to branches, the trunk and other leaves. But once that leaf had the courage to let go

the wind could carry it and gently carry it to the soft grass.

He knew how the leaf felt. There were many times when he wanted to give up and let the winds carry him wherever they wanted. He could shrivel up inside and let the winds of the world blow him off of the Oak. Away from Tulla. Away from Alpha Mu Epsilon.

During those times Boxer was there to teach him. The cold winds would blow across his bare arms and the dry leaves would flutter down in the moonlight. They would blow away. Boxer would lay close to Logan and keep him warm.

Aunt Tulla taught him about following the rules. Boxer had taught him about loyalty.

Aunt Tulla wanted him to grow to be a good boy.

"Is fo yer own good, chile. Gotta get the wicked out cha."

Aunt Tulla wasn't fond of spanking. Said hands were made for loving. Love was very important to Aunt Tulla. Each night whether he slept in his bed or with boxer under the Oak she needed him to be sure and say "I love you."

Only time Aunt Tulla really tanned his hide was the day he refused to say "I love you."

It was the day boxer died.

It was the day he wanted to blow away.

A siren blaring down the road startled Logan out of his memories. Memories were good things. They showed you where you came from. They were a person's strength. Don't know

where you came from and you won't know where you're going.

He was going to Rachel.

He drank down his glass of white milk and set it in the sink. He always drank white milk.

Chocolate Milk was for gluttons.

Alpha Mu Epsilon was about persistence. It was about avoiding excess.

It was about Rachel.

Her name warmed his insides. God had brought Rachel to him.

The way they had connected. Things were moving along faster than he could have hoped

they would at that first meeting but then he had a feeling Rachel had been waiting for him all

along too.

She had been created for him like Eve for Adam.

Theirs would be a love story for the ages.

He'd see her again in a couple of days but the time drug when they were apart.

That was how he knew she was the one.

Info dumping—Backstory, only WORSE!!!

At the end of the last section we talked about back story. That is where you share information that is really outside of the story. When someone puts in a large amount of back story—or when they simply share a large amount of excess information—that is called an info dump. These are extremely common in the manuscripts I edit for clients. All of us have a tendency to want to make sure the writer 'gets it'. The problem is that an info dump is a lazy way of showing that information.

As you're reading, watch out for large sections of back story or information. Flag them and rework them.

Five

Rachel arrived at the restaurant at six-twenty. They had decided on a steakhouse that she

had heard rave review about. She stepped in to the dim entry way. To her right the bar was full of

women on barstools. There was only one man and he was at a table for two with a woman she

assumed was his husband. She walked to a wooden podium where an equally wooden woman

stood.

"My date isn't here you. Do you have a menu I can look at while I wait?"

"Sure." The woman handed her a menu. Rachel thanked her and sat down on the padded

bench along the wall. Despite the packed bar Rachel was the only person who waited to be

seated. She scanned the choices. As she imagined there was mostly beef, and surf-n-turf. There

were also quite a few items at "Market Price". She checked her wallet. When she picked the

place she hadn't realized how expensive it was. She had enough money to cover if she had to.

"Sorry to keep you waiting." Drew said when he walked in the door. He wore suit pants

and a white shirt with no tie. His top button was undone and as he walked toward her he began to

roll up the sleeves of his shirt.

"It's fine. I was a little early." She stood to greet him. He leaned in and kissed her on the cheek. She was startled by his advance but when he turned away as if nothing had happened she

concluded that maybe he was just very European.

The hostess motioned for them. "Right this way." Drew touched the small of Rachel's

back and she complied by stepping in front of him. They followed the hostess past what

appeared to be four separate dining areas, before entering a fifth room, holding five tables, with

only two of them occupied. Candles burned on each table, soft music wafted around them and

the whole place was elegant.

"Is this table all right?"

"Fine, thank you." Rachel said as she sat down in the chair Drew pulled out for her. The

hostess opened her menu and gave it to Rachel then did the same for Drew before setting the

wine list on the edge of the table and leaving them.

"This place is really nice. I'm glad you suggested it." He said.

"The girls at the office rave about the food here. I had no idea it was this fancy, or

expensive."

Drew opened the menu. "Wow, how much are you paying your employees?"

"I pay them well but I have a feeling they're paying on plastic if they eat here very often.”

“Did they have any suggestions from the menu?”

“Almost everything here is great they said but the most popular was either prime rib or

fillet mignon, medium rare.”

The server came out a few minutes later and took their orders.

Rachel gave the server her menu then placed her napkin across her lap. “Do you like

working in real estate?”

“Usually. The hours are long some weeks.”

“I think that can be true with any job.”

He nodded his head. On the table a small oil lamp threw a soft glow on his face. His

deep, smooth voice reminded her of a radio personality who hosted the all love song show from

eight to eleven every evening.

“Have you ever considered a job in radio?” She asked during a short lull in the

conversation?

He smiled and took a sip of his drink. “No, why?”

“You have the perfect voice for it.”

He chuckled, "Thank you. I've never had anyone say that before."

"I mean it." He looked away for a moment and Rachel soaked in his features. Shannon

was right, as usual. Drew was what she'd been looking for. She wouldn't need to go home and

read her romance novel with the radio on at night if Drew were there. His voice could be the

radio and his touch the romance novel.

The server stepped up to the table, "I have one rib eye with a potato and one rib eye with

asparagus." She set the plates in front of them.

Rachel cut her meat. It was the perfect shade of pink and the tender cut melted in her

mouth.

"I don't know how I've never heard of this place." He said before putting another bite in

his mouth.

"Do you find working in real estate affords you the opportunity to hit on lots of women?"

He finished chewing and started to cut off another piece as he spoke. "Not usually. I deal

with a number of couples or divorcees. I don't have many beautiful, single women pass through

my office."

"Good." She cut off a small piece of asparagus. "I wouldn't want to be jealous of all your appointments."

"You'd have nothing to be jealous of." They chatted between bites throughout dinner.

"Would anyone like dessert?" The server asked as she cleared the plates. They ordered cheesecake and coffee.

"Tell me about your family." She asked.

He shifted a bit in his chair a bit. "I'm not really close to my family at all." A flash of anger registered on his face but quickly softened. Rachel stiffened a bit. His eyes were wild when he was angry. "I volunteered for years at the Red Cross and Alzheimer's wards of Nursing homes. They are really my family, if you'd want me to point to the people I love and who support me."

"I'm sorry I didn't mean to bring up anything painful."

"Hey, you didn't know. It's a fairly normal question." His expression softened further. "I'd rather hear about your family."

"Well, I guess we have the All-American" family. Mom, Dad, Son, Daughter, I'm the baby of the family."

"And that is why your mom was house hunting for you?"

"No, my mom likes to nose in my life. That is why she was house hunting for me."

"Ooh, I sense some animosity." His voice reminded her of a school boy taunting a chum on the playground.

"No, just *issues* I guess. Everyone has them."

He nodded in agreement.

The server came back out with their dessert and coffee. The vanilla bean cheesecake melted in her mouth. She scooped up a bit of the raspberry sauce drizzled around the edge of her plate and took a second bit. "This is incredible."

"I will have to come here again." He looked around the room they were in as he spoke.

"Let me know when you do." That had sounded pretty forward.

They finished their cheesecake and ordered a refill on their coffee before they decided to call it an evening. The outside are was cool and damp.

"Smells like rain." She said.

"I was thinking the same thing. I like the damp smell of leaves in the fall." He inhaled deep and let it out slow. "Makes me want to jump in a pile of leaves."

She reached down and took his hand. He stiffened for a moment the interlaced his fingers with hers.

What was she doing? It was too late now. If she let go it would be rude. She'd gotten

caught up in the moment again. Why was she always doing things like this? She was going to

take this one slow but the evening, the food and-

"I had a great time tonight." He said and pulled her in front of him to take the other hand.

"So did I."

"I guess I'll be talking to you soon on the house."

"Yes." She shifted on the other foot and looked in his eyes. She hated first dates. They

were nice to look back on and remember your first date but that was only because you could look

back and laugh at all the dumb things you'd done.

Right now there was the first kiss question. The timing of the first kiss usually set the

entire pace for Rachel's relationships. Kissing on a first date and less than a month he'd be

spending the night if history was any indication. But if she put him off she was only postponing

and would have another awkward-

His lips brushed lightly against hers before he gently kissed her. As if flipping a switch

her body instantly took over and all reason and logic left. She kissed him back passionately losing herself in the touch of a relative stranger. Like the heroine in her current romance novel a

strong hero was snatching her out of her mind and causing her to live in her heart.

The kiss ended and she looked at him again but now with new eyes. The tension of first

kiss was gone and the tension of when to invite him over was a least two or three weeks away.

Right now she could live in the moment.

Six

Adam would be there any minute. Rachel raced around her apartment to put the food

she'd bought at the deli on to nice plates. Thankfully mom had agreed to drop him off and not

stay. She needed to talk about both of their relational issues.

The buzzer sounded and she let Adam up.

"When should I be back for'em?"

"I'm not sure." Rachel turned to Adam and signed. "When you want mom come back

you?"

"Doesn't matter."

Her mom put her fist on her hip. "Then how to I plan my afternoon?"

That wasn't Mom's issue at all and it only made Rachel madder. Adam was in his mid-

thirties and she still wanted to mommy the man. No wonder she hated Yvonne. Yvonne didn't

put up with it.

"Do whatever you had planned and if it isn't convenient to come get him I'll drive him

back out."

"I need rent car I think." Adam signed.

"Maybe good idea."

"No." Her mom both signed and spoke. "There is no need for him to rent a car."

"He here." Adam signed. "And he man can rent car."

Wow, Rachel couldn't remember Adam snapping at Mom like that before. She didn't think kids should be rude to their parents but it was a two way thing. Mom left and the two of them ate club sandwiches and chili at Rachel's dining room table.

"How has your visit been?"

"Good, I miss friends here and Ohio. People where I live not talk a lot. Don't know neighbors. People busy." He signed slowly as if carefully choosing each word.

"Why you not come back live Ohio?"

Adam watched her sign the question then turned away. He stood up and walked across the room. Rachel watched him. "Adam why won't you talk to me?" She said out loud but of course he didn't know. He had left for California with such joy ready to do 'God's work' as he put it but now he was back broken. That happened fairly often in Rachel's life. Oh, it was fine to get excited thinking you'd had an encounter with an all powerful being that was going to make sure life worked out for you.

The reality never fit the dream.

No, people ended up like her brother Adam. They go chasing some notion that they attribute to God and they give up a fine life to do it. Then when their marriage falls apart, their job gets cut or their life is destroyed they come back broken like Adam.

Then they blame themselves for some 'sin'.

Thankfully Rachel only beat herself with that stick once before she learned. She didn't spend her life trying to be perfect, whatever that was.

She walked to Adam and gently touched his shoulder. Adam turned to face her with tears in his eyes.

"Adam, can I ask you something?"

"Yes."

"Since we talked at Wendy's we haven't really gotten back to why you are back in Ohio."

"Why do you think Yvonne stopped loving you?"

"You never understand."

Of course she understood. Maybe she had never been married but she'd had enough relationships to understand giving yourself fully to a person only to have them decide they didn't want you any more.

"Explain me." She said to him.

"We go California I work hard." His gestures were exaggerated but Rachel didn't need to see the large gestures to know how passionate he was about this. "I talk lots of people and every, every I go talk pastors, I talk ministries share my vision but no one listen. Yvonne go with me, interpret. I day she say 'No, I stop go with you.' I mad, tell her she my wife I need with me. She tell me God no say come California."

"When that happen?"

"Two week before I come." He signed it then walked to the couch and sat down. "I tell her I know God. I hear God. She say not sure I can hear God now."

Rachel sat beside her big brother and put her arm around his neck. She was so sick of hearing about God and what He did and did not want. People blew up shopping centers for God and people stayed in loveless marriages. God wasn't a benevolent dictator, that is if the Christian God actually existed. No, this religion that had been used for centuries to keep women oppressed and men in power was now becoming every person's excuse or crutch.

If it hadn't been for Shannon helping Rachel escape from the guilt of that life she would

probably be in the same situation as Adam. Worried sick that she was going to miss what some

voiceless mist wanted and being willing to give up the love of your life, your hopes and dreams

for the illusion of a hereafter.

At least in her confusion over her love life she only had people to contend with. Between

her mom and Shannon trying to choose Mr. Right for her she had enough to worry about. If she

had an elusive being to add to the mix…no wonder people went postal. Their trying to read a

two-thousand year old book to figure out a twenty-first century world and apply it using gut

reactions, of course attributed to spirits in competing factions. She wanted to scream thinking

about it.

Adam tapped her leg. Rachel turned to face him. "Mom tell me you date man who find

you house?"

"The realtor?"

"Yes."

"I went on one date. I not sweetheart."

"Oh, mom try make you fall love again." He smiled and poked at her like they did when they were kids. He understood better than anyone how mom liked to pry. "You like realtor."

"His name is Drew. I think I like him."

"You no sure." His smile was gone. "Rachel, you be sure. Need love if you make marriage work. No love it too hard and not fun."

"I know but Shannon and Mom think Drew wonderful. I like fine. He good kisser."

"Awww" he vocalized. Rachel laughed. When it was the two of them vocalization was reserved for the biggest shocks. Her brother knew she wasn't 'pure' any longer but he didn't judge her and with each relationship he acted as if she were a little girl who wasn't familiar to the ways of the world. "You careful kiss boys. Good boys respect you. Bad boys take you further."

"Drew bad boy." She signed

"Awww, Way chall." he vocalized. She loved how her brother said Rachel. He could speak clear enough to be understood when in an all hearing environment that required it but since they both signed they never used their voices together. It also cut down on their mom eavesdropping when they were younger. He always called her Way chall though. To her it was a term of endearment, not a mispronunciation.

"Adam, I so happy you back Ohio. I wish you live here, have family near me."

"When God tell me live Ohio again I come home."

Seven

If only life could be as simple as a spreadsheet. Rachel could make an equation, set the if

then question then plug in values. The computer would run the program and every time a new

variable was introduced the spreadsheet could make adjustments. Even with the spreadsheet she

was working on that morning returning error messages over and over she had found solving that

problem far easier than her emotional woes.

Why wasn't she attracted to Drew?

Here she had a man who was handsome, funny, successful, and had the voice of a radio

announcer and it wasn't enough. Worse yet she knew he was going to call some time this week,

probably today. She'd put in the offer almost a week ago and still hadn't heard back. He'd

emailed but she had her auto-reply on so he had no idea if she was reading them or not.

Each email was about the same. He was thinking about the fun they'd had and the

goodbye kiss. She'd thought she had a month but this guy was looking for a physical relationship

almost immediately. Even in the romance novels those things took time. Shannon thinks he is a

great guy and she usually is dead on with these things but it's not there.

What about love and romance and slowly wooing a woman. Rachel pushed back from her desk and paced in her office. She had no idea what to do. Shannon was clear and Mom was clear

but Rachel wasn't. She wanted more than great looks. How dumb did that sound? She decided to

call Drew and check on the house. Maybe she'd hear what she needed in his voice.

She called his cell.

"Hi Rachel I have some bad news."

"What is it?"

"The owners rejected your offer."

"They didn't have a counter offer?"

"They said no. I think they are trying to hold out for asking price. Which if that's the case

in the market right now it is going to be a while."

"I like the house but I can't go up any more than two thousand dollars."

"And I'm sure that won't be enough to make them budge. I found out this morning but I

was waiting because I was hoping they'd go ahead and offer something back but their realtor

didn't return my calls."

"That's fine. Like I told you before, I wasn't really looking. It was more window

shopping."

"I'll go ahead and run properties like that one for you if you'd like."

She thought for a minute. "I'd like to be no more than thirty minutes from work and forty-five minutes from my parents ideally."

"I will see what I can find. You want to keep the same search parameters?"

"Yes. I like that house, except the teeny master bedroom. If you can find something similar to that one, in the right location around my offer price we'll be all set."

"Great." The line went silent for a few moments. "I had fun the other night."

"Yes, I've been kicking myself for never checking that restaurant out before. I need to listen to the office chatter more often."

"I'd like to see you again." And there it was.

"Drew." Shannon passed by Rachel's door and stopped. "I was thinking." Rachel spun her chair away from the door in an attempt to get a bit more privacy.

"Don't you dare." Shannon whispered from the doorway. She walked in to the office and stood toe to toe with Rachel.

"Maybe we should stay on a professional level right now."

"What are you doing?" Shannon scolded.

"But I thought you enjoyed yourself."

"I did."

"Then what's wrong?"

"Don't you dare dump that guy."

"Was I rushing you? It felt to me like you wanted that kiss as much as I did."

"No, I mean yes. No you weren't rushing me."

"Don't tell him no."

Rachel shot a glare at Shannon. "No, you didn't offend me at all. I had an incredible time with you and I'm not ruling out seeing each other in the future." She said that part for Shannon's benefit the tried to shoo her away with her hand. Shannon only moved back a few feet and stood with her arms folded in front of Rachel. "I think it wiser until we are done with our business dealings that we should hold off on a relationship. I'd hate for a personal relationship to get in the way of our professional relationship."

"You're assuming something would go wrong." She knew he would be agitated but his tone put her on edge.

"I don't want things to be awkward."

"And this isn't?" Shannon said a bit louder than a whisper. Rachel swatted her hand at

Shannon.

"Drew, all I'm saying is until we are done house hunting let's stay professional and we

can examine our feelings after that."

"It was nice of you to tell me this now and not string me along or anything." The

agitation was blending with sarcasm to create one very unattractive package.

"I-."

His tone was firm "I'll email some properties to you. When you're ready to make an

offer, let me know. We can handle it all by fax if that will be easier for you."

"Ok, I-."

"You'll hear from me soon." There was a click then the dial tone.

"What in the world are you doing?" Shannon said when Rachel put the phone back in the

cradle.

"I don't have time for a relationship right now."

"You don't have time?"

"No, I don't." She snapped. The bitterness in Drew's voice had her wondering whether she wanted to even maintain a business relationship with him at this point.

Shannon sat down. "We've been friends for almost ten years now. You never have time. First you needed to concentrate on school. Then it was graduation. Next it was starting this business and now it is maintaining this business."

"Wait, there was a pretty significant exception in there that you're glossing over."

"That was an anomaly."

"But he-."

"My point is you have found a man who is successful, handsome and who seems to really want to start something with you. Why are you going to throw it away?"

"But I'm not attracted to him, except physically."

"So have fun for a while and see what happens."

"I'm done having fun, I want a relationship." Shannon laughed and when Rachel realized what she had said she cracked a small smile. "I'm trying to be serious. I want to have a relationship where-."

"Never mind Rachel, I'm not in the mood to fuss with this right now. You want to throw this away for some fantasy that ain't gonna happen then do it. But I do not want to hear about how confused you are or any of it.”

“It was one date.”

“But it was going to be two.”

“I hear you. Now I have work to do.” Rachel spun her chair back around to her desk. “I

never asked you to come in in the first place.”

Preaching isn't for books.

How many times have you been reading a book and suddenly the story paused to force some political, social or religious view on you? Was it irritating? Distracting?

While it is sometimes more common for a character in a Christian/inspirational book to preach, the fact is that I've seen NYT best selling writers of main stream suspense stop the entire action to give me a lecture on the environment or their thoughts on a political party. Readers read for entertainment, not to be lectured.

It is logical for a politician in a book to talk about a bill or a pastor to share scripture, stopping the story in order to lecture is poor craft.

The characters in this book are Christians and sometimes preachy. How could this be rewritten to be more organic without stripping that part of the character completely?

Eight

"Rachel, I haven't seen you for a couple of weeks. Why don't you come over Saturday

for lunch?" Her mom's call came just as Rachel was sitting down to a fast food dinner for one.

"I'm not staying over mom."

"I'm not asking you to. We have a turkey your dad got from the company for Christmas.

The thing is eleven pounds and that is too big for the two of us to eat by ourselves. Now Fall's

coming around again and they'll be another turkey so I thought I'd have you and a few others

over for lunch Saturday."

"What others." Rachel was suspicious. She didn't want to walk in to some sick dating

game.

"A few of my friends from church."

"Mom."

"I invited three people."

"And how many are young men?"

"One."

"Who?"

"Curtis."

"So what you are asking me is if I want to come over so you can fix me up with while you guys watch?"

"I'm thinking one o'clock. You can come over Friday night or first thing Saturday morning. Adam said he'll have the chessboard set up when you get here."

"Tell him I'll be over Saturday and that I've been playing against the computer so he'd better be ready."

They hung up and Rachel returned to her meal. It was no longer good enough for her mom that Rachel was dating a man. She needed to have a spare. It was fine. Curtis was a nice guy and fun to talk to. He knew Lisa, Mom, well enough to know he was being set up as a love interest for her daughter and he took it in stride.

As far as church people went Curtis seemed about the most normal of any of her mom's friends. He didn't put on airs or look down his nose at Rachel.

She ate another French fry. If she was going to keep her weight in check during the holidays she'd have to cut back on her Wendy's French fries. But that was still a touch over six weeks away. She bit another fry.

She'd have to talk to Adam before everyone got there, oh and Mom too. Even though she was only friends with Curtis she didn't want him to know she'd gone out with Drew. Mom would probably keep her mouth shut without Rachel saying something but she preferred to play it safe.

It was better to keep the conversation with Curtis on things that didn't go anywhere near relationship or dating. All her mom would need was a small crack and she'd try to connect the two of them.

Nine

At eleven-thirty Saturday morning Rachel arrived at her parent's house. Both of their cars were parked on the street and the garage was empty. Rachel pulled her car in to the garage and closed the door.

"Good. You're here." Her mom said for hello when Rachel came in the kitchen. "Adam has been waiting for you. He has the Chess set up in the other room."

"He doesn't waste any time does he?"

"Neither do you." Her mom laughed. She picked up a potato and cut the peel off with a knife. "Oh, when you're done playing Chess could you help me with a few things in the kitchen?"

"Yeah, call me when you need me." Rachel walked out through the kitchen and in to the living room. Adam was on the couch reading a book. Over on a small wooden table near the bay window he had set up a chess board with mahogany and artificial ivory pieces. She tapped his shoulder and without looking back walked straight to the board.

"Ready to lose?" She signed.

"Never."

The two of them sat in complete silence. Their focus was on the chess board and nothing else existed.

"Hey you two I hate to interrupt but everyone will be here soon." Rachel looked up at her mom. After forty-five minutes of playing neither was in check.

"Finish later?" Rachel signed.

Adam waved her on and Rachel followed her mom in to the kitchen.

"Wash your hands then will you get the mashed potatoes finished up?"

"No problem."

"The mixer and everything else is there." Rachel poured the warm mixture of melted butter and evaporated milk into the blended potatoes. Her mom made the best mashed potatoes. The secret was to using baked potatoes or cook off some of the water of boiled potatoes before adding the rest of the ingredients.

"So who is the other couple?"

"I don't know if you know them. They're some newlyweds your dad and I have taken under our wing."

"So you can show me how great married life is?" Rachel smiled to her mom.

"I think it's great. Your daddy and I are best friends."

"But most marriages aren't like that."

"I know." Her mom looked toward the living room where Adam was sitting with daddy.

"Most people don't have a marriage like your daddy and me but my concern is the two of you. I want you and Adam to have happy marriages." She paused again to put the corn casserole in the oven. "That's why we want you to meet a nice man."

"I will but it has to be in my time mom. Can't you be happy for who I am now instead of thinking once I've-." Rachel paused. She was getting agitated and that wasn't the point of today. She came over to see Adam and Curtis. Today was for fun not tension. "Mom, I promise when I find the right guy I am ready to settle down. Okay."

Her mom nodded her head and turned but not before Rachel saw her mouth "Thank you, Jesus." Oh well, if her mom felt better thanking a dead philosopher Rachel wasn't going to fuss.

They finished up in the kitchen and greeted the guests as they arrived. Curtis was the last there.

"Hello again." Rachel said when she opened the door.

"Hello."

She held the door open for him. "I don't know if my mom warned you but this is a dating ambush."

"A what?"

"Mom invited over another couple and you. Presumably to create a third couple for the afternoon."

"I see." He said and he nodded his head. "So this is an unofficial first date. And what about Adam?"

"Oh he's here but his job is to report to mom later on what everyone was whispering since he reads lips so well."

"Good to know."

"Come on in and make yourself comfortable." She motioned to the living room. They had arranged a couple of folding chairs between the couch and daddy's lazy boy recliner. The seats were full when they walked in.

"Do you mind sitting on the bricks in front of the fireplace?"

"You mean the hearth?"

"Is that what you call it?" Rachel laughed and squeezed in the circle formed by the couch and chairs.

"I think so."

"There's no fire burning so we won't get hot."

"Good to know."

They sat down and leaned up against the glass front with a sizable distance between the

two of them.

"Have you had a chance to talk to Adam?"

"No." Curtis replied. "Just a few passing words. I don't know sign language and I think I

still make old hearing people mistakes."

"Talking slow and over exaggerating your words?"

"Yep."

Rachel pounded her foot on the floor twice. Adam turned and looked. So did Daddy.

"Rachel, I could have tapped him for you." Daddy said, in his 'Father Knows Best voice.'

"I know but I didn't want to interrupt."

"And stomping wasn't an interruption?"

She waved Adam over to the Ottoman next to her.

She turned to Curtis. "I'm going to sign and talk at the same time. ASL is not exactly like English so sometimes I slow down a bit or stop talking. I will look at you when I've finished interpreting what Adam says. Then you can start."

"How is ASL different from English. I thought sign language was English."

She signed what Curtis had said to Adam then told him to read the people's lips until she was done explaining ASL to Curtis. He laughed and waited.

"What's so funny?" Curtis asked looking from Rachel to Adam.

"I told him to eavesdrop on everyone else while I'm talking to you."

"Oh. I saw a show once where a woman was in the FBI and her job was to read lips."

"Sue Thomas, FBI. Great show. That's a real woman you know." Rachel tucked a bit of hair behind her ear.

"Yes. She's a Christian." Curtis again looked between Rachel and Adam as he spoke. He had clearly done some research on the deaf community for his business. She hated when people pretended Adam wasn't a part of a conversation.

"Yes." Adam said in his nasal voice. "I went to hear her speak at a church once. She's very funny."

"I was amazed in her trust in God." Curtis turned away from Rachel and focused on Adam. "I haven't actually met her but I saw her talking in a church on tape once. You're right. She is really funny."

Adam started to laugh. "Yvonne and I went together when I saw Sue Thomas." Adam bent over and held up a finger. He laughed harder and tears started to run down his eyes. "Rachel, interpret." He signed.

"He wants me to interpret."

Curtis turned back to Rachel.

Adam began. "Tell him when I see S.T. there long line see her. I want hurry and I ask Yvonne interpret for me so I not slow read lips."

She told Curtis what Adam had said. Curtis started laughing.

"That is the most ridiculous thing I've ever heard."

"What's so funny over there?" Daddy called over.

Rachel told the rest of the group and there was a mild chuckle but nothing link the belly laugh going on with Adam and Curtis.

"Okay boys." Rachel both said and signed at the same time. "Did you want to talk or not?"

"Yes." Curtis said. "But you were telling me about ASL."

"Real quick there are a few different kinds of sign language. There is SEE which is Signed Exact English. There is ASL, American Sign Language and then there is Pidgin sign. SEE is obvious. It's English. ASL is more like French in its structure and it also leaves out words like to, at, the."

"Didn't know that."

"So how do you keep the two straight when you are talking to him and hearing people."

"It's funny. When I watch his signs I don't really pay attention to what I'm saying. I say what I see. Like you can read a book and not remember the words even though you said them out loud."

"I never thought of it like that."

"Y'all can come on out en eat." Her mom called.

"Adam, eat." Rachel signed.

They walked to the table, where her mom made certain Rachel and Curtis sat next to each other. They had the blessing then started eating. The meal was pleasant with everyone chatting back and forth at the table. After she helped mom clear the table Rachel went back out to the

hearth where Curtis was already sitting with Adam.

"We were talking some business. Could you ask him a few questions for me?"

"Sure." Rachel scooted closer to Curtis so they were both across from Adam.

"Ask him if he'd come by my place this week to look over my ideas for the new

business."

She interpreted. "Adam says that would be fine and that we make a really cute couple."

"What?" Curtis said.

What had she done? Her cheeks started to burn. "Um, I'm sorry." She wanted to slink up

the steps. She felt like she had walked in front of the whole school with her skirt tucked in her

pantyhose.

"It's fine. He was paying you a compliment." Curtis said. "Can you finish for me?"

Rachel nodded and interpreted the rest of the conversation. Adam left to talk to the other

guests leaving Rachel and Curtis alone on the hearth. She now felt awkward sitting next to him

on the bricks but sitting on the ottoman and facing him would be equally as uncomfortable.

"Thank you for your help on the pre-approval." She finally said.

"You're welcome. How is house hunting?"

"Well the offer I made on the first house was turned down flat but Drew is looking for other places."

"Who is Drew?"

"The realtor."

"Ah, how far do you live from here?"

Rachel turned back to Curtis. "About half an hour or so."

"Are you looking to move closer?"

She laughed. "Not really. Mom is trying to move me closer against my will."

He smiled back at her. "You know, your mom speaks very highly of you." His voice held a soothing quality which surprised Rachel because it was so much higher pitched.

"My mom? Really?"

"Yes. I hear updates on you and Adam fairly regularly."

"My mom is a matchmaker." She laughed. "She means well but unfortunately she lays it on a little thick sometimes."

"No. She doesn't talk like that."

Rachel turned toward him and folded her arms. "How does she talk?"

"She is very proud of how you've created a successful business at such a young age and that you have the confidence you do."

"She said that?" Rachel looked out to the dining room where her mom and Adam were busy setting out mini-cheesecakes out for dessert. Curtis continued to speak.

"Yes. She's told me she worries about you being on your own but she knows you are a strong woman."

She turned back to Curtis. "I had no idea my mom felt that way."

"She has good reason to. You're a wonderful woman."

She looked straight at him. His playful smile was gone replaced by intense blue eyes that were fixed on her, searching. He was putting out a ping. At least that was the term she had given it. A man put a compliment out in the air to see how she would respond. If she smiled and blushed he would be emboldened. If she deflected it he didn't have to feel rejected. She felt heat burning in her face. Despite her best efforts she was blushing.

"Thank you." She smiled then turned away.

"I know your mom kind of threw us in an awkward position today but I'm glad we had a chance to meet socially.”

He wasn’t anything like Drew but she felt a tug on her heartstrings. Maybe that was why she felt that way. “Me too.”

“And thank you for helping me with Adam.”

“My pleasure. You are going to have to learn some sign language if your going to run a business.”

“Yep, I’ve been trying to avoid it since I’m awful with languages but I need to bite the bullet and start learning.”

“It’s not that hard.”

It felt awkward now. Their light-hearted banter was now forced questions and stilted replies. Despite that she wanted to keep talking. She enjoyed sitting with him this afternoon sharing fun stories and laughing. Years ago this was life: Saturday afternoons with mom, dad and Adam playing chess or scrabble and laughing at old stories.

It was like the first couple of years of college when Yvonne, Adam and-.

She stopped before the pain got a foothold again. Those memories needed to stay tucked away with all their hurt.

It was enough to say it had been a long time since she had felt so light. And almost as

long since she'd felt so much heartache. That was back when she did pray.

Ten

Logan watched her get in her car and start down the road.

"Yes, Rachel, Yes." He whispered. He knew she could sense his presence. He was

drawing her to him. She wanted to move here, to Woodhaven, where she would be closer to him

and their life together. Of course she was the one. "You'll say yes to me won't you Rachel?" She

drove down the road to her other life but soon, soon she'd be here. In his territory. He was

drawing her in closer to him. Patience was all that was required. After love was patience.

Eleven

Rachel wrapped a plate in newspaper and set it down in the cardboard box on her counter. She reached for the next plate and the muscles in her neck groaned. Hopefully she could get out of the office early enough for a massage one day next week.

"How in the world did you get them to close on the house so fast?" Shannon asked as she taped a box of books shut in the next room.

"The house had been empty for four months and they were ready to be rid of it."

"Drew didn't have anything to do with it did he?" Shannon still kept his name in at least two or three conversations a day. Rachel hadn't forgotten how perfect people thought he was for her, even after only a couple of dates. It wasn't only Shannon. Her mom also made it a point to remind Rachel how wonderful he was. She put the last two plates down in the box and climbed off her step ladder.

"Shannon can you tape up my box too and I'll label them."

"Averting the question."

"No, I'm not. He only helped me find the house. I don't think he did anything to try to get me a better deal." Rachel wrote "books" with a thick black marker that smelled similar to nail polish remover. "We need a new marker. This one is making me light headed."

"That's why I like it." Shannon took the marker out of Rachel's hand and sniffed it.

"How did it go when you saw Drew again?"

"Fine. I've talked to him quite a bit." Drew was his usual charming self but Rachel was a

bit more reserved on the few occasions they'd been together, professionally, since the night at his

house.

"I know but you put him off until after you got the house. Now you have the house. Do

you think he will still be so easily put off?"

Shannon had plenty of reasons why Rachel had overreacted to his…aggression that night

at his house. She was probably right. Rachel didn't like to be led on either. On the other hand his

reaction was only part of the reason she didn't feel comfortable there. She felt, unsettled, there.

But for the sake of peace she had learned to keep her opinion to herself when she was talking to

Mom and Shannon. Those two matchmakers saw wedding bells in their eyes and she wasn't in

the mood right now to go through why it wasn't going to happen.

"Who said I was going to put him off now? I never said I didn't like him. I said I didn't

think it was smart to date someone who was helping me find a house."

"Which makes no sense."

"Whatever."

Shannon picked up the box of books and moved it to the other side of the living room.

There had to be at least three dozen boxes that needed to be moved in to the truck still sitting in

this front room. Things were multiplying. There was no way she'd had all this stuff in her

apartment. She picked up a long narrow box and started loading DVDs in to it.

"So are you going to go out with him again?"

"Who? Drew?"

"Of course." Shannon brought CDs off of the music rack and stacked them next to her.

"I'm not sure. That Curtis guy is kind of cute too."

"Right."

"You don't think so?"

"He's not your type, remember."

"Yes."

Of course she remembered what happened before but Curtis was different. Curtis was

kind, gentle and funny.

Just like last time…

But this was completely different. He did nice things for no reason. Never once had they mentioned relationship but he brought her a dozen roses at closing. They were different colors and when she asked him why he'd said "Because I wasn't sure which color would go you're your new house better."

Shannon wouldn't see that though. All she remembered was when she had been hurt, in college. Shannon picked up the pieces. She had no idea how she would have gotten through those first couple of years without Shannon supporting her…watching out for her.

"So are those the only roses you've gotten recently?"

"Huh?"

"Remember the little gift on your car."

"Why in the world would you bring that up?"

"I noticed the flowers over there on your table."

"Curtis gave those to me."

"Ah."

"Nothing like that. He was at Mom's when I stopped in to see Adam and he-."

"No need to explain to me."

Rachel's cell phone chimed across the room on the end table. Shannon picked it up and looked at the screen.

"It says unknown."

"Give it here." She took the phone and flipped it open. "Hello?"

"Rachel?"

"Yes?"

"Jeremy Wright. Our cars met about a month ago."

"Oh Jeremy, hello."

"I hadn't heard from you on a bill. You aren't going through your insurance are you?"

His voice was at once concerned and scolding. It wasn't a combination Rachel liked.

"No, I haven't had the time to get it fixed. I'm in the process of moving."

His voice softened. "I didn't know you were moving. When will that be?"

"Right now."

"Oh, your moving at this moment. I'm really sorry to interrupt. Give me your new address when you get settled and I'll send your check as soon as you get a quote."

"You can send it to my address on the business card."

"I'd feel better knowing that you got it and it wasn't intercepted at work."

"It's fine. I'm co-owner so I usually open all the mail. You can use that address."

"Oh, well then good. I see the address right here. I'll wait to hear back from you."

"Okay, bye." She flipped the phone shut.

"Guy who hit your car?"

"Yep." Rachel put the phone back on the small wooden end table and resumed packing.

"Drew will be there today with my keys so we'll have to call him when we get the first load in the truck."

"Why's that?"

"The old owners forgot one set of keys so I didn't get them all at closing. Drew offered to bring them by when we moved in."

"I'll bet he did."

Heavy-Handed foreshadowing

Watch out for Heavy Handed foreshadowing. While this can be as obvious as the clichéd "Little did he know there was an axe murderer on the

other side of the door", sometimes it is more subtle and shows up with the writer taking a clue one step too far.

As you read, look for places where the clues were well placed as well as places where they were overly obvious. Note them in the story and look for them in your own writing.

Twelve

Rachel eased her car on to the side street that led to her new house. The things her dad strapped to her cars roof rack clicked again. "We're almost there. Don't fall off now." The area was much more Suburban than the nice apartment she was leaving behind but Woodhaven was a sweet little town where kids could ride their bikes at dusk on the sidewalk.

It was much quieter too. The trees and tall shrubs that lined the streets and yards help cut down on traffic noise considerably. She turned in to her new driveway and pulled to the back of the house. Shannon pulled her car in front of the detached garage and her dad parked in front of the house. She got out of the car. Everything on they'd put on the roof rack was still there by some miracle.

"You must be the new neighbor."

Rachel turned to the direction of the chain link fence that ran the length of her back yard. A man with white hair, white mustache and squinting eyes stood with a small pair of hedge clippers in his hand.

"Yes." She walked to the fence and stretched out her hand. "I'm Rachel."

"Names Wade." He dusted his palm on grubby trousers before shaking her hand. "Nice to see someone in this place again.”

“Thank you. I-.”

“Didn’t want to keep you none. Wanted to be a bit nosey is all. I’m sure we’ll have lots

of time to get to know each other after you’re settled.” He turned and walked back to his house.

“Nice neighbors.” Shannon said behind Rachel.

“Be nice.” Rachel turned around. Did you see Drew?”

“Drew, Curtis and your dad are all three on the front porch exchanging guy talk.”

She walked along the hedges that separated her driveway from her neighbor. The yard

was narrow along that side of the house but the back yard was deep enough that Rachel expected

summer entertaining wouldn’t be too much of a problem. She rounded the corner of the house

and walked across the grass. The men saw her and abruptly finished their conversation.

“Rachel welcome home.” Drew’s footsteps echoed on the wooden porch. He reached out

a small metal ring that held the rest of her keys.

“Thank you.” She looked at the three keys. “Which one goes to the front door?” She held

out her palm.

“This is the key to the back door” he lifted a silver key with a round top. “And this little brown one goes to the front door. You also have this one that goes to the garage if you want to

lock the overhead door but the former owners said the lock is a real pain." He lifted the ring by

the brown key and handed them to her.

"Great." She took the keys from him and unlocked the door. The large wooden door

groaned open in to a large living room. She stepped in to the living room her footsteps echoing.

"There's a white shag rug and pad in my car. That needs to go in the living room before

any of the furniture comes in."

To her right an archway stretched nearly the entire length of the wall separating the

dining room and living room. Through the dining room to the other side a staircase that led to the

second floor was open on the left. From the front door the kitchen was straight ahead and then

the basement steps. She could have fit her entire apartment in half of the first floor of this house.

"This is a really nice place Rachel." She turned to see Curtis standing almost directly

behind her.

"I was thinking the same thing." She stepped further in to the house. Her footsteps

echoed on the wooden floors. She needed to remember to buy a rug for the living room and

dining room to cut down on the sound.

"Your dad and I are going to start hauling in furniture. Is that okay with you?"

"Yes, Adam will be here soon too."

"Hopefully he's not chatty." Curtis let out a small laugh.

"Why's that?"

"Hands." Curtis wiggled his hand around as if to imitate sign language.

"Where do you want this box?" Rachel turned and saw Shannon standing on the other side of the screen door holding a small box. Drew was standing next to the truck while her dad piled boxes on top of the one Drew was already holding. Curtis opened the screen door for Shannon then continued out to the truck. Rachel looked at the top to check the label. "The kitchen is straight through there." She set the slider on the door to hold it open.

Rachel walked out the door for a box and passed Curtis and Drew. "Thank you for helping guys. I'll have to refer you to my friends." Both laughed. She lifted a small box and walked in the house.

"This isn't a bit awkward is it?" Shannon mumbled in to Rachel's ear.

"Keep your mouth shut and everything should be fine."

Shannon nodded and walked back out to the front. Rachel put the box along the wall of what was now her dining room.

"Your brother's here." Shannon yelled in the house before coming in and plopping down

another box.

"It looks like you have quite a crew going here." Her dad motioned to Drew and Curtis

hauling in boxes. "I guess Adam and I can go down to the ice cream shop."

"Or, you could help and maybe all of us can go." She scanned the boxes in the back of

the U-Haul. "These boxes here look like first floor stuff. The living room is to the left, dining

room to the right and kitchen is straight through." She turned and signed the same to Adam and

went back to unload her car.

"Rachel," Drew walked up to her as he slid his phone in its holder. "I'm going to have to

run. I got a call from someone on another property."

"Thank you so much for your help. You didn't have to do it."

"Not a problem at all." Drew looked around then said quietly. "I'll call this week to check

in and make sure everything is all right."

"I'll look forward to it." When she turned around her dad was smiling a crooked smile at

her. "Quite the customer service at that realty agency."

"Okay dad." She grabbed another box. When her mom joined them two hours later the truck was emptied except for a few pieces of furniture and they were beginning to fill the kitchen cupboards with dishes and the canned goods she'd brought from the apartment.

Her mom scanned the room. "You've got this about wrapped up."

"Not really. We still have to unpack everything." Rachel set three square pillar candles on her dining room table.

"I can help unpack if that will help." Her mom said and she started for the kitchen.

"Actually mom, can you unpack my clothes." Rachel grabbed a box then hesitated. "I'm trying to organize my kitchen as I go but if you can put the things in the upstairs bathroom-."

"Sure. Whatever you need done."

Rachel took a box and led her mom up the steps. Her feet sunk down in the plush carpet. "Isn't this carpet great mom?"

"Yes it is. Good pad."

"After ten years of dorm carpet and apartment carpet this feels like a slice of heaven."

"It is nice."

They turned down the hall to the main bathroom. "Mom, put the taupe towels in here for now until I get out to buy others.”

“Are you sure you want those nasty older ones in your bathroom?” Her mom crinkles her nose and bent over to open a box.

“I certainly don’t want them out for everyone to see when they come over.” Rachel dug through the towels in her box. “Why don’t you stick the older towels in the back of the linen closet. It’s this door here.” She tapped on a small door in the hallway. “Put out a set of the taupe on the towel racks and put the rest in my bathroom. I’ll try to get out sooner and get the new ones bought.”

“That will be better.”

Beige walls met her in every room. Taupe was a fairly decent color to make the bathroom look a bit better until she could get some paint. Rachel lifted the corner of peeling border behind the bathroom door.

“What color should I paint this?”

Her mom never looked up from the box. “You don’t wanna go too dark. Room’s much too small for deep colors.”

“I know that. I was thinking taupe walls and amethyst towels and accents.”

"That'd be pretty. Nice contrast but soft and feminine."

"That's what I thought."

"Rachel." Someone bellowed from downstairs.

"Be right there." She yelled back. "I should have four or five sets of those towels so put out one and put the rest in my bathroom. My rooms down there." Her mom looked up to see the direction Rachel pointed then pulled out more towels.

"Better get on downstairs, now. I got this handled."

Rachel walked down to her new bedroom and stepped in. The room felt like it could go on forever. There was not a piece of furniture in it yet and she could enjoy the size. The carpet was soft like the rest of the upstairs but it was brighter. A large southern window splashed sunlight across the carpet. Everything was fresh and clean, like a new outfit, and she was anxious to see her things make it comfortable.

"Rachel." The voice downstairs called out again.

She glanced around the room again and shuffled down the steps. "Sorry, I was looking around to figure out where to put furniture."

"Good because your dad and I were going to bring in the last of the furniture so he could take the truck back." Curtis spoke as Rachel moved down the staircase.

"Okay." She looked at her watch. "That should work out fine."

"And I was hoping maybe you'd be up to some dinner."

She crinkled her nose. "I'm not in any shape to go out."

"I was going to bring it in."

She looked at her watch again. By the time the truck was empty she'd be ready for something to eat. "Sure. I'd like that."

"I'll help your dad finish up then."

"Where's Adam?"

"Not sure. Last I saw he was helping Shannon with something."

She walked through the dining room. The cardboard boxes that were empty sat in a stack on the far side of the living room but newspaper covered the floor. Adam was in the kitchen talking to Shannon in a nasal voice.

"Adam. I want eat with Curtis. It okay you go, take mom dad." She signed after she had his attention.

Adam looked at Curtis then back at her. "You eat dinner sweetheart?"

"No. We talk."

Adam nodded and gave her a thumbs up.

"Shannon, Adam is going to get mom and dad home. Curtis and I are going to eat some

dinner here."

Shannon looked at Adam then turned away from Adam. "Do you think that's wise?"

"It's nothing like that. He wants to hang out and eat. We're friends."

"Uh-huh." Shannon nodded and pursed her lips.

Thirteen

Rachel stepped out of the shower and quickly toweled off. She was still miffed with

Shannon's attitude. Why was it everyone thought they had the right to tell Rachel how to live her

life?

Curtis had left twenty minutes ago to pick up their Chinese take-out. She wasn't sure how

long it would take him to get there and back. Probably had another twenty minutes unless they

were faster than the one she liked to stop at on the way home.

The sticky sweat was gone and she felt human again. Most of her clothes were still in

boxes. She dug around in a couple marked "clothes" but found mostly shoes and some clothes

she had no reason why she had moved to the new place.

The towel was not providing much protection against the cool fall air that nipped at the

moisture on her skin.

"This is taking forever." She walked to her bedroom door and locked it then flung her

towel on to her bed and dug as quickly as she could through the clothes. She saw the edge of a

pair of jeans and pulled those out then she dug around until she found enough clothes to make an

outfit.

Fifteen minutes later she was dressed, her face painted and her hair dry enough to be presentable. Curtis still wasn't there but a huge mess was. She gathered a few boxes from the hallway and started down to the living room. The boxes that remained were mostly odds and ends. She found places for those she could but some just moved to a new box she'd label "why did I move this?"

Curtis knocked on the back door and Rachel opened it. "Sorry it took a little extra time. I stopped at the grocery to get some paper plates and plastic ware."

"Thank you." She took the bag of food from Curtis and set it on the dining room table.

He pulled open the plates and set the table.

"Place looks really nice." He lifted out a large white folded box. "I think this is your General Tso's Chicken."

"I love this stuff." She set the box by her plate. "I'm going to have to do something with all these boxes. They're going to drive me nuts."

"You can collapse them and put them in your basement."

"That will work for about a week. I hate clutter."

"So do I." He pulled out the last of the food and dumped out little yellow, orange and black packets of sauces. "People say I'm a neat freak but I like to know where things are. I have

to mess with so much paper and chaos all day when I get home I want to have order."

"Yep."

They filled their plates with food and ate in near silence. Rachel's body ached. She put

down her fork and rubbed her shoulder trying to ease the knot on the right side of her neck.

"Stiff?" Curtis asked.

"Very." She bit in to her spring roll. She crunched through the outside but then shredded

cabbage and vegetables went all over her plate. She covered her mouth with her hand and tried to

catch some of the food that was falling out.

"Do you want me to get you a napkin?"

Rachel shook her head no. Had this been a date she would have been crawling under the

table or hiding in the bathroom. Curtis put her at ease.

"Does it feel like home yet?" He asked after she finished her spring roll.

She looked around the room at all the familiar furnishings that filled the walls of a

strange home. "A little. It feels a little funny to be in such a big place after living in a two-

bedroom apartment the last five years. I think I need more stuff." She laughed.

"Don't worry. Houses have a way of filling themselves."

"I know. Every time I've ever moved I've told myself that finally I will able to keep the clutter down but then I find all kinds of things on sale and I fill the shelves with knickknacks and other things until it's finally bulging at the seams.

"How far do your parents live from here?"

"About fifteen minutes or so."

"I think it is great that you have such a close relationship with Your mom."

"Yeah, it's nice." She didn't want to say anything that could be misinterpreted and reported back to her mom. "Sometimes she can be a little pushy but I know she means well."

"You mean like that dinner date she set up?"

"Exactly like that." Rachel tried to gracefully eat a long noodle but then bit it off rather than slurp it in. Hopefully he hadn't noticed her poor table manners.

"I'm glad she did it though. It's been nice to get to know you through this home buying process."

"You're not at all what I expected." She pushed food around with her fork as she spoke.

"Usually when mom wants to introduce me to someone…They're…uh…Not my type." She said trying to be a bit diplomatic.

"So I'm your type?" He sounded more playful than interested.

"No I didn't mean that."

"Really?"

"Oh stop." She laughed. "Yes, you're funnier than I expected a mortgage broker to be."

"What did you expect?"

"You know different professions tend to attract people with different quirks. I guess I figured you to be more uptight."

"Fair enough. I do have some quirks. Loyalty is huge to me. I find it can be hard to trust people." His face turned serious. "Before I found this church I didn't have the best experience with people who called themselves Christians unfortunately."

"I really don't get in to organized religion. You have to be careful. I prefer to live in the moment; grab life by the horns and enjoy the ride."

"For me I like to know who holds the future."

Rachel shifted nervously in her chair. "Life is about more than a bunch of dos and don'ts. I like to enjoy life."

"That's a great perspective. Enjoy life. I agree. Life isn't always exactly the way we'd like for it to be but we can accept it for what it is and enjoy it."

She relaxed a bit in her chair. "Exactly. People spend so much time trying to figure everything out. On the one hand you've got people reading horoscopes and on the other hand you've got preachers on TV screaming about the end of the world." She took a sip of water. "Live today. If a belief works for someone then I guess it's good. Some people need something to believe in to make sense of the rat race."

He put down his fork and pushed back his plate. "Is that how you see life? A rat race."

"Sure, I'd say for the most part we live in a rat race." She leaned back in her chair. "You know like my family. They find goodness in church. More power to them. I think that's beautiful."

"But not for you?" He leaned toward her a bit in his chair. He wasn't judgmental which was a nice change for religious people. He asked questions and she was pretty sure he heard the answers too.

"No. I went to church when I lived at home but people at church are no different than anyone else. Most of them just think they're better."

"Do you feel that way about me?"

"No, you're cool." She moved her hand and the tension that seemed to be building wafted away. "You aren't closed minded."

"So you don't have a problem with me since I believe Jesus is the only way to get to heaven?"

"Nope." She didn't mind him at all. He at least lived what he said he believed. She could respect a person with other beliefs as long as they respected hers too.

He looked around her dining room. "I don't feel right leaving so many things still in boxes. Why don't I help you get some of these things unpacked before I leave."

Fourteen

Logan flipped through the digital photos in his camera. Rachel at various angles and in various places. His favorites were the ones where her shoulder length hair blew in small loose strands around her chin. There were only two but they were the cream of the crop.

He printed an 8 x 10 and put it in a silver vase. He traced the curves of her face on the print with his finger. Rachel was his perfect flower. A thing of beauty that could withstand the harsh winters and grow in to a delicate bloom at the first hint of spring sun.

He laid a stack of 5x7 and 8x10s on the table by his photo album and crossed to a wooden bookshelf with three shelves. Across the bottom shelf were eleven white photo albums. Each of them were identical. He'd bought them for the other women but they'd betrayed him. After they were punished he-.

He looked at the large black Xs of electrical tape on the spines of those photo albums. Bad memories in those white books. Didn't want to think about that any more.

At the end of the shelf was a wooden jewelry box. He sat on the floor and put the box on his lap. This was where he kept his special treasures. Trinkets from all the women he had loved before. Jenny had come the closest to fulfilling him. Memories stung him. Everyone betrayed him. None had been loyal. Not Aunt Tulla, Not Jenny not-.

He lifted Jen's class ring and the lock of red-brown hair that he'd put in the box days before the ring. He rubbed them against his cheek. Despite their betrayal each had touched him in a special way. He picked a piece of lint out of the bottom of the box then placed the ring and lock of hair back. He lifted out the small diamond ring and held it up. Large hands squeezed his heart. Rachel would love him.

He put the ring in a black ring box then placed them on top of the other trinkets before closing the lid and sliding the box back on the shelf. Rachel was going to be different. She didn't throw herself at him like other women did. There was a challenge to her. She was a mature woman who knew how to get what she wanted. He would give it to her all right. He walked to a bouquet of roses sitting on his table and slid a single white rose from the cluster.

The white rose was a sign of purity to many. A rose was a delicate thing of beauty that should be reserved for women who were both beautiful and pure. He picked up a black ribbon from the second bookshelf and began to tie it around the rose. Ten ribbons each cut exactly six inches long were stacked on the shelf. He stopped for a moment.

"Twelve." He whispered.

"Twelve apostles."

He looked at the books. "Twelve women."

Then back at the ribbons. "Twelve roses."

Of course. He had known she was the one but now he understood why. There had to be others. He had to purify his perfect one through blood. Without the shedding of blood there is no remission of sin. Yes the Bible said that. Aunt Tulla had talked about the blood sacrifices in the Bible. Twelve was the perfect number. He sniffed the flower. His heart thudded in his chest.

"But wait."

He stopped and held up a single finger as if telling an invisible guest to be still for just a moment. "These things take time. They must be developed slowly." He thought for a moment. "One, only one a week." His excitement rekindled. "Yes, one rose a week. Make her want it. Build her desire to know me better." It all made so much sense. Why hadn't he seen it before? All the lies and betrayal of all the other women were leading to this moment. He walked to the close up of Rachel sitting on top of his stack of pictures and brushed the rose petals up and down the photograph.

"I know you're anxious. but soon."

He said/She said

When you write dialog watch out for a few common issues.
    • Ending every, single piece of dialog with 'Said' or some derivative [commented, sighed, yelled, screamed, etc.]
    • Flipping the said. This is a recent thing I've seen and it is so irritating. It looks like this. "I was going to the store." Said Elliot. "Not without me." Whined Susie. It just feels awkward
    • Writing like we talk [with lots of uh, or um]
    • Writing long speeches or 'monologing' or phonetic writing [more on that in other sections].

Fifteen

"Are you sure you want to go out with Curtis?"

"I told you, Curtis is a friend. It's nothing physical. I enjoy talking to him." Rachel

gathered a small stack of papers and put them in her folder to go home then followed Shannon

out the door.

Shannon turned her key to lock the door to the suite their office was in. "And if you

weren't friends with Curtis you could have a real relationship with Drew."

"I haven't ruled Drew out completely. You've made it very clear you don't approve of

me hanging out with Curtis."

"Drew may rule it out if he finds out you've been having friendly dinners with the

mortgage broker." They walked to their cars parked beside each other.

"I would tell him the same thing I told you." Rachel beeped the lock open on her Toyota.

"Curtis doesn't think of me like that anyway. We enjoy talking."

"If you're ditching Drew I want him." Shannon smiled and tossed her purse across her

seat to the passenger seat.

"I'll see you tomorrow." Rachel climbed in her car and turned in the direction of the highway.

She'd been somewhat surprised when Curtis called to ask her out to dinner. They'd had a

pleasant enough time eating take out on moving day but they hadn't met socially without a

family member around other than that night. Maybe she should have called Adam to see if he

wanted to come along. More than likely he needed some professional advice on his business

venture.

She turned in to the parking lot of the Stable and cruised up and down the full aisles

looking for a spot to park. She parked finally along the back row. She pulled her thin white

sweater around her arms in an attempt to block some of the evening air. Curtis was standing in

front of the wooden front door with his hands in his pockets.

"Rachel you're going to freeze in that." He when she was a few feet away.

"I hope not."

"Our table is ready and waiting for us." He pulled open the front door and gently touched

the small of her back as she walked ahead in of him. She walked to the podium and glanced at

him nervously. He motioned to a table without saying a word then pulled her chair out for her.

Was this a date?

She placed her cloth napkin in her lap and looked around. She had been to the Stable a few times over the years. The food was excellent for the price but she mostly came to enjoy all the horse things on the wall.

"You know" She started. "This place was a nineteenth century horse stable that they converted in to a restaurant."

"I'd heard that from someone before."

Then they were both quiet again.

Curtis cleared his throat and looked over the menu. Neither one was saying anything.

This *was* a date.

How could she have agreed to a date with Curtis? Well, in reality she hadn't. He'd called and asked if she'd like to get together for dinner and she agreed. There was really no reason to think that they would be on a date.

Was there a way she could gracefully excuse herself without hurting his feelings? She closed her menu and looked up.

"Why are you staring at me like that?" she asked covering her nervous smile with her hand.

"I was enjoying the way the light moves around your face. You look very mysterious."

He sat back in his seat and smiled.

"Yes, I'm an enigma." She said and she reached in to the breadbasket. She didn't like the way his looks made her feel. He wasn't creepy, no. These were feelings she hadn't experienced for a long time. Those were the kinds of looks and feelings that left her alone in her bedroom crying. And why would she feel them for Curtis and not Drew?

"You really are a bit of an enigma. You're nothing like most women I know."

"How so?" She leaned forward and put her elbows on the table. What are you doing Rachel? She was absolutely asking for trouble.

"I can't put my finger on it quite yet. You're an interesting combination of self-assured and searching. That's the best way I can describe it." He paused and put his finger to his lips. Then as if solving a puzzle he said "You're a bubble."

She laughed. "I'm a bubble?"

"Yes. That's exactly what it is."

"Why in the world do you say I'm a bubble? Am I round and air headed?" Some of the camaraderie was returning.

He shook his head and leaned on the table. "Rachel, think about a bubble." He motioned as if there were a bubble floating by their table. "What is a bubble like?"

"Light? Full of air? Made of soap?" She had no idea what he was looking for.

He rubbed his chin then began to speak. "A bubble is beautiful and delicate. You love to watch a bubble. It floats by you and changes colors in the light. It is lifted up on the slightest of breezes-." He smiled and looked beyond her as if watching one float by them as they spoke.

"Thank you…I guess." What should she say when a guy called her a bubble?

"But there's another part to a bubble and that's the part that hurts me to see."

"What is that?"

"Inside a bubble is hollow, empty and the slightest outside force will cause it to pop, shatter. Then there is nothing left."

Rachel's breath caught in her throat along with her voice. Tears burned her eyes and threatened to spill all over the table. Curtis didn't speak with a hint of animosity but tenderness, like her daddy's voice. He reached across the table for her hand.

"Rachel, I'm not saying this to be…well,…I'm saying it because I care about you and I want you to know that if you need someone. I'm here."

"Are you trying to say I'm going to pop?" One tear managed to escape. Curtis saw it. He looked down at the spot on the table where it landed. He squeezed her hand just a bit.

"Only you know if you're about to pop." He smiled just a bit. "I see a delicate, beautiful woman who has everything going for her but you don't feel complete. You wonder if there isn't more than this."

Now she understood. She straightened a bit. "Is this your lead-in to try and get me saved?" She cursed herself. Stupid Rachel always following her heart around like a doggy on a leash. She thought about getting up and storming out.

"No. Not at all. I promise-."

"You know nothing about me." There was that old spunk she'd had. "How can you presume to know all the-."

"Here are your salads." The server reached in to the middle of their conversation and placed white ceramic plates full of lettuce down on the table. "Can I get you anything else while I'm here?" She looked between the two of them. How was it possible for this woman to be so dense as to not see they were in the middle of something?

"No, thank you." Curtis said and she walked away. "Rachel-."

"What?" She picked up her fork and began stabbing at uncooperative lettuce leaves.

"I promise I only invited you because I had so much helping you move and eating take out in your dining room."

Images of the two of them than night softened her armor a bit but she was still ready.

"Okay but I want you to know I like my life. I really do."

"I'm sure you do." He still hadn't picked up his fork.

"I, unlike you, don't seem to feel the need to find a deeper meaning in everything. I'm happy to live for the moment, enjoy today and not worry about tomorrow."

"What are you feeling at this moment?" His voice was gentle.

Scared and vulnerable were the first words to come to mind but she wouldn't say those.

"Hungry comes to mind."

Curtis relaxed and picked up his fork. "Well we came here to eat so let's do that."

She picked at the lettuce leaves looking for the cucumbers and tomatoes. That bubble thing was-. Well, everyone was a bubble. We all clean up the outside to look great but inside we're different people with secrets that hurt people.

"So Curtis. Are you a bubble too?"

He put down his fork and wiped his mouth with the cloth napkin. "Do you believe in God Rachel?"

"Yes."

"Do you believe in right and wrong?"

"Of course." She picked up a sugar packet and flipped it with her fingers then remembered she was drinking Coffee and not tea. She put it back with the other white, blue, pink and yellow packets.

"How do you know what is right and wrong?"

"What does that have to do with being a bubble?"

"Answer my question." He kept his voice calm. It was inquisitive, not the least bit confrontational.

"You just know, in your gut."

"Tell me some things that are right and wrong."

"Helping poor people is good and killing is bad."

"Is that always true?"

"Yes." Then she stopped. "Wait, why am I on the hot seat? What about you?"

"You already know I believe the Bible is true and everything else is false."

"Yes and what does that have to do with being a bubble?"

"I was a bubble when I used to go with the flow. I bobbed up and down with every new trend but inside I was empty."

"Then you found Jesus and it was all fine." She'd heard this tired worn out story a million times. Life falling apart with no hope for anything, homeless and hungry then a street preacher gave them a Bible and life is perfect.

"Nope. My life got so much worse."

"Really." She stifled a laugh but a bit of it trickled out.

"It got better for a few months but after that there were a couple years of hell on earth."

"Then why do you still go and try to get other people to go to church."

For a moment he seemed to be thinking, formulating an answer. "Because this time…I knew there was someone rooting for me and even if things got worse they'd turn out in the end."

"Have they gotten better yet?"

"A little but they still aren't quite to where I was before I let Jesus get a hold of my life."

She no longer tried to hide her shock. "Then why do you still do it? Go to church I mean.”

“I’m not talking about church. A church is just a bunch of people. I’m talking about the church, the body of Christ. I have peace. I sleep better at night. I don’t worry. I may be thirty-something, single with some financial woes but now I have hope that things will get better.”

“I guess it’s not enough for me to hope something will be better when I die. I want it to work here or I ain’t buying. I don’t believe in a God who would send me to hell if I slept in on Sunday mornings.”

“What if you’re wrong?”

What did some financially struggling, plain looking man have to tell her about her life. He had no idea what she believed or why and here he was judging her. “What if *you’re* wrong? It would shatter your world.” A voice inside told her to stop, not to say the words bubbling inside her but it would feel so good to let them out. “The little perfect land you’ve created for yourself where you are the right ones with your big floppy Bibles and old men in flowing robes. If you would open yourself for just a moment to the idea that there could be another way to look at things it would make your head spin.” She was starting to spit as she spoke.

“And if you’re wrong, and I’m right, then you’re headed straight for hell.” His voice was somber.

"I've had enough of this conversation. I wanted to have a nice evening but…"

"Wait…" He reached forward for her. "I'm sorry. I don't often get to have stimulating conversations with beautiful women. I'm sorry I got carried away. Please stay. Let's have a nice evening."

She looked down at his hand, still on top of hers. "Okay. Why don't you tell me about you?"

"Umm, I think that's what got us in trouble in the first place. Let's talk about Adam."

Sixteen

Rachel turned the air conditioning vents so they blew straight in her face. The sun

beamed in the driver's side of her car. Sweat ran down her back. Slowly her car crept along

through the miles of construction zone that appeared a few weeks after she moved to her new

house. She sipped on her large coffee. The morning commute was now forty-five minutes

because of the orange barrels. She had yet to find that perfect balance between enough coffee to

keep her awake the whole trip without sending her running to the first gas station restroom after

the construction zone.

She hadn't slept well the previous night so this morning she was failing at both. Her cell

phone rang.

"Hi Shannon." She said when she flipped it open.

"Quite the night owl. You on your way in yet?"

"How did you know I was up late?" She reached over to turn down the fan so she could

hear better.

"I saw you sent me an email at two a.m. Sorry your date didn't go so well."

"I wouldn't say it was a total waste. Especially for not knowing going in that it was actually a date."

"I told you to stick with Drew."

"I'm starting to think I should stick with being single. You know he called me a bubble."

"Why did he call you a bubble?"

"It was some metaphor for how beautiful I am on the outside but lost on the inside. Some

church analogy I guess."

"Is that the only reason he asked you to dinner?"

"Nope. I guess he was inviting me on a date."

"Told ya."

Rachel craned her neck to try to see over the pickup truck in front of her but her car was

too low. "What do you say to church people who want to impose their beliefs on you?" It was

one of three questions that had pounded in her head until sweet sleep came sometime after three

in the morning.

"Nothing. I don't usually talk to them at all."

"You believe in God though don't you?"

"Sure but there is more than one path to God. I'm kind of cafeteria style. I think there is beauty in all faiths so I pull from each. That's make me more spiritual than religious I'd say." S

She turned the fan up a little more. The sun was baking her arm. "I'd say I believe the same thing. I see so much beauty in nature and the world around me. I don't need to go to church to feel God."

"It takes a strong person to go through what you did with Nate and still be willing to see beauty in God."

She didn't blame God. Well, God as she defined him. Not entirely. If the God of the Bible was real then it wouldn't have happened. As much as she prayed it never would have happened. "You know it was good for me."

"How in the world could it have been good?" Shannon sounded disgusted.

"I didn't spend my whole life like some people following vapors. I saw without a doubt that I was in this world alone and -."

"A-hem."

"Yes and with you." Rachel added. "But I was headed down this same blind path as my family and Curtis are."

"You should be the one saving them."

Rachel edged on to the shoulder and accelerated around the semi that had blocked her

exit. "You know, I would, but I respect their beliefs and if it helps them deal with the world to

think there's some big guy upstairs then I'm not going to take it away."

"You're a better person than me. I'd throw it in their face the next time they tried to judge

me. When do you think you'll be here?"

"Should be by nine from the looks of traffic. I got around this semi so I'm finally starting

to make some headway." She accelerated around a minivan then hit the cruise control. "I'd say if

not nine then nine-thirty."

"This might cheer you up on your long commute." Shannon's voice was at once happy

and ornery.

"What's that?"

"I have a message here that Drew called and would like for you to call him on his cell."

"And you waited to tell me this?"

"Yep."

She hung up with Shannon and stuffed her phone down in her purse. She had no idea

what to do. She could go out with Drew again. Things had been pretty intense in the parking lot and it was definitely too soon to spend the night.

She felt around in her purse for her lipstick then used the rearview mirror to be sure she got it on straight. If she was honest with herself she wanted to be with a handsome man who acted a bit more like Curtis. Minus the church stuff.

Actually that wasn't quite fair. Curtis had never acted like some crazed fanatic around her. That could change if they started dating though. Then there'd be the expectation that the little lady defer to her man. He'd never said any of that really. He might be open minded and willing to allow her to have beliefs that were different. There were people of different faiths that got married-.

See, right there was why she hadn't gotten in to a relationship like this. Things get sticky, people get hurt and there's no reason for it. It didn't really matter who was right or wrong because it had nothing to do with life today, here, in this car.

She picked up her phone and scrolled through the phone numbers and keeping one eye on the traffic around her. A good God would not send a good person to hell. Her hand shook as she scrolled down through the Cs.

She couldn't be with a man who made her uncomfortable.

Through the Ds.

She needed a man who could make her feel like a woman. Someone who could take away

the pain. Who could erase all memory of what Nate had done. Some one who could fill her

bubble.

Of the two men only one had offered that possibility.

She pushed send on her phone. He picked up on the second ring.

"Could we meet for dinner? I have something I need to talk to you about."

In the previous section I gave some common issues seen in writing dialog in a book. One common error I spot is Monologues and Speeches by characters. This is long sections of speaking by a single character without a break of any kind.

What do I mean by long? A few lines or more.

Think about it. If you stopped to read a paragraph of 4 or 5 sentences without stopping to take a breath, without touching your face, adjusting the paper or hearing someone in the room shifting, it isn't very natural. We gather information constantly. You can create the scene and the tone simply by breaking the dialog to let us in the mind and body of our POV character.

So, what if the POV character isn't talking? Interrupt the speech to let us hear how the point of view character perceives what is said or what they observe in their environment.

For more on this I strongly urge you to pick up a few books on dialog, read them and then study people as they talk. What do you notice when you're listening to others. Do you take notes? Look around? Notice the sun coming from behind the clouds?

How do your own emotions skew the perception of what is going on around you?

Write some notes here, note it as you edit this story and then look for it in your own writing.

Seventeen

"What am I doing here?" Rachel said to reflection in the bathroom mirror. It had seemed

harmless enough when she asked him dinner. She thought he was a nice to spend time and they

had fun together. She'd never told either man about the other. Really there was nothing to tell.

Her and Curtis had only been on a few dates. That wasn't really dat*ing*. Dating implied

some kind of steady relationship. Theirs was more of a strong friendship.

Besides any feelings she may have for him could not compensate for their radically

different worldviews. She smoothed down her blouse and went back to the table.

Drew walked around and pulled out her chair. He'd been extra attentive this evening and

she was glad that she'd given him a second chance.

"The server was just out with the dessert tray. I told her you'd be back in a minute."

"Thank you." She placed her napkin across her lap. "Are you getting something?"

"The pie a la mode looked really good."

"How in the world can you eat ice cream now?"

"You cold? You could use my jacket."

"I'm fine. I have my sweater but it's so cold outside I couldn't even think of having ice cream.”

“Would you like to see the desserts?”

Drew looked at Rachel as he ordered. “I’ll have the pie a la mode. And could I have

coffee?”

“Sure. And you ma’am?”

“What do you have chocolate?”

“We have brownie a la mode, dark chocolate lava cake with Raspberry sauce -.”

“I’ll have that.” She jumped in.

“I’ll be out in a moment with your desserts.”

They sat in silence Rachel sipping on her coffee and Drew his Pepsi. The restaurant was

fairly dark with three small chandeliers casting a soft glow over the tables directly below. The

rest relied almost entirely on the oil lamp on the side of the table.

They served the desserts. Both were much larger than Rachel had expected them to be.

Drew cut down in to his as if he hadn’t eaten an entire meal with appetizer. Which he

had. “I’m glad you agreed to see me again.” He squeezed in between bites of pie dripping with

white ice cream.

She nodded, not quite sure what to say. You're welcome sounded ridiculous but that was the only answer that popped in her head. She picked off small nibbles with the corner of her fork.

The chocolate melted in her mouth but her stomach pushed back when she tried to swallow.

"What's wrong?" Drew asked after he'd wolfed down another bite.

"I guess my eyes were bigger than my stomach."

"We'll get it to go. You can come back to my place."

When he said it her stomach squeezed in to a knot. Curtis' face flashed in her mind. "Oh, I don't know. I…"

"I rented a comedy. I was hoping you'd come see it with me."

A comedy did sound nice. It was certainly better than going home and waiting to be tired enough to fall asleep. "That sounds fun." She smiled. "I'll follow you over."

"Great. I don't live far from here."

Rachel had her dessert put in a to-go box and went out to her car. After she pulled out behind Drew she called Shannon.

"Hey, how was your date?" Shannon's voice was up beat.

"It's not over yet. I'm following him back to his place."

"Nice, you will give me *every* detail tomorrow." Shannon's hunger to date Drew through Rachel bordered on nuts.

"Don't know if there will be anything to tell."

"Why?"

Rachel would have preferred a little less disappointment. "I don't know how I feel for Drew. He just….*it* isn't there."

"Don't you feel anything with him?"

"Sure, there is a bit of physical attraction like any woman has for a handsome man but all I do is compare him to Curtis."

"Well, then go with it. Don't tie up a great guy like that if you aren't serious. But if I were you I'd stay tonight just to be sure."

"That is so shallow. I will talk to you tomorrow."

Rachel followed his car out to the edge of town and in to a new subdivision. She could make out homes under construction near the entrance and there were For Sale signs on the empty lots. Drew's name was on most of the signs she passed as they wove their way to the back of the subdivision.

Drew turned on a gravel drive that led to a large cluster of trees. The moonlight splashed down on the roof of a two-story A frame home that was nearly in the trees. He turned in to the smaller driveway that went to the back of the house and parked the car. A floodlight clicked on illuminating the yard. There were flowerbeds along the house and hedges across the front, at least as far as she could see.

"You admiring my landscaping?" He walked back to her and put his arm around her.

"You certainly have a green thumb."

"I put in perennials all along the sidewalks then bushes across the front. In the spring I put in a few annuals when I mulch the beds. It doesn't take much time to do and makes the place look neater."

"Oh I agree, if I didn't have such a knack for killing plants I'd have some in my house."

"I have a gazebo with a swing in the back. I spend a lot of time out there in the summer watching birds and squirrels in all of those trees."

"This isn't at all what I expected a single man's house to be like."

"I'm an outdoorsman. I don't like being stuck in a house but I also don't like looking at a bunch of grass. My grandparents taught me about plants and gardening brings back a lot of happy memories."

"I thought you weren't close to your family."

He started to walk her around the back of his car. "The door is this way." He took her

down a sidewalk that went past a picture window and to the door on the side. "My grandparents

are gone." His voice was low, near a whisper. Rachel stilled her breathing to hear him. "They

were good people. Others in my family weren't. I don't talk about, or to, them."

He stepped in the back door and put his shoes on a black mat. "You can put your shoes

here." He pointed. She took hers off and set them on the same mat. He walked through the

archway to the next room and turned on the light. His kitchen was neat, not a single dish or

spoon was anywhere in sight. Even the towels hanging by the sink on a hook were neatly

centered.

The colors were quite bold. She followed him through the house in to the living room.

The walls were golden yellow with army green trim.

"Your couch looks like one I saw recently in a decorating magazine."

"Oh yeah, which one?"

"I'm not sure. I get three or four different ones but I remember the light green couch because I was surprised a green couch would look so nice." She walked around the corner. "Oh

and look at this chair. This pattern really pulls out the green."

The carpeting was plush and it felt inviting under her stocking feet.

"You're house is absolutely beautiful." She said when he walked in to the living room.

"Thank you. I like to have an oasis when I leave work."

"Did you design all of this yourself?"

He handed her a drink. "No, one of the designers that worked at a parade of homes did

some work on one of the models. Her name is Brenda Swartz. I was impressed so I asked her to

design my place too."

"She does great work." Rachel walked in to the dining room and admired the shelves full

of books and trinkets.

"Thank you." His voice was deep, serious. It made Rachel catch her breath. "I'm really

glad you like it." He came up behind her, put the glass that was in her hand on the table and

gently kissed the back of her neck. Rather than surrendering to his touch she thought of how

secluded this house was. Guilt mixed with fear and she swallowed hard.

"I value things of beauty. When I find them I want to hold on to them." He kissed her on the ear then down the back of her neck.

Rachel turned slowly to face him and he kissed her deeply. Fear melted away and she was sucked in to the moment. Her heart was no longer in control.

"You're all I think about from the moment I wake up until I go to bed at night." He spoke the words straight from a romance novel. "I've tried not to rush things but I need you."

As if he anticipated her every desire he pulled her in close and kissed her gently. Every primal impulse raged through her body and all thoughts of Curtis vanished. She was here, in this moment. And in *this* moment every cell of her body screamed to give in to Drew.

He lifted her feet off the ground and carried her the few steps to the staircase. Her breathing quickened. It had been so long since she had a man find her desirable and clearly Drew found her desirable. She didn't want this to be only physical.

"Are you looking for commitment or a physical relationship?"

He kissed her cheek then whispered in her ear. "I don't care. I only want to have you. Whatever level of commitment you want."

Oh she melted. This was much too soon to go this far. She was no virgin but she wasn't easy either. What if this was all he wanted all along?

And what if Curtis finds out.

The thought crashed in her head. She stepped back from Drew, and sucked in a deep

breath, fighting for control. What was she doing? He looked like a clown with her lipstick

smeared all around his mouth. Her fingers running through his hair had made little spikes all

over his head. His chest heaved, and he gulped in a deep breath as if he'd been running hard.

How did she let things get this far, this fast?

She slowed her breathing down even more. Her body calmed down a bit.

"What's wrong?" Drew asked, as he ran a hand over his hair, smoothing it back. He

reached out and took her wrist.

"I shouldn't be here." She looked away.

"You're right, let's go upstairs."

"No I mean this…us…now. We are moving too fast."

"Too fast? What, do you think I'm looking for a one night stand? I'd hardly say this

relationship has moved fast." He took a step toward her. Icy fingers of fear needled at her.

"Drew…I-."

"What are you a tease?" He began to make large gestures with his arms as he spoke. "Did you think you'd come over and kiss for a while on the couch and I'd be fine with that?"

"Actually, I thought we were coming for a movie."

"Oh come on Rachel." He took another step to her, she took one more back. "You know that after a few dates when a person invites you over for a movie there is more implied."

She bumped in to a wall. He continued to walk to her. The wild look she'd seen the first night was back and he was now inches away. He took her face in his hands and pressed his lips hard on her mouth.

Then he was calm.

"You are the most wonderful woman I've met." He kissed her forehead and looked in her eyes. "If you want to watch the movie we can watch the movie." He took her hand and walked back to the living room and picked up a DVD.

She followed him in the room. If she stayed was she safer than if she tried to leave? She couldn't run fast in pantyhose and he could quickly out muscle her.

But if she stayed he could change his mind at any moment and force himself on her if he wanted.

She began to speak but the words caught in her throat.

"Did you say something?"

The charmer was back. She would try now. "Maybe we can see a movie some other time. I think it would be better if I went home now."

"Are you serious?" He tossed the movie down on the coffee table and took a step toward her. "You really want to leave." He stomped out to the kitchen, ripped the door open, and spun around. "Fine, leave." His eyes were small slivers of blue behind red eyelids.

She needed to leave. Why had she even come here in the first place?

"I'm sorry. I had a nice time but I need to get home."

"Oh, so you had a nice time. I wish I could say the same."

"I, uh."

He marched right over her words. "I was hoping to spend a nice evening here with you but tonight you were interested in playing the part of the tease." His voice was harsh.

He was going to grab her. She braced herself.

"I'm sorry. I was too embarrassed to tell you. This week is my…well…"

He looked at her for a moment then started laughing. "Oh, it's…" He laughed some more. "I'm sorry. I…" He walked to the door and pulled it open for her.

"Thank you again." Her voice trembled and she bent down to put buckle her shoes.

"You're still welcome to stay and watch the movie with me if you'd like." His voice was calm again.

She looked toward the living room for a moment, considering his offer. He wouldn't force himself on her tonight and she wouldn't have to risk his anger.

No.

Something inside of her though wouldn't let her stay. She couldn't remember ever having a gut feeling so strong. She needed to get away from the house and Drew as fast as she could.

"Thank you but no." She touched his cheek and quickly scooted out the door before he could reply. She walked around the house and paused for a moment outside the large window she'd passed on the way in. As she looked through it Drew came in to view. He clicked on the television with his remote then turned toward her.

Their eyes locked and she froze. For a few moments she was powerless to move. Drew turned and walked toward the direction she'd exited. That gave her the boost she needed to get her legs moving again. She walked quickly, nearly a run. Her healed books clanking steadily on the sidewalk.

Fear wrapped around her throat and her heartbeat thudded in her ears. She jumped in the car and started the engine. The headlights threw their glow on Drew standing where the sidewalk met the driveway less than twenty feet away. His eyes were dark and while she was sure he couldn't see her past the high beams her blood ran cold.

She backed in the turn around and cranked the wheel without making eye contact again. The floodlight in the driveway showed his silhouette as she pulled down his driveway and out of the subdivision. She watched for head lights in her rearview.

Her heart didn't slow down until she was out of Drew's neighborhood and back on the main roads.

Eighteen

Rachel turned into her driveway, skin still tingling with fear. She had glanced at her review mirror every few seconds searching for any sign Drew had followed her. Of course that was ridiculous, after tonight he'd never want to see her again. She parked in the driveway behind her house. A few houses down the neighbor's dog barked in their front yard. The hair on the back of her neck stood up and she scooped up her papers from the office with her purse and closed the car door with her hip. The sound echoed around her yard and for a moment the neighbor's dog was silent.

The trees along her yard cast long shadows from the streetlight. She turned trying to catch a bit of light to figure out which key was gold and which was silver. She tried three keys in the lock before one finally spun and she pushed in to the back door. She locked the door then tossed her papers on the counter.

The light from her living room lamp cast a swatch of brightness in to the otherwise dark kitchen. She hadn't expected to be gone so long and only one light was on. She put her shoes by the door and quietly padded in to the next room flipping on the kitchen's overhead light as she went. She stepped in to the great room. To her right the lamp was casting a dim glow around the room. She turned to her left and turned on the light in the dining room. The answering machine

blinked three times.

She pushed the play button. The first two messages were nothing but silence. Then the

third message "Hi Rachel, Shannon. If you come home tonight call me. If not, I know what you

did tonight." Her voice sang. Rachel flipped her phone open and dialed Shannon.

"So you did come home. That was quick." Shannon said. "I only talked to you, what, an

hour ago?"

"Yes, about that." Rachel continued walking through the house as she spoke opening

closets and checking locks on windows and doors "The strangest thing happened when I was

there." She hesitated for a moment. "Things were going great. He was saying all the right things

and we were kissing." The tingle of fear poked harder as she thought back.

"And?..."

"Well, I thought of Curtis and went cold."

"How in the world did that dweeb pop in your head when you were kissing a hottie like

Drew?"

"I don't know. Adam, Curtis and I were having a good time at mom's and it reminded me of back before, well, back before everything happened in college."

"And you started remembering old thoughts and tied them to Curtis?"

"No, I think Curtis popped in my head…well, I don't know why he was there but when he did come in my head the moment was gone."

"And…" Shannon sounded disappointed. How was Rachel supposed to control every thought that entered her brain?

"I told him I wanted to stop. That was when he changed."

"Well duh. You can't lead a guy on like that."

"I wasn't." Rachel yelled in the phone. Then calmer she continued. "I wasn't in the mood any more but when he cornered me and acted like…Well, it gave me chills. I had to get out of there so I left and came straight home."

"Are you okay now?"

"Yes, I was almost in tears on the way home but I've calmed down." Rachel rubbed her arms hard against the cold inside her.

"Was it a panic attack?" Shannon sounded really concerned. It was about time. Rachel had begun to wonder who Shannon was rooting for.

"Have you ever felt like…I don't know…a bad feeling about something and you don't

know why?" Rachel's shuffled back and forth on the wood that separated the living room rug

from the dining room rug. Her slippers drug on the hardwood and made the only other sound in

the house.

"Yes, you start to remember every horror film you've ever seen."

"I didn't remember any horror films."

"You know what I mean."

Rachel picked up a white sweater she had hanging on a chair and wrapped it around her

shoulders. "I don't know what it was. I'm really scared though."

"Still?"

"Yes. I can't put…I feel like I can't breathe"

Someone knocked and Rachel squealed in surprise.

"What is it?" Shannon asked, fear evident in her voice too.

Rachel took a few moments to catch her breath. "Someone knocked on the door and

about made me jump out of my skin. It must be mom."

She walked over to the front door and opened it. "No" Rachel said, barely able to get her voice above a whisper. "Please no." She started crying.

"Rachel what is wrong?" Shannon's voice was shrill in Rachel's ear. "Rachel, answer

me."

She didn't answer, couldn't answer.

"Rachel? Rachel!"

Talking to the Reader

Don't talk to the reader!! Unless this is a book written in 1st person or 2nd person, do NOT talk to the reader! That is just as bad as breaking the 4th wall in theater. Don't do it. It can be subtle when it is done, but watch out for it. If it doesn't seem a logical thing to say in a conversation, don't say it. NEVER say, "As you know, we've been friends for 12 years and our moms are cousins." That is talking to the reader and doing it using an "As you know" statement. Double bad!

Watch out for places this happens in this book and in your own writing.

Nineteen

Logan stood across the street hidden by a large oak tree. Rachel was standing on her front porch looking at the rose he had placed there. He smiled with satisfaction. She was completely surprised.

"I know there's another man, Rachel." He whispered. He watched her step slowly on to the porch and pick up the rose and take it in the house. "Do you think you can leave me? You are mine, Rachel." He watched her pull the blinds closed on her front windows. His smile widened. She got the message.

Normally she'd have to be punished for her betrayal tonight but he knew she'd make it right when they were together. She knew she belonged to him now. Every ounce of manhood within him screamed out to charge in the house right now, don't wait.

"No." He hissed. Patience. Love, patience and long-suffering. Slowly. He had to follow the plan. She had the message now. She would think twice before betraying him again.

Twenty

Rachel sat erect with her back against the headboard, legs drawn up against her chest.

She started at her bedroom door, ears alert to every sound. Each time a dog barked or the house

creaked the hair on her arms stood up. He was out there. He knew she was alone.

She reached under the pillow beside her and ran her fingers along the handle of the knife

she had taken to bed. A baseball bat was propped against her night stand. If he came for her

tonight she wasn't going without a fight. The police said they would patrol her street and keep an

extra eye on the house.

She should try to sleep. The alarm was set and the police were patrolling. If he wanted

her dead he'd have killed her tonight. He was scaring her. Tears ran down her cheeks. Loneliness

enveloped her. Her bedroom was silent except for her breathing. She slid down under her

blankets. Her eyes were heavy. It was two-thirty in the morning. She only had to last four hours.

Then this night would be over.

Twenty-One

Rachel sat quietly in the corner of the coffee shop with her back to the wall. She sipped at a double espresso and nibbled on a bagel to try to calm the waves of nausea in her stomach. Was he here in this coffee shop, watching her? Two tear drops leaked from her eyes. She wiped her cheeks dry and tried to calm down with deep breaths. Deep breaths did nothing to calm the shaking inside her.

"Excuse me miss?" A lanky young man walked to her table and stared down at her.

She looked up at him without speaking.

"Is this seat taken?" He pointed to the chair to her right.

"Um, I."

Her mom walked to the table and plopped her large purse on the table. "Sorry I'm late. Had a devil of a time finding a parking spot."

"Are you expecting others?" The man said again, this time to her mom.

"No, please. You can have the chair." She said and pulled the edge of the chair out for him.

"Thanks." He lifted the chair just above the floor and took it to a table full of high school or new college students. She wasn't sure which.

"Rachel!" She spun and looked at her mom. "Honey, you feelin' alright? You look pale."

"Didn't sleep well."

Her mom eyed her for a moment then dug a ten dollar bill out of her wallet. "I'll be right back. I need to get my coffee. You want me to get something for you?"

"No. Thanks."

"You look completely exhausted."

"Yes, I am. I think I'm taking the day off to try and get some rest."

"Glad to see you taking some time to yourself." She scooted her chair up to the table. "If you're not feelin' well how bout you come on over to the house? Stay with your dad, Adam and me. There is nothing worse than being all alone when you don't feel good." She smiled and patted Rachel's hand. "I best get up there. Coffee's not bringing itself over here." Her mom turned and walked over to the line in front of the counter.

Rachel wanted to tell her mom what was going on. She mouthed the words "Mom, the fratboy killer is after me." Tears caught the words in her throat. Her body ached. Rest was what she needed. Uninterrupted sleep for more than thirty minutes at a time would do her so much good. She wiped her eyes again.

No she needed the creep caught. She needed some peace. She pushed her coffee cup

away and concentrated on the people around her.

Any one of these people could be the killer. She looked around at the tables of guys in

their twenty's and thirty's. It was close to half of the people. She turned and looked over her

shoulder then quickly turned forward again. No less than eight men were looking in her direction

or stole a passing glance.

Her mom walked back to the table, her coffee in a to-go cup and sleeve. "So you want to

follow me home?"

"Uh, I, no. I need to swing by the office for a few things first." Rachel tried to wipe the

fatigue from her eyes. "I'll be by in a little while."

"Rachel, I don't think you're in any condition ta go drivin' all over."

"I'll be there soon mom."

Her mom hugged her, first time she'd done that in quite a while, then walked to her own

car. Rachel climbed in her car and locked the doors behind her. Her body melted in to the seat. If

she could close her eyes for two, maybe three, minutes she'd feel so much better. She blinked long blinks and allowed her body to soak up the moments or rest.

Her cell vibrated in her hand. She jumped and fumbled with the phone.

"Hello."

"You sure you don't want me driving you?" Her mom said. Then Rachel heard to honks

on a horn outside her window. "Caught you nappin'" Her mom said through the phone. She was

about four car lengths from Rachel.

"I'll see you later this afternoon, mom." Her mom waved and slowly pulled her car on the

road.

Rachel felt a little guilty for calling off but she would have been completely worthless in

the office. She couldn't concentrate on anything. She only needed to stay awake and alert for

another hour and then she could rest.

Twenty-two

Rachel turned in to the gas station and groaned at the price. It had jumped up six cents since the day before. It was like the lottery and she kept picking the wrong numbers. She closed the gas tank and looked at the dent. She didn't feel like messing with that thing but she was only going to get busier moving in to fall.

The repair wouldn't take long at all and then she could go get a nap at mom's house. She scrolled through the contact list on her cell phone until she saw Jeremy's name. He answered on the second ring.

"Jeremy, this is Rachel. With the car." She pulled in to the parking space next to the gas station.

"Hi."

"I wanted to go try to get this thing fixed since I'm off work today. I was wondering if you could give me the name and number of that body shop you like." She was trying to mask her exhaustion with an overly happy voice.

"The one in Woodhaven?"

"Yes." She started to look for something to write with. It would have been smart to have that ready when she called for a phone number.

"Here it is." He gave her the number and the shop name. "Then mail the bill to the

address on my card and I'll get you paid back."

"I will. Thanks." She flipped the phone shut after he said goodbye and then called to see

if the body shop had an appointment open for a small dent. Fifteen minutes later she was sitting

in the corner of the repair shop's lobby. She slumped down in a seat and closed her eyes. She

wouldn't fall asleep, no just a small rest from the noise and lights going on around her.

Her cell phone hummed against her hip. She glanced at it, Curtis.

"Hi Rachel."

"Hello."

"I called the office and they said you were sick. Are you okay?"

"Exhausted. I've had trouble sleeping the last few weeks."

"Oh, I'm sorry to hear that. Having a hard time adjusting to the new house?"

His voice was soothing. She fought to keep her voice from cracking into tears. "I've been

under quite a bit of stress. I'm going to my parent's later to try to rest at their house. Right now

I'm getting a dent fixed on my car then I'm heading over there."

"I'm going to come get you and take you to lunch."

"You don't have to do that." She said it but the thought of his company was starting to appeal to her.

"No, I feel bad after dinner the other night. I want to make it up to you."

"Okay, I guess you do owe me."

He laughed. "Where are you at?"

"Smitty's in Woodhaven."

"Really, I know the owners. They're great people."

"That's reassuring." She looked around the three other dirty chairs that made up the waiting room. It had to be pretty difficult keeping a place clean when everyone there had their hands in oil and grease all day.

"I'll be over there as soon as I can. How long is it going to take them to fix the car?"

"They told me it shouldn't take more than a few minutes to do but they have a few cars ahead of mine. I have to be back before five."

"I won't keep you that long. You need your rest but I would like a chance to see you again."

She hung up the phone and walked in to the restroom which consisted of a toilet, sink and small mirror. A dried out air freshener in its white column couldn't overpower a windowless bathroom that lacked ventilation and a roll of paper towels sat on the back of the sink.

She looked at her reflection in the mirror and groaned. When she drug herself out of bed to meet her mom she had barely bothered to clip her hair up. The mop of brown hair on top of her head resembled a fountain.

She dug around in her purse and pulled out her lipstick. She couldn't tell in the dim yellow light if this was making things better or worse. She pulled her hair down out of the clip and tried fluffing it with her fingers. That was even worse. Her eyes were puffy from sleep deprivation.

"This is a lost cause." She combed her hair back with her fingers and flipped it back up to the fountain hair-do.

He wanted to see her again.

Rachel put everything back in her purse and went out to the waiting room. When had everything changed? She had fun with Adam and Curtis at her parents house. He was like a friend of the family who was as comfortable talking business with her brother as she was the church calendar with her parents or Chinese food with Rachel. But somewhere along the line something changed and now he called because he wants to see her again.

She looked out the front window to see if his car was coming yet. The scariest thing was she wanted to see him again too. Despite their differences there was enough sameness in the two of them that she smiled more when he was around.

There was nothing that would have made her stop in a bar and talk to him, not that he'd ever step in to a bar. It was little things. Her mom told her when she used to cry about a boy at school not liking her that Rachel needed to look for little things.

Rach, honey, you can't go lookin' for some guy who's handsome, or popular or any of that. You need to find a man who's got the little things. Gentleness, genuine, respects you, those are the little loves that when they're all together make the big love. You go looking for the big love without those other little loves then your love'll die.

But she wasn't talking about love here. No it was vulnerability. Her happiness could be affected by something as simple as lunch with Curtis now and she didn't know when it happened.

Twenty-three

Rachel pulled a long French fry out of its box and dunked it in ketchup.

"You know you didn't have to pick Wendy's for lunch." Curtis said for the second or third time.

"Don't you like Wendy's"

"I do but when I invited you to lunch I didn't expect to bring you some place where your food was served on paper. I would have sprung for more."

"I know." She looked up at him. "This doesn't count. You still owe me dinner."

"I see." He picked up his cheeseburger and started eating again.

Shannon would not approve at all if she knew where she was today. And a couple months ago she probably wouldn't have been here either. Possibly she would but she wouldn't be here feeling the way she did. Curtis balled up the paper his burger came in and set it off to the side of the table.

"You're awfully quiet." His hand moved toward her side of the table then hesitated. She desperately wanted his hand to cross the invisible line down the center of the table and touch hers.

"Sorry. Not much of a conversationalist today I guess."

"I wish I could do something. Do you want to talk about it?"

Of course she did but talking wouldn't help, especially not with Curtis. She couldn't risk Curtis getting upset over her date with Drew and there was no way to tell him about the roses and not tell him who she thought could be leaving them.

"Not really. I don't want to think about it right now." She moved her hand closer to the invisible line down the middle of the table that separated the two of them. She, of course, couldn't stop thinking about 'it'. 'It' had been her all consuming thought since last night. Before that there was a lingering voice in the back of her mind warning of danger but that danger now had a face. A face her mother had brought in to her life. A face that knew her address and all about her.

Curtis reached across the line and touched the back of her hand. "Why don't I take you to your mom's house and you can come out and pick your car up another day. You look exhausted."

She heard the sounds of his words but her attention was on the searing heat below his fingertips on the back of her hand. Tingles ran up her arm and straight to her heart. Her muscles relaxed in a moment and she knew that this was one of the little loves penetrating the armor that

had surrounded her heart since Nate hurt her.

Since Shannon had helped her erase the pain.

Since the days when she had stopped praying.

Twenty-four

Rachel hoisted a bag on her shoulder. "I've been counting down for this Chicago trip. I'm going to make my MasterCard groan under the weight of my shopping spree." She loved their fall excursion to Chicago. The weather was cooler this year than last year so they wouldn't spend as much time peering in to shop windows as they usually. Instead they'd booked a spa day, well spa afternoon really, to get pampered before returning to the chaos leading up to the holidays.

"No you won't. You'll agonize all day over a few purchases, decide on one and then put it back because it's too expensive." Shannon held the screen door open so Rachel could lock up the house. Then they walked down to the car where Shannon already had a few bags leaning against the back tire.

"I've got to be smart with my money. I want to settle down in a few years and I hate stories of people getting married and having all those credit card bills." Rachel pushed the unlock button on her key ring.

"And that is why you handle the books at the office."

"I wouldn't go in to business with you if I didn't." She raised her eyebrow in a motherly scold and set the bag down by the car. Shannon's lack of responsibility with money was legendary. "Do you ever think about starting a family?"

"Where in the world did that come from?" Shannon put her bags next to Rachel's.

"Thoughts pop in my head sometimes…So do you?"

"Sure I dream about it sometimes. Then I wake up screaming in a cold sweat."

Rachel folded her arms and glared at Shannon.

"Where'd your sense of humor go?"

"I'm not trying to be funny right now. I really want to know."

"I'd say with the right guy I'd love to start a serious relationship and maybe have a kid or two. But I haven't found him yet so I'm not too worried about someday."

"I wonder if I'll recognize him when I find him." Rachel dug her toe in the dirt.

"We're only thirty. I have a couple more good years of freedom and I want to enjoy them without longing for something I don't have or worrying about whether I'll find him." She pretended to swoon like the women in black and white western reruns.

"I wonder sometimes if I did things in the wrong order." Rachel folded her arms across her chest. "I wonder if I should have looked for a family and then started a career."

"It's not what you did so why worry about it?"

"I don't know."

"Rachel, I know this guy's got you freaked with the roses. I'm pretty freaked about it too. The police are watching the area and watching your house. Those other girls…" Shannon's voice trailed off. She took a deep breath and continued. "None of them had a chance. If he wanted you dead hc would have killed you." Her eyes were intense. She touched Rachel's shoulder. "I am not entirely convinced that it is really him. The news didn't make any mention of him leaving flowers along the way. He left flowers on dead bodies."

Rachel wrapped her arms around her waist and tears burned in her eyes. She wanted to believe every word of what Shannon was saying but how could she? Who could understand a crazy killer? And even if it wasn't the guy on TV, what if it was Drew. The crazed look in his eyes as she pulled out of his driveway gave her chills.

"Rachel. You are going to be fine. We are going to Chicago. There are no white roses there. No relationship issues or any of that. There are only clothing stores and massages. Let's go and relax."

Rachel nodded her head in agreement and walked around the car to the back. Shannon followed her with the bags. The release latch clicked and she lifted the lid. Inside was a single white rose, with a black ribbon.

Twenty-five

An owl hooted on a branch. Logan sat crouched in his hiding spot from which he could clearly see Rachel's house. During his nights under Aunt Tulla's Oak he'd heard owls hoot. He pushed the button on the side of his digital watch. A small light brightened the LCD face. It was after nine and she wasn't home. He balled his fist, trying to defeat the urge to pound it into the tree at his right."

"Rachel what do you think you're doing." He whispered through clenched teeth. "Didn't you learn your lesson?" He was going to have to teach her. The message last week hadn't been enough for her. He turned to watch a cop car drive up the street. The next one wouldn't be through for a few hours. Slowly he stepped out of his hiding place and crossed the grass to the back door. He pulled out his key ring and fingered her house key.

The key slid in the lock and turned the knob. After he put them in his pocket he wiped down the door handle and slid on his black leather gloves.

Street lights illuminated her kitchen. The counters were impeccably clean. Not a scrap of paper laying about. Bananas hung from a wooden holder and papers were stacked neatly in a basket. He removed his shoes and left them by the back door then walked through the kitchen stopping from time to time to open her cabinets. He shined a flashlight in the cupboards and admired the rows of canned goods. Each was grouped with its own kind and the labels were lined up facing out.

"My beautiful Rachel is neat and tidy." The cupboards had various canned and boxed goods neatly arranged on paper covered shelves. The refrigerator had little more than a calendar and a few magnets in neat rows. It was perfect.

He stepped in the living room but quickly moved in the dining room so the small lamp on her end table wouldn't give him away. He wiped his white handkerchief along the wooden piece of furniture that held her linens. Not a bit of dust and the linens were neatly folded and arranged in the drawers. A group of wicker balls in a ceramic basket sat in the center of her dining room table. He'd seen these before. They were overpriced cat toys that decorators used to pad their commissions. Poor Rachel had fallen for the scam.

He left the dining room and tiptoed up the steps. These were the steps Rachel walked up and down every day. His mind drifted to images of her in her night clothes on the steps wrapped in a fluffy robe. At the top of the steps a hallway opened to the left and to the right. He walked down the hall and peaked in to each of the rooms ending with her room. Soon that would be their bedroom where they would be one together. Where they would start their perfect life.

He walked in to her bedroom, clicked on the light looked at her bed. Waiting had been good for him. In the past he had always taken what he wanted, what was owed to him. This time he was doing it right. He would slowly romance her. Heighten the desire so when they were finally together it would be.

Perfect.

Her bed was a bit more modern then he would have chosen but he knew she was a modern girl. He walked around the bed but didn't touch any of the things on her dresser.

"Which side of the bed is mine?"

He looked and saw the alarm clock on the right.

"I guess I'm on the left."

He went back to the left side of the bed and knelt down. His body vibrated with excitement. What would she do if she came home and found him waiting in their bed for her? Would that make her happy?

"No, Alpha Mu Epsilon." He whispered. "Stick to the plan, Alpha Mu Epsilon." Of course that was right but he couldn't leave quite yet. He went back around to her side of the bed, noting the way she tucked in the sheets. They were in tight with the blankets turned down at the top then tucked under the mattress. Two pillows were at the head of the bed with a round pillow and two tootsie roll decorative pillows leaning against them. He reached behind the decorative pillow, lifted her pillow to his face and inhaled deeply. Laundry detergent mixed with the Vanilla scent of her perfume. It was the smell of desire.

"Oh Rachel, how predictable." He reached down and touched the blade of the knife she kept under her pillow. "A small piece of metal won't keep us apart." He laughed and shook his head while he put her pillow back and smoothed down the blankets.

"I am growing weary of your disobedience Rachel but in time all will be amended."

He stepped away from the bed and opened the small top drawer of her dresser. Satin night gown in jewel tones were lined up next to pantyhose. He lifted out the top night gown. It was sapphire blue. This is the one he would pick for her to wear. He tossed it on the bed. The spaghetti straps landed near the pillows and the end draped over the edge of the bed. He walked to the side of the bed, moved the decorative pillow and repositioned the gown. He looked over to the nightstand where a photo of Rachel and that other woman sat is a black wrought iron frame.

He layed the photo down and put the gown on top. She smiled up at him much like she would their first night together. He walked to the bathroom. Her toiletries were all gone. No toothbrush. No perfume.

Who was she with tonight?

His skin that had burned with lust now burned with rage. She tried his patience. Rachel would learn about loyalty.

He snatched up her gown and put it back along with the picture. He would leave her a message, this one unmistakable. Next would have to be punishment.

God required punishment.

Alpha Mu Epsilon required it.

How are your main characters developing?

We're solidly in the story now and it is time to evaluate the characters a bit. How are they developing? Are they changing as the story continues or are they staying pretty much the same? We may even see them get worse before they get better (personal development can be like that), so have we seen any of that movement yet?

These are important questions to consider because the ideas, circumstances and actions of a character must change during the course of a book in order for us to see movement in the story. It isn't just the plot that moves the story, but how the plot impacted the characters. Both of these things are important.

Take time now to evaluate the growth of the characters in this book and in your own story. Make adjustments as needed.

Twenty-six

"It is great to see you. How was your trip?" Curtis leaned forward with his elbows on the table as he spoke.

"Relaxing. I need to get away more often." Rachel sipped her water after she spoke. She had enjoyed two nights of restful sleep. In Chicago there was no fear of roses appearing and noises that go bump in the night. She had shopped and ate out and enjoyed girl talk with Shannon well into the night.

"I'm glad to hear it. You've been pretty uptight the last few times we've talked."

"I have a lot on my mind. It's been an eventful couple of months."

"How?" He asked and reached out to put his hand on top of hers.

She looked down at their hands as butterflies flapped in her stomach. She wanted to be comforted by his touch but right now it made her uneasy. It made no sense for them to be attracted to each other at all. Curtis was the kind of guy a woman would settle down and start a life with. Before they met she didn't think she was ready yet to be that kind of woman.

"I find myself thinking a lot about the future these days."

"You do?" He gently squeezed her hand. "Am I in it?"

The truth was always nice but that would require submission that was beyond her ability right now. It would mean allowing him to not only penetrate but remove the armor she wore. She couldn't allow a man that close.

On the other hand, life without Curtis in it would be unbearable. She had figured that out while in Chicago. For all the glitter and fun she had more than once wished it was Curtis rather than Shannon at her side.

"You might be." She made her voice playful. Coy was always best.

"Good. I want to be in your future." He lifted her hand to his lips and kissed it, then he gently sat it back down on the table. "Rachel, I'd like you to come to church with me on Sunday."

"Why?" She hadn't meant for her voice to sound so disgusted but the request had surprised her.

"I want you to get to know me better." He sounded defensive at her response.

"That is what we're doing right now. We are taking time to know each other."

"Yes but Rachel this is only the smallest, most superficial part of me. I want you to know who I am at my essence, my core."

"Has this whole thing been some evangelism device for you?" It wasn't how she planned to bring up the subject but now there it was. She wasn't going to retract them.

"Do you think that poorly of me?" He leaned back and folded his arms. His eyes were intense. It was something she hadn't thought he was capable of and it made her feel like a naughty child who'd gotten mud on her good clothes. "I don't prostitute myself for the gospel."

"I'm not sure what I think. I'm not trying to change you, Curtis, but every time I think I may have feelings for you, you throw church at me." Her voice was steadily raising. She looked up. They were beginning to get an audience. She leaned in slightly and lowered her voice. "I want to have a good time with you but I'm not interested in church stuff."

"Fine." He sat up straight. She knew that pose. It was the same one she used when she knew there was no further debate.

They sat in almost complete silence until the food arrived then the silence was only broken by the occasional slurp or fork squeaking on the plate. They finished their meal, passed on dessert and walked to the parking lot.

Curtis pulled his keys out of his pocket and folded his arms. "I'm glad you got home safe."

“Thank you.”

“I’ll call in a few days if I don’t hear from you first.” He fidgeted with his keys.

“Fine.” She wanted this fight to be over but she wasn’t going to be the one to make the first move. The fact that he wouldn’t admit that he had ruined their afternoon by brining up church again. “I’ll talk to you later then.”

“Yep.” He turned and walked away from her.

She watched him walk away. As much as her body cried out “Come back”. Her pride wouldn’t let her do it. Why couldn’t he accept her answers? Some people have reasons for not going to church. It didn’t make them bad people.

He put his car in reverse and pull out of the parking lot. In her romance novels this was the moment that her phone would chime and he’d apologize… She reached in her purse for the phone. He didn’t understand her reasons. Maybe she should apologize now, not let him go. She flipped it open. A silly picture of her and Shannon appeared on the screen. She closed the phone and climbed in her car.

She turned up the CD that on the way over had made her skin ache for Curtis’ touch. Now as the final notes played it was more a haunting reminder that some people out there were happy and in love. She brushed away a tear and pushed the back button to start the song over

again.

The pain felt good, familiar and tangible. The sweet first words of the song talked about

the freshness of new love. Rachel let them wash over her as she began her short drive home.

Slow teardrops rolled out of the corners of her eyes. Loneliness gave way to anger and

frustration. Why would she date him knowing he'd want to change a chunk of her?

When they were together she felt safe, truly alive. Curtis made her want to strive to be

better, as if, in some way, all her accomplishments weren't quite enough.

But if she wanted to change then why was she mad at him?

The song ended and she pushed the repeat button. The music cleared her thinking. He had

something she wanted. He was genuine. There were no ulterior motives when she was with him.

They didn't have awkward moments because she knew that they wouldn't spend the night. He

wouldn't give himself fully to her yet which only made her want him more.

Even with all that she wasn't about to find religion for him. Frustration rose up in her

again. Just this past spring she had it all together and now everything changed. Of the two men in

her life the decision should be duh-simple. One is was successful, handsome and passionate for her. The other is was successful, cute and passionate for her soul.

As the song started up for the fourth time she turned in to her driveway and pulled behind the house into the garage. She popped the CD out of the player and carried it in the house. The evening was cool and she averted her eyes from the long shadows made by the streetlights. The dog a few houses down barked. She jumped.

"Stupid dog. Can't they hear that thing barking every night." There always had to be one neighbor that ruined it for the block. She knew she'd be home after dark so this time she'd left every light on in the house. She reached in and pulled the mail out of the box then felt around to be sure she hadn't missed any and locked the door. After she placed a mug of water in the microwave she walked to the counter next to the trashcan to go through her mail. The stack of papers turned in to three bills after throwing out the solicitation and credit card offers.

She ripped open the credit card bill. Might as well get rid of the worst one first. She scanned down the page and saw the body shop charge. "There is *how* much in new charges? I'd better call Jeremy." She scrolled through the contact list in her phone and pushed send after highlighting his number.

"Hello."

"Hi Jeremy, this is Rachel."

"Hello Rachel."

"I got the car fixed and I realized when I got my credit card statement that I never mailed you the statement. Can I get your address again?"

Her call waiting beeped. She'd let it go to voicemail.

"Sure thing it's-."

Her other line beeped again.

"I'm sorry. Jeremy, can you hold on just one second. My other line keeps beeping."

"Of course, no problem." His voice had a hint of hesitation.

"Hello?"

"Rachel, it's Curtis."

"Um...I-."

"I want to talk." He sounded more like 'Let's see other people.' Than 'Let's work things out.' She wasn't ready for that.

"I have someone on the other line. Can we maybe talk tomorrow?"

"I really think we should talk now." No, she couldn't hear this right now.

"I can't. I've got to handle this on the other line." She choked back tears.

"Fine. I'll talk to you tomorrow." The tone in his voice didn't give her much hope.

"Bye."

"Yep."

She punched back over.

"Jeremy?"

"Yes."

"The address?"

"Do you still have my card?"

"Yes."

"It's on there." He hurried her with clipped answers. It was just as well. She wasn't in a chatty mood.

"Okay, thank you."

"You're welcome. Good-bye."

"Bye."

Twenty-seven

Logan hung up with Rachel and slammed his phone down. Thankfully it hit a cushion and bounced.

"Who does she think she is, talking to me like that?" He paced from one side of the room to the other. "She doesn't know who she is dealing with here. I don't put up with disrespectful women." His voice echoed in the empty house. He walked to the bookshelf and stared directly at the 8 x 10 of Rachel in the frame.

"I could have any woman I want but I *chose* you. You were the one, the perfect one." His jaw was tight. His teeth were pressed so tight together his head throbbed.

"And you would dare to speak to me in that way?" He slammed his fist on the table as he walked past. Pain surged up through his wrist in to his arm. He yelled out a foul word then rubbed his wrist. "Who do you think you are speaking to me like that Rachel?" He said again wagging his finger at her picture. "We'll get that spunk out of you right away. You'll learn submission to me."

He lifted her photo and set it on the floor by his feet. "You'll learn to submit." He kicked the picture over with the side of his foot and went to the bouquet of roses in the kitchen. It was time to contact her again. Leave another message to her, let her know he was close. He pulled

out the white one and tied it with a ribbon. The roses fragrance wafted up and desire

overwhelmed him. The anger drained from his body and all that remained was the need to be one

with Rachel. He walked back to the other room and bent down to the photo on the floor.

"I'm sorry, Beautiful." He lifted the photo, wiped the glass and placed it back on the

bookshelf. "I didn't mean it. I get angry sometimes. Don't worry. I'm not really like that."

"I have a flower for you. It's a rose. You know what that means? We are one step closer

to being together." He inhaled the rose's fragrance again then laid it down in front of her photo.

"You're right. I do need to learn a bit more patience. I'm working on it." He smiled at the photo.

"I shouldn't be so hard on you. You're just nervous about being in love."

Twenty-eight

Rachel placed the bill in the envelope, sealed it and placed it in the basket with the other

outgoing mail. Then she called Shannon.

"What's up hon?" Shannon said without greeting.

"Is there something wrong with me?" Rachel tried to sound funny but it came out

pathetic.

"What is it now?"

"Men."

Shannon laughed. "I know there are so many of them in your life. Most women would be

thrilled with your problem."

"They would not. It is one thing to have a man in your life. It is quite another to have two

different men in your life when you're not sure if either is right for you at all."

"Date didn't go so well?"

"Not really."

"What happened?"

"He invited me to church."

"Rachel, it was bound to happen."

"I know but…"

"Do you like him?"

She groaned and plopped down on the couch. "I don't know. I think so."

"Well do you or don't you?"

"Yes. I really like him."

"Then go with him to church. You go with your mom and she's not a good kisser."

Shannon laughed.

"I can't believe you're telling me this after-."

"After Nate?"

"Well…yes."

"Curtis isn't Nate."

"Yes, but-."

"No, but. Church is nothing but a social group. There's a support structure with people

who have a common interest."

"But we don't agree with that." Shannon had never wavered in all the time Rachel had known her. She gripped the phone tight. "Why would you tell me to go?"

"My thoughts. Do what feels good. If right now it feels good to date Curtis then church is part of the deal. If you two don't work out then you do things with your new lover. It is no different than going to football games with a sportsman."

"But Nate didn't leave me for football." Rachel screamed in the phone. "He left me for church."

"He left you for one of those freaky commune things Rachel. That is why I told you to stay away from religious people. People get fanatical about things. But you kept this Curtis thing going."

"I can't help it. He makes me happy."

"Well go with it. If he makes you happy do what you gotta do to stay with him. If that means go to church then go every once in a while. As long as you don't start to buy in to their con you'll be fine."

"But-."

"Go once and see what he's like there. Make an appearance if you really like him. It's not like you're signing up for church or anything."

How could Shannon be the one who suggested she do this? "But what if he wants me to start going all the time?"

"I guess you'll have to make that decision then but if he only asked you to come once then go for it."

They talked for a bit longer then Rachel hung up the phone and put her feet up on the coffee table. She wanted to do this and still save face. Curtis couldn't think that he'd won anything.

Twenty-nine

Saturday morning Rachel woke up and looked at the clock. It was 10:30? She hadn't slept

that late since college. She picked up the romance novel from her nightstand and went down to

the kitchen. The coffee pot had automatically shut off at some point and now the coffee starting

to cool off. The timer was set for 8:30 which was when she was usually up on the weekends. Her

head was throbbing. Most likely the headache was from all the crying she'd done the night

before. Hopefully coffee would help but if not she'd need medicine for this one.

She stretched out on her chaise lounge and opened her book. After reading the same page

for the third time she set it aside. The book was no more help this morning in getting her mind

off Curtis than it had been the night before. He was foremost in her mind. What Shannon had

said made a lot of sense. He was only asking her to go to church once. She wouldn't be this upset

if he'd asked her to a hockey game. Though she had no desire to do that either. Really it was the

principle of it. He knew her feelings about church but yet he still tried to get her there. If she

could cut that part out of him things would be great between the two of them.

She lifted her mug and sipped at her coffee. It was only warm so she took a gulp and set

the mug down on the table beside her. When had her life gone so out of control? She closed her eyes and laid her head back against the large pillows of the Chaise. Relationships were so

complicated now. None of her friends wanted to go out and have fun. They suddenly worried

about where everything was going. Except for her and Shannon, everyone's clocks started

ticking at once and now there was a mad dash to find "the one". There was no sense of enjoying

the moment.

Now even Shannon was starting to turn on her. Since when did she become a Bible

thumper? Maybe the roses had given Shannon a Jesus experience? Rachel wasn't sure what to

think now. To be honest she would love to go back in time before she ever met Drew or Curtis or

any of this mess.

"There were no roses before all this."

She couldn't listen to the questions pounding in her mind over and over. There were no

answers to them. People were confusing and relationships were messy. She wanted to scream in

frustration but that was reality. All this was not going to fit in a neat package.

She stood up and went to her kitchen for a dust rag. A sense of order would make her

feel better. There was something soothing in the scent of pine and lemon in a sparkling clean

house. At 2:15 the phone rang. She picked it up and pushed the talk button as she walked up to her bedroom.

"Hi Rachel, it's Drew."

"Hi." She forced her voice to be calm.

"I was wondering if you had plans for the afternoon."

"Right now I'm dusting." She walked in to her bedroom and moved things off her dresser

and on to her bed. She swiped the surface and tops of the drawers with a disposable dusting

cloth.

"Is that a brush-off like washing your hair?"

"No it's what I'm doing."

"I should have known you were a neat freak. I like that. You're welcome to come to my

place any time and clean up."

"I've seen your place. It is cleaner than mine." She had no plans to ever step foot in his

house again.

"If you say so." He cleared his throat. "I was calling to see if maybe we couldn't get

together this afternoon and talk a little."

"I don't know if…"

"Before you say no hear me out. I don't like the way things ended the other night. I feel really bad about my response. I should have respected your feelings more." He paused. When she didn't fill the dead air he continued. "I was a real jerk and I want to make it up to you. I'm really a nice guy. I don't know why I acted like that."

"I shouldn't have led you on like that."

"You didn't lead me on. I thought we had a great time together and that we clicked."

"We did. I don't know why I acted so weird."

"So will you meet me then?"

He was calling to apologize. That had to count for something. It was more than Curtis had done. Typical. She didn't want to ruin any salvageable part of her relationship with Curtis but didn't look like much of a priority to him at the moment. It was better to have a man who desired your than one who wanted to baptize you.

How would he feel if she went out with Drew? He probably wouldn't like it. But she didn't like what he was doing to her either. He was supposed to call today and it was mid-afternoon and she hadn't heard boo from him. If he wanted to act like this he wasn't worth worrying about.

"Rachel?"

"I'm thinking." What if Curtis called when she was with Drew? Guilt grab hold of her.

"Today isn't good. Can we get together on Monday after work?"

"Are you sure? Dinner sounds a lot more serious than coffee."

"I'm sure. Today doesn't work well for me. I need a down day to be grubby. Work's been really hectic and I was looking forward to living in sweat pants this weekend."

His voice brightened. "I can understand that. I'll meet you Monday after work at Sofo's is that okay?"

"Sofo's at 6? Will that work for you?"

"Perfect."

She hung up the phone and started pulling pillows off her bed. She picked up the knife under her pillow and set it on the nightstand. Was she making a huge mistake by seeing Drew? It didn't matter. She was living in the moment. Sticking to *her* princliples. Enough worrying about every little decision. Time to be carefree like she'd been before these guys entered her life. She shook her pillow out of its case.

Her mistake was over-analyzing every aspect of her relationships. Just roll with it and stop trying to figure everything out. She turned on the radio in her room to drown out her own thoughts.

Rachel walked around the bed pulling the sheet loose and rolling it in to a ball to take to the washing machine.

Pain shot up through her toe. "Ouch." She yelled then plopped down on the bed and looked at the bottom of her foot. She'd stepped on something sharp.

"What did I step on?" She looked down on the floor. There was nothing there. Moving carefully, she checked the floor. Nothing. She knelt and lifted the dust ruffle. With her heart pounding in her chest she pulled out a rose stem with the bloom cut off. The ends were dry and the thorn that had poked in her foot was snapped off.

She took the rose and threw it in her trash can. Was there any other way a rose could have ended up under her bed. No. There was only one way and it meant somehow he'd gotten in her house.

Without another thought to the pain in her foot Rachel jumped off her bed and ran from room to room. Somewhere a window had been left open. He would not get in again. On the second floor everything was locked. She ran down to the first floor and checked the windows and doors. Every window was latched and the doors were locked.

The door to the basement stood open an inch. She was certain she had closed that door

before she went to bed. Did he come in while she slept? The hair on her arms rose as she thought

of the image of a silhouetted man standing by her bed watching her sleep. She grabbed a knife

and flipped on the light to the basement. It was still except for the hum of the heater. She stepped

on to the first step. No rustling or foot steps.

Second step, still no sounds.

Her ears were tuned to any sound that may be in the basement. Slowly she moved down

the steps pausing to listen for movement of any kind. The naked light bulb showed a stack of

boxes she hadn't yet unpacked. The curtain was drawn across the sliding glass door. Her socks

allowed the cold in the cement floor to soak in to her foot. The hair stood up on the back of her

neck. She scanned left and right as she crossed the basement to the door. Nothing to give her an

indication that he'd been there.

She reached the door and pulled the curtain back. Overhead something clacked and rolled

across the kitchen floor.

Development of our Antagonist
Writing bad guys are the best part of writing! I love it!! You can do

things with a bad guy that a person would NEVER let you do with a good character.

The problem with writing bad guys is people want to make them pure evil and that just doesn't work!! I'm not afraid of a burned up school janitor invading my dreams and killing me as I slept. I am afraid of the nice guy in town who turns out to be a serial rapist. It is because we trusted them. We let our guard down and they were evil.

The key to writing a great bad guy is that crazy people do not think they're crazy. They find their desire to kill, maim, attack and control to be totally rational. When we can find the rationale in our antagonist we can create chilling and memorable characters.

Right now take some time to evaluate the rationale of the bad people in this book. Why is it logical and permissible to do the evil things they do [in their minds]? Now look in your own story and come up with a reason why it is okay to do all of the evil they do in your book.

Brainstorm here

And now, while you're at it, find a weakness in your GOOD guys and let them rationalize why they don't need to change. Build that in to the character arc.

Thirty

Rachel got out of her car and adjusted her new jacket. The fine wool pantsuits had been one of her purchases on her trip to Chicago with Shannon. It was a snappy black jacket that turned sapphire in the right light. Shannon wouldn't let her leave the store until Rachel bought it.

"Hot date?" Shannon said when Rachel walked in the office.

"No, I hate the idea of wasting money on an outfit that sits in the back of my closet."

"What time are you meeting him?" Shannon said seeming to have not heard a word Rachel has just said.

"I said-"

"Yes, I heard what you said and I don't believe a word of it. I'm looking right at you and the hair and make-up scream date." Shannon folded her arms and cocked her head to the side as she spoke.

"I'm meeting Drew after dinner to talk."

Shannon took Rachel by the arm and led her back to the conference room.

"What are you doing?" Shannon said as soon as she closed the door.

"Don't start. I'm not doing anything wrong."

"Does Curtis know?"

Rachel glared at her. "What do you think?"

"I thought you had something with Curtis."

"I don't know if I do or not."

"So what? You're having a last fling?"

"Don't you get judgmental with me Miss On-the-first-date-Shannon."

Shannon's eyes narrowed. "I was trying to be a friend. You're the one who called me torn up because Curtis was mad at you."

"When did you join the Curtis fan club?"

"I don't know, I guess he grew on me." Shannon paused only momentarily. Typical. Do what Shannon says no matter how irrational.

"Then you date him."

"He loves you. Although at the moment I'm at a loss for why."

"I am not going to commit to something until I'm sure." Rachel focused on adjusting her outfit again to avoid eye contact.

"What more do you need to be sure?"

"I'll just know." Rachel took her purse off her shoulder and set it on the conference table behind her.

"Fine. Whatever Rachel." Shannon threw her hands up in the air. "You have messages in your door. I have an appointment with a potential new client at two but I'll be back by end of the day." She turned and opened the door.

Rachel sat alone in the room for a long moment. Shannon of all people should understand not wanting to settle. Rachel picked her purse up off the table and dug out her cell phone. She scrolled through her contact list but there was no one to call? Shannon was the person she always talked to when she had a problem.

She jammed the phone back in her purse and jerked the strap over her shoulder.

"Shannon." Rachel yelled down the hall as she turned in her own office. "Can you come in here for a minute?"

Shannon stopped in the doorway, arms folded. "What?" She said and folded her arms.

She wasn't quite sure how to start. She couldn't stand to have one more thing wrong in her life. Why had she been so defensive? Shannon was trying to protect her friend.

"Do you have the expense reports from last week?" She tried to make her voice normal.

It came out stiff.

"Folder on your desk." Shannon said pointing then folding her arms again. "Is that the only reason you summonsed me to your office?"

"No, I…uh."

"What Rachel? Do you think this office stops when you have a problem?"

"No."

"The expense reports are on your desk."

"Have you looked them over yet or am I the first one?"

"Looked at them already. That's why they're on your desk."

Rachel unlocked her desk and turned on her computer.

"I don't want to fight, Shannon."

"Fine. We're not fighting." She turned and walked out the door.

Rachel had not handled that well at all. She lifted the expense reports and flipped through them. Some of this was going to have to go home to get it done in time for monthly budget work ups. She ripped open the bottom drawer of her desk to toss her purse in. She froze. Another rose.

"Shannon, who has been in my office."

"Why?" Shannon came around the corner into Rachel's office. "I put everything-."

Shannon's stopped the moment she made eye contact with Rachel.

"A rose."

"Don't touch another thing in this office." Shannon waved Rachel to her. "I'm going to

call 9-1-1 from the front desk."

Rachel stood up and picked up her purse and walked out of her office. Shannon was on

the receptionist's phone confirming the office's address.

"Get them out of the office." Shannon said pulling her chin away from the phone to say it

quietly to Rachel.

"C'mon guys. Let's get out." Rachel walked to the door and opened it.

"What's going on?" People started turning to each other.

"Go on out, please." Rachel held the door for everyone to go in the parking lot then

closed the door and stepped back in with Shannon.

"Thank you, goodbye." Shannon said in the phone. "They're on their way."

"Check your keys."

They both pulled out their keys and went through them. The only person who had keys to the office were the two of them and the building owner.

"What about Walt?"

"Yeah, but he doesn't have keys to your desk."

So much for the building owner.

"Rachel, have you been here with anyone?"

"No, you?"

Shannon shook her head no. "Let's go outside." Shannon put her arm over Rachel's

shoulder as they walked out the door. "Are you okay?"

"Not really." She smiled through tears.

Shannon hugged her tight.

"We'll get all this straightened out. Don't worry about a thing." She pushed the hair back

from Rachel's face. "The police will get this handled."

Rachel shook her head as her breakfast roiled in her stomach and threatened to come

back up.

The police arrived twenty minutes later and ran down a list of questions. Who had keys?

Anything else strange? What did you touch? Rachel answered all their questions in a fog. Who was doing this? They finished checking things out then allowed a limited staff back in the

building to work. Around lunchtime Drew called.

"Rachel, would it be all right if we move things up earlier in the day?"

"That shouldn't be a problem. Why?" Someone had been through her desk and looked at

everything there that was private to her. Nothing was private and things would be much less

private soon.

"I have to go out of town tomorrow morning so I need to meet earlier in the day."

"What time were you thinking?"

"Is three too early?"

"No three is fine."

They finished talking. Down in her office the police were still talking amongst

themselves and photographing everything they could fine. Rachel tried to focus on her expense

report. She filled in the expense sheets and balanced the books with one eye to her office. He had

been in here. He may have gone through her things or sat in her chair. He knew her intimately.

He had seen her home and her office and her car. She wrapped her arms around her waist and

pressed her back to the wall. There was no place he hadn't been.

At 2:15 she left the office and drove to the restaurant to meet Drew. This whole thing at the office likely ruled out Drew. He knew where she lived but someone from the office would have noticed him walking in her office.

Maybe the stalker was gone. There were no more reports on things happening and while the police were diligent in helping her they no longer seemed overly concerned with the roses. It had to be a copycat or someone's misguided notion of romance. The ideas did little to sooth the fear that lingered on the edge of her every conscious thought.

She arrived at Sofo's a bit early so she fixed her hair and makeup before walking in to the restaurant. The smell of tomato sauce and garlic greeted her. The bar to her right looked like a European outdoor café. Straight ahead was a wooden podium and a park bench.

"Will there be anyone else joining you this afternoon?" The host asked when she put in her name.

"Yes. He should be here any time. Could I look at a menu while I wait?"

"Of course." He gave her the menu then returned to rolling silverware in white linen napkins.

She sat down on a bench near the hostess station and read over the menu. The food smelled good but she wasn't sure if her stomach could hold anything.

"Rachel, glad to see you." Drew walked in with his arms outstretched. She put down the menu and stood up. He gave her a quick peck on the cheek. It was a once kiss greeting she'd seen on European movies. "You been waiting long?"

"Only about five minutes. I got here early."

The host led them to a corner table near the back of the room then read them the special off a white card before leaving them.

"Thank you again for meeting me." Drew said over the top of his menu.

"You're welcome. I rarely turn down free food."

"I thought you were buying." He winked at her and returned to his menu.

After they placed their orders Drew folded his arms and rested them on the table.

"You look absolutely beautiful."

"Thank you." She smiled.

"I've been thinking about you quite a bit."

"You have?" She tucked a bit of hair behind her ear. "Why?"

"Because I really care about you Rachel." He reached over and touched her cheek with his fingers.

Drew knew what to say to her and how to look at her. A few moments with him and all was now forgiven. Why had she doubted his sincerity? Any person had a right to be upset when they got led on. She was mad at the way Curtis had-.

Curtis.

She once again saw his face in her mind's eye. His sincerity and his charm. She looked up at Drew. His hazel eyes were intense.

Drew cocked his head to one side. "Do you have any feelings at all for me?"

The server set down her tray on a stand and placed a salad in front of each of them. Rachel was relieved. It only bought her a few moments though. She got a few lettuce leaves on her fork and took a bite. Drew picked at his salad across the table from her.

"I'm not sure how I feel right now, Drew."

"Do you feel anything?" His voice didn't betray much emotion. He was trying to save face.

"I find you attractive."

"But?" His voice sounded amused as if physical attraction should be enough.

She picked at her salad and took another bite.

"But I don't know. What are you looking for in a relationship right now?"

"Depends on the woman."

"What are you looking for in a relationship with me?" She set her fork down and looked straight at him. He pushed tomatoes around his plate.

"I want to take this relationship as far as it will go." She didn't reply so after a long pause he continued. "I am done with purely physical relationships with women who are only looking for fun." He lifted his head and stared straight at her. When she didn't say anything he continued. "I'm starting to think long term. Maybe live together; see what happens. Hopefully, eventually, I want to settle down."

How many nights over these last couple of months had she longed to have someone beside her for protection and comfort. And how many of those nights had she needed protection from images of Drew? "What makes you think that I'm that woman?"

"I don't know." He wiped his mouth with the linen napkin and placed it back in his lap. "I guess I can only say there is something in your eyes when you look at me. You have an inner strength I don't often see in women."

She smiled. Not for the compliment he paid her but for the irony. Her life was crashing in on top of her and she couldn't figure out which man held her heart. Now Drew was looking her in the eye telling her it was her strength that attracted him to her.

"I'm really not that strong."

"But you are." He reached out and took her hand. "You have taken life and squeezed every bit of opportunity out of it possible. You are successful. You know what you want. And you are going to be a wealthy woman one day. You mark my words."

She moved her fingers and Drew released her hand. "Can we stop talking about me for a bit?"

"If that's what you'd like."

"Tell me about you Drew. When you aren't selling houses what do you do? What do you want to be?"

He picked his fork back up and took a bite of his salad. After he chewed it he started.

"You know I'm not sure. I'm a man who loves to live in the moment. The moment is all we've really got."

"And the future?"

"The future is going to happen whether or not I do anything about it. I try to live and be the best person I can be today and trust that tomorrow will reward me for it." He shrugged his shoulders and took another bite.

Hadn't this lunch been all about the future? "What do you plan to do with your real estate career?" Rachel asked.

"Well, the market is really slowing down but these things go in cycles. I am going to ride it now and when the market goes back up I'll be doing quite well for myself."

"Sounds like a plan." She thought he was a professional like her.

"Hey, Rachel. You still awake."

She blinked her eyes and looked at him. "Sorry. So are you a real estate investor?"

"No." He crinkled his nose. Not a good look for him. "I sell houses. I don't mess with all that other."

"How was it you came in to Real Estate?"

He smiled. "Interesting story." He put his fork down and moved his hands as he spoke.

"My brother who is a few years older had read about people making big money in selling houses. At the time we were working various minimum wage jobs and I'd just had to move back with my parents." He smiled. "Quite embarrassing."

"I can imagine."

"Well that was during the big real estate boom and they were almost begging for agents. People couldn't keep up with the demand. I took the classes to get licensed and started selling houses. Within two months of selling I moved out of my parents' house and got my place. I got a great deal on it because I knew the listing agent. I never thought I'd be in to selling houses but here I am. It's a paycheck."

"Wow, you did well right off the bat."

"Yep, I had to. I have expensive taste." He tapped to a gold watch on his left wrist.

The server brought out their main courses. Rachel pushed noodles around on her plate occasionally scooping up a small pile and eating them. As if a light switch flipped the attraction that had bubbled inside her was gone.

Drew bored her. Curtis had ideas that challenged her. He had business sense she respected.

"Rachel, you're awfully quiet today." Drew smiled but there was no ache or pull. Simple acknowledgement.

"Sorry. My mind is on a marketing client I've been working with." She wanted to be with

that marketing client right now instead of running back to the same kind of man she'd wasted all

these years chasing.

The server brought out the check and set it next to Drew. Rachel reached across for it.

"Let me pay."

He pushed his plate to one side. "Why would you want to do that?"

"You've paid the other times."

He straightened his back. "I invited you to lunch. I will pay." His tapped one finger on

the table as he spoke through tight lips.

"I would feel better if I paid for this."

"What has gotten in to you today? I am a perfect gentleman, I invite you out and talk

about the future with you. What exactly are you looking for?"

"It's not you. It's-."

"Oh I know it's not me." He pushed the plastic folder holding the check over to her side.

"It's you. Do you really think you can buy me off by paying one lousy twenty dollar lunch tab?"

Rachel put her credit card on the tray and set it on the edge of the table. "What do you mean buy you off?"

"Come now. We both know you are fairly wise to the ways of men and women." He

scanned her up and down. Rachel pulled her sweater across the front of her. "When a man goes

out with a lady for a bit it comes with certain…expectations."

"Drew, I appreciate the meal but I don't think right now is a good time for me to be in a

relationship."

"Fine. If you don't want to make some kind of long term commitment but I've invested

quite a bit of my time in you." His tone was steady as if he were explaining to her why a charge

was so high. "And you've been leading on pretty strong."

"I've been confused."

"Oh, you've been confused." The server walked out and handed Rachel the receipt.

Rachel signed it and handed it back. "Then let me clear things up for you a bit. I don't have time

for women who want to play games."

"I have a lot going on in my life right now. I thought this was what I wanted." She

motioned between them with her hand indicating the relationship.

"I'm fairly accustomed to getting what I want Rachel."

"I'm sorry."

"Whatever." He stood up and bumped the corner of the table with his thigh. Drinks

sloshed and coffee splattered on Rachel's outfit. He didn't say a word of apology but stood up

and snatched his jacket off the back of the chair and walked out of the restaurant.

She looked down at her watch. It was almost 4:15. She should try to beat rush hour home.

False Clues

When constructing your story don't forget that these characters are REAL PEOPLE. That means they don't have a perfectly developed sense of what to do in every situation. They'll do things wrong. They'll perceive things wrong. They'll act on those wrong assumptions.

In the spaces below brainstorm a few false clues you can use in your own writing.

Make sure you label false clues in this book after you've finished reading. And if you think you've found a false clue, label it and see if you're right.

Thirty-One

Logan lifted a ribbon off the bookshelf. Not many left, soon they'd be together. A surge of desire swelled inside. He looked at the open photo album on the table. Rachel on every page.

Whenever they spoke every bit of manhood inside fought to drive in to her house, not to wait. He had to discipline himself. He needed patience if he was going to do it right. She was battling within. She had two men fighting for her affections. The poor thing couldn't know which way was right.

He would show her.

But now wasn't the time. Everything had to be perfect. There were still ribbons on the shelf. He still had roses to be given. Win her slowly. Take her slowly.

It was the anticipation of the revelation that kept spice in relationships. Most often what isn't said and what isn't shown that keeps the relationship refreshing. She had to suspect by now it was him leaving the gifts for her. Who else could it be?

He smelled the bloom. Each one was sweeter than the last because it brought him one step closer to touching and loving his beautiful Rachel.

He walked to the picture of Rachel on the shelf that was on eye level. "Are you excited?"

He asked it. "You have it figured out, don't you?" A shiver ran down his body. "You're playing along. I like that." His voice was low and soft. It was the voice he was going to use when he stepped from the shadows and in to her life.

Forever.

He was going to be her fantasy. They would be like a couple in a romance novel. He would be her dream man who would show her things she never realized she wanted or needed.

When they spoke now there was always a spark. They had a connection that continued to draw her to him. No matter how many times she wavered she always came back to him. She'd come back this time too.

She had hurt him with her rejection when they last spoke. Her voice was cold and she was distant. She was lucky he was a man who was committed to her. All was forgiven.

Alpha Mu Epsilon.

Thirty-Two

"Rachel." Curtis' sounded genuinely happy when he answered the phone. "Good to hear

from you." There was no hint of the terse words they'd shared the last time they spoke.

"Sorry. I've needed some time to sort a few things out."

"Anything I can help with?"

"No, thank you though." There was a long silence on the phone. She searched for a

thought but nothing seemed to be appropriate, or even interesting. "What have you been up to?"

It seemed a safe question.

"I've started a new Bible study at the church. It is on the book of Hebrews."

"Oh." Not what she was looking for. Reluctantly she continued. "What are you talking

about?"

"This last time we were talking about Faith." His voice trailed off. "The book deals a lot

with our faith in God and his faithfulness to us."

"Oh." She used the most interested voice she could muster.

"Rachel, I'm sorry about how things ended before."

"It's okay."

"No, I'm not trying to push anything on you. I wish that you'd want the joy and peace

God has given me but that is something you have to work out yourself. I can't force it on you

and I shouldn't have pushed you."

"Really, don't worry about it. I was a little touchy on it."

"I was a bit overeager because I want you to be a part of my life. My relationship with

God is a huge part of who I am and I didn't feel like you could really understand me if you didn't

understand where my faith comes from."

"You have to understand that my parents drug me to church my whole life. It was fine

when I was little but once I was a teenager it got old. They finally left me alone and let me stay

home when I was in high school. Then a few years ago they started a new church, the church you

go to with them. Then they started bugging me *all* the time."

"Sometimes when God gets a hold of us we get really excited, and possibly a bit over

enthusiastic in some people's opinion."

She softened a bit. He was really listening to her and what she thought instead of

jamming a bunch of verses down her throat. "I understand. My parents, especially my mom,

really changed when they started at the new church. I think it is great for them. If that is their truth and brings them happiness then they should do that."

"But it doesn't bring you happiness." He sounded disappointed.

"I don't feel I need a set of rules imposed by man to live a good life."

"Maybe that is where the two of you aren't connecting. You think you're talking about the same thing but you're really talking about two different things."

Rachel stood up and walked around the living room, geared up for a discussion that was surely coming. "We're both talking about church."

"No, you're talking about religion and they're talking about relationship."

"Fine and speaking of relationships, let's get back to ours so we don't get another fight brewing."

"Okay, I want to see you."

Rachel smiled. "When?"

"Ideally now, but I'm on my way to a business meeting in about twenty minutes."

"You have meetings at seven at night?"

"You have them whenever you need them to get the business."

"I guess that's true. We could meet after work tomorrow." She wrote it down in her calendar.

"That will be fine." He paused for a moment before continuing. "You've asked a bit about me. Besides working through a few things how are you, Rachel." When he said her name it caused her voice to catch in her throat, a ridiculous reaction.

"There's been a lot going on. I want things to calm down so I can breathe again."

"Do you want to talk about it?"

She did want to desperately. "I do want to talk to you a bit but now isn't a good time. You have your meeting."

"Are you sure I can't do something to help before I have to get there?"

"No. We can talk about it tomorrow."

"I understand." He paused for a few moments. "I missed you these last few days."

She'd tried not to think about him but he had lingered in the corner of her thoughts since the last time they were together. He was opening the door. Why did she keep playing this safe game of not telling him how much she needed him in her life?

"Why's that?" She tried to sound playful. That was the safest route. Keep playing the game.

He laughed a little bit. "Why do you miss people? I wanted to see you and you weren't around."

"In that case I guess I missed you too."

"I'm glad to hear it. For a minute there I thought I'd made a huge faux pas."

She got a bottle of water from her fridge and sat back out on her chaise. "Why would you think that?"

"I thought maybe I was reading too much in to this relationship."

Rachel's mouth was dry. She took a slow sip of water. Every muscle in her body tensed up. "Um," she began, trying to form the words that were sticking in her throat. "How do you see this relationship?"

Silence on the other end. She scolded herself for sounding judgmental when she said it. Curiosity was the tone she was after but clearly he had heard something very different. How could she continue now that she had stuck her foot in her mouth?

"Right now I guess I'd say we're seeing each other. Does that sound vague enough?" He laughed.

She exhaled the breath that, until that moment, she didn't realize she was holding. "You don't have to be vague. You can be honest." Her voice sounded a bit more natural. Curiosity

overcoming fear.

"How do you see it?"

"No," she laughed nervously "I asked you first."

"I hope you're the one but…" He stopped abruptly. Rachel tensed up again.

"But, what?"

"But, that isn't a decision I can make on my own."

"We can start investigating together tomorrow at dinner." Her curiosity now giving way

to excitement. What if he was the one?

"I'll call you tomorrow and let you know when my last appointment is and we can make

arrangements then."

"I'm looking forward to it."

"I have to make my appointment now."

"Okay, bye."

Rachel hung up the phone and sat it on the end table. Maybe he was the one. She let out a

squeal and grabbed her phone again.

"Shannon." Rachel said her name almost before Shannon had finished saying Hello.

"Is everything all right?"

"Yes, why?"

"What do you mean why? Today. The rose."

Rachel had chosen to forget the events of earlier in the day. She was no longer interested in being controlled by fear. For the moment she could smile and be excited and she was going to do it as long as possible. "I'm past that, for the moment. I just had the best conversation with Curtis."

"With Curtis? I thought you were having dinner with Drew." There was a clear I-told-you-so quality to her voice.

"I decided that Drew had some qualities I couldn't deal with."

"Such as?"

"A rather nasty temper."

"What happened?"

Rachel briefly recapped the evening.

"I can't believe he was like that. If he got so worked up in a public place I don't want to think about what could have happened in a long term relationship."

"Those were my thoughts."

"So you ended it tonight."

"I don't think he'll call back. He left in a huff after I paid the bill."

"You paid the bill? What a winner."

"I'm a 21st century lady. I can pay my own way but he is the type…never mind."

"What type?"

"He just…No, I don't want to talk about him. I want to talk about Curtis. That's why I called in the first place."

"Tell me about it."

Rachel jumped out of her chair again and paced from the dining room to the living room and back. "I felt a connection with him tonight I've never felt before."

"Like?"

"Like when we talked about church. I didn't feel like I was going through the inquisition. He didn't act like he was the be all and end all on wisdom."

"Why don't you go to something at church?"

314

Rachel took a sip of water and planned her words very carefully. "Why would I want to do that?"

"Same reason you do it for your mom. Look like you're making an effort."

"What's wrong with him accepting me for who I am?"

"We've already talked about this."

"But-."

"Do you go on a date looking like you rolled out of bed?"

"No." Her voice was flat.

"Then you try to impress him even though you know that is not who you really are."

"That is absolutely not the same thing." She sat on her chaise and scooted back in its cushions.

"Fine. All I am saying is if you went to some church event you will look like you're really trying to understand him and you won't have to deal with all the church stuff."

"What, you mean like a picnic." She could tolerate a social event with some church people. That would not be awful.

"Something like that. Find out if there are any social gatherings you can go to and do that. I think that's your best plan. You're bound to have to go to some of these if you get serious anyway so why not start them on your own terms."

Rachel let the idea roll around in her mind a moment. "The idea isn't awful."

"Is that supposed to be a compliment?"

"If you want it to be. I know my mom has some women's professional seminar going on soon. There's a woman speaking I read about in *Fast Company* magazine. You know, Carol Adnaw, I could get a chance to talk to her and score brownie points at the same time."

"Well there you go."

They chatted for a few minutes about how Rachel could casually ask about the event without letting her mom think she was going to start coming to church.

"The best way will be to tell her you want to go see the speaker."

"She'll ask why you're not coming with me." Rachel picked at her fingers as she spoke. She was way overdue for a manicure. "Then what will I tell her?"

"Tell her I don't want to come. We don't do everything together."

"Wish me luck."

"Thinking good thoughts." Shannon lifted her voice an octave or two in exaggerated excitement.

Rachel clicked the phone off and snuggled down in her chaise. A day of listening to a top woman executive wouldn't be bad at all. They'd throw in a few things about Jesus and likely talk about how it's all because of God that she is where she is today then the real teaching would begin. What women do to impress the men they love.

She didn't necessarily think that love described her feelings toward him yet. It was more of eager fascination or strong interest. He knew how to make her heart jump in her chest. Many times he also knew how to infuriate her as well. She enjoyed challenge and Curtis represented a real challenge. He was different then other men she'd dated, which was part of his charm. The sting of lost loves ate at her. Life for Rachel marched as a series of regrets, what-ifs and if-onlys.

Let the Reader Discover with you

In the previous section we talked about false clues, now let's talk about real ones. Readers like to discover the story along with the characters in the book. Make sure you're leaving enough information to be discovered SUBTLY [without a character saying, "Oh, looky there!! A clue!"]

Watch throughout the story for clues that point to you a new discovery in the book. Label them.

Thirty-three

"Where would you like to eat?" Curtis whispered into Rachel's ear. His cologne was woodsy. Not what she had expected from a straight-laced man. His 5 o'clock shadow scratched the back of her ear when he spoke. The office was empty except for the two of them standing in the lobby trying to decide where to have dinner. Curtis leaned against the wall when he arrived and Rachel slid in his arms. They'd stood there, chatting about their day for over thirty minutes.

"No where." She leaned back on her heels and pulled his arms tighter around her waist. Her fingers were laced between his and she resisted the urge to kiss his hand. "I want you to come back to my place."

"You aren't hungry at all? My stomach is eating my spine." He squeezed her.

"We can grab some Boston Market on the way."

"If you're sure that's what you want."

She laid her cheek against his arm and watched the cars pass by on the road outside her office. "That's exactly what I want. Boston Market at my place. A quiet evening in."

"I suppose we could be classified as an old dating couple now."

"Why because we're eating in?"

"We're eating take-out."

"Well if you want something else-"

He pulled her in close to him and rested his chin down on her shoulder. "If that is what you want then that is what you're going to have. My lady gets what she wants."

She reached back and touched his rough face. His stubble gave him a rugged look Rachel tried to resist.

"If we're going to get it though we should go."

She laid her head against him one last time. Even with him standing behind her holding her close there was distance between them. She wanted more of him. Her heart ached to hear his deep voice or to feel his soft fingers caress her skin. He wasn't willing to start a physical relationship with her, which only made her want him more. Slowly she turned to face him.

"Do you want to pick up the food or should I go?" She held his hand while she spoke. She didn't want to let go of him until they were each in their own cars.

"No reason for you to go. Head home and I'll be there soon." He leaned down and kissed her tenderly. She released his hands and slid her arms around his waist. Why wouldn't he start a physical relationship? Her insides screamed but she knew on that point he wouldn't budge.

"I'll wait while you lock up." He said and led her by the hand to the front door. She locked everything and kissed him again before she got in the car. Rachel drove through town to the tree-lined streets leading to her home. She had never noticed how many kids lived on the block closest to her house. Today she watched elementary aged boys running around the yard and girls off to the side chatting in small huddles. She heard a familiar song on the radio.

A familiar tune played quietly on the radio. She turned it up a bit. "Woo-hoo, I love this song." She cranked the volume button to the right and screamed out the words of the song while tapping out the rhythm on her steering wheel.

It didn't matter that the woman she let cross the street in front of her car crinkled her nose and smirked a bit. Singing opened her up. At least the woman didn't see her waving her arms around at the next stoplight. Throwing off inhibitions and cutting loose was good for a person every once in a while. She wasn't going to live every moment of her life in a stiff, regimented schedule with no time to decompress.

She turned in her driveway and gathered her purse, sweater and satchel from the passenger seat. Curtis said she'd have about twenty minutes before he'd be there with the food.

She came in the back door and set her things on the counter then walked to the front of the house and got the mail from the mailbox on the front porch.

"Junk, Junk, Junk." She tossed them in a pile. The rest went in the wire mail basket. The

clock in the kitchen clicked out the seconds and the refrigerator hummed to life. She scooped up

the credit card applications to shred and pushed the answering machine.

A robotic voice said "You have no messages." She switched on the shredder and

shredded those few things.

"Oh no, my lilac sweater is still at the cleaners." Rachel turned off the shredder scurried

in her stocking feet from the kitchen up the steps to her bedroom. That lilac sweater always drew

compliments and the weather was cool enough today that she could have wore it. Not that it

mattered that much. What she had on was just fine.

"But these pants aren't comfortable."

Would Curtis worry too much about her outfit? It wasn't a first date by any stretch. When

they'd met she was in jeans and an Old Navy T-shirt.

"Where's the blue one?" She scanned across her closet from left to right. Her finger

stopped on her blue top. It looked great with jeans. She pushed the hangers to the side and pulled

out a sweater then her favorite jeans. The outfit flattered her figure without being sensual then slid on her house slippers. She was attractive but relaxed. Curtis had a knack for being early. She

shot a glance to the clock and dashed downstairs to tidy up before he arrived.

There wasn't much to do after her weekend cleaning spree so instead she lit candles

around the room, turned on a CD of piano music and set two places at the dining room table.

This was a real relationship. Not since her breakup with Nate had she had an adult meal at home.

Instead they'd eat out someplace and then end the evening at one house or the other. The Chinese

takeout her and Curtis had shared on moving day didn't count. She felt more like a woman, an

adult.

And now her man was here.

She watched him get out of the car with the bag. She went through the kitchen and out

the back door. "Anything I can help you carry in?"

"I left something in the car." He said.

She grabbed the one small bag, closed his car door and held the door for him. He put the

bag he was carrying next to the one Rachel brought in and went back out the door. She lifted the

food out and started scooping potatoes, vegetables and baked apples in to serving dished.

"I thought the point of eating take out was to avoid a mess." He said when he walked back in the house and saw what she was doing.

"It's our first meal in as a couple. I want it to be nice." She said then she smiled and looked up at him.

"Here." He handed her a bouquet. "Put these on the table too. They'll look nice."

She took the bouquet of mixed flowers and smelled them. She loved the way different flowers always seemed to blend to make a fragrance as beautiful as the blooms. She'd yet to find a combination of blooms that didn't smell great together.

"Thank you." She said, still not putting them down.

"You're welcome." He kissed her then started collapsing the bags. They carried the serving dishes out to the dining room.

"Music, candles and flowers. Rachel are you trying to seduce me?" He said when he walked in.

She laughed at his movie reference. "I won't tell." And she set the bowl down. They filled their plates and ate without saying much for the first few minutes. It was Rachel who first broke the silence.

"Beyond being a Mortgage Broker what do you like to do?"

"This."

"Eat?" She smiled.

"Exactly. I love to eat. It keeps me alive."

"Boston Market sustains you, huh?"

"I like spending quiet time at home. My workdays have crept from eight or nine to more like ten to twelve some days. After all that time with people, ringing phone and paperwork it is nice to come home and have a quiet dinner and put my feet up. What about you?"

"I love to read. Give me a romance novel and I'm a happy woman."

"Oh, you don't read those things do you?"

"Those things?" She put her fork down. "Those things can be great."

"But you always know what's going to happen in the end."

"And you don't know in a movie that they'll live happily ever after?"

He shrugged in response.

"That's what I thought. The fun in them is the adventure. You know that the good guy will be handsome and perfectly romantic. Then one or the other will feel intimidated by the relationship or have a personality problem. There will be attraction; a wrench will be thrown in the works. *Then* they will live happily ever after.”

“And yet you read them?”

She smiled and shook her head. “I like predictable.”

“Somehow I knew that about you.”

“Is that a bad thing?”

“No. Predictable.” He smiled at his joke.

“Ha, ha.”

“What was the most unpredictable thing that has ever happened to you?” Curtis asked.

Icy fingers of fear pricked up and down her skin. Curtis looked up at her and his smile dropped.

“Are you okay?”

She needed to get a grip. Don’t ruin this moment with that. Don’t let the Fratboy ruin this

moment. She cleared her throat. “I’m fine. I’d have to say the most unpredictable thing I’ve done

was one summer during college instead of getting a summer job I pulled some money out of

savings and spent two weeks in southern France near the French, Italian, Swiss border.”

“Impressive. What was it like? I’ve never been over there.”

“It was a bit intimidating to tell the truth.” She took a sip of water. The fear was fading but she hadn't yet regained her carefree mood.

"Did you know the language?"

"I spoke French pretty well. Unfortunately I had studied French all through high school

and college but everyone failed to tell me that in France they don't speak French."

"What do they speak then?"

"Verlan."

"Verlan?" He pronounced it with a hard American accent.

"No, it's Ver, like in Very. Ver-law. But you have to talk through your nose at the end."

She smiled and demonstrated. He repeated back with an increasingly bad American accent.

"Okay, I can't say it. What is it?"

"French slang."

"Then why didn't you just say French slang." He laughed and tried to say Verlan again.

"Because it's called Verlan." She smiled. "It is a crazy language. They flip the syllables

around and use different verbs. It's like French pig Latin but people use and understand it."

"Guess you learn something new every day." He pushed his plate back.

Rachel stood to clear the table. Curtis stopped her by putting his hand on hers.

"Go sit. I'll clear these up."

"You don't know where they go."

"Go sit down." He pointed to the couch then stacked the plates and serving dishes.

Rachel scooped up the napkins with the last bowl and followed him to the kitchen.

"I thought you were sitting."

"I can't sit down in the other room while you clean my kitchen." She rinsed the plates

and arranged them in the dishwasher.

"I still get credit for being a nice guy." He gave her a bowl and she put it in the top.

"Yes, you get credit."

In five minutes the kitchen was picked up and the leftovers were in the fridge. They

walked back to the living room and sat down next to each other on the couch. She leaned her

head against his chest and listened to the thudding of his heart. Curtis squeezed her against him

and she tilted her head up to look at his face. The last of his aftershave or cologne filled her

nostrils. She pressed her face in to the side of his neck.

"What are you thinking about?" He said.

"Nothing. I'm enjoying the quiet." She was thinking about how she was living a romance novel.

"I was thinking about you."

"What about me?"

"I was thinking that when I met you there would have been no way I would have imagined I'd be dating you."

"Why's that?" He pulled his arm tighter around her.

"You aren't really my type?

She laughed. "That's fine because you're not my type either."

His cell phone chirped on his hip.

"You need to get that?"

"No, that is a business call. There aren't mortgage emergencies after seven so it can wait until morning."

"You don't answer your business phone after seven."

"Not unless I'm expecting a call."

She couldn't imagine ignoring any call, whether business or personal. What if there was an emergency that needed to be handled before the next morning. He didn't budge. It was as if the phone call never happened. Until a couple of months ago it was rare when she left the office

before seven.

"You're not even a little curious who called you." She said.

"Nope." He kissed her forehead. "Not a bit."

"I can't imagine."

"It takes a lot of practice but now I don't think twice about it. I even have two cell phones

with two different numbers. I forgot to take my work one off and leave it in the car. Usually I

don't carry it when I'm with you."

They sat in silence again for two or three minutes.

"Curtis?"

"Hm?"

"I'm going on the women's retreat at your church with my mom."

He leaned back and spun to face her. "Are you really?" He was beaming.

"I talked to her about it yesterday. I think it will be fun. I've wanted to hear Carol Adnaw

speak for some time."

Curtis grabbed her face with both of his hand planted a kiss square on the lips. She held on to his arms and kissed him back.

"Thank you. It means a lot to me that you would do that." He said.

"You're welcome. I had no idea you'd be that happy."

"I am." He leaned back on the couch and pulled her head back against his chest. She stretched her legs out and propped them on the coffee table and snuggled down against him.

"Hey, have you talked to my brother much?"

"I'd say we've talked a couple times a week plus I see him at church."

"Has he talked about his wife at all to you?"

"Yvonne? Yes a little."

She sat up and leaned forward on the couch and spun her rings. "My mom doesn't like Yvonne at all. I don't get in to it but there's no reason for Mom not to like her. She isn't doing anything to mess the two of them up is she?"

"No, I don't think so."

"Then what happened with them?"

He took her hand. "They're fighting all the time. She wants to come back to Ohio and he won't."

Her brother was the most pig-headed person she knew. When he thought he was right there was not changing his mind. "Then why is *he* in Ohio?"

Drew shook his head. "I asked him the same question. Adam said it was different because he was here to work some things out. It wasn't the same as moving."

"He's the only one who thinks they need to be out there." When they'd left Adam had been so sure he was doing what God told him to do. That was the danger in taking the God thing to far. Now he was willing to destroy his marriage rather than admit he was wrong. Of course, if that happened it would be God's fault too.

"I'm praying for him and we've prayed together quite a bit." Curtis continued. "He's starting to come around.

"I might call Yvonne and see how she's doing."

"That would be a big help. I've only talked to her once and that was because she happened to call your parents on the voice phone when I was there. She told me the thinks your family wants them to split up-."

"I don't."

"Call her and check in with. That will mean so much to her.

What is your impression of the character? What is that impression based on?

On the lines below, write some of your impressions [positive and negative] of a few of the characters in the story. List both primary characters and minor characters because all of them are meant to influence the story and the way you perceive it. All of them add flavor to the story. Sometimes secondary characters serve to reflect the qualities of the primary character. How well is that working? Write your notes in the book and below.

Thirty-four

"I'll call you in the morning." Curtis said before climbing in his car to leave. Their few hours had flown by so quickly. Rachel stood in the driveway behind her house with a leather jacket to keep her warm. Despite everything she said he insisted on leaving by eight p.m. He didn't want to steal her beauty rest. She waved as he turned to go down the road but it was too dark to see if he'd waved back.

Thirty-five

Logan pulled his car to the curb at the end of the block. Rachel's house was halfway back

along the street. She couldn't see him from here. A large blue spruce tree blocked the view. He

sat for a minute, thinking about Rachel, his lovely Rachel, just a short distance away. She'd be

going about her evening ritual, not dreaming he was here. He climbed out of his car and walked

down the street toward her house. The sky had darkened and the evening air was cool and damp.

The scent of her perfume lingered in his nostrils. He'd bought her brand and smelled it whenever

he was lonely for her touch.

He looked around at the dark splotches that blanketed the neighborhood. The shadows

formed when the street lights hit the trees. The sun was gone. "It's shadow time." He whispered.

He crossed the street and walked on the sidewalk opposite her house. Today was a special day

for the two of them. They had passed the two-month mark. He deserved a pat on the back for

patience and spending so much time with her, thinking about her but still unable to satisfy his

inner hunger.

"That's what Alpha Mu Epsilon is all about." He reached down to pet the dog in the yard

down the street from Rachel. He'd given the dog the name "Guardian" since he would alert

Logan to danger and because the dog guarded Rachel's house from across the street.

"I got something for you tonight boy." He stuck his hand in his jacket. Guardian walked as close to him as he could stretch. He whimpered and strained against the chain. Logan remained just out of reach until he'd found the treat in his coat pocket.

"There you go boy." He gave Guardian a pig's ear dog chew. Guardian grabbed it greedily and plopped down on the grass a few feet away and chewed on it. He was a smart dog. He almost never barked at Logan anymore when he came. "That should hold you until tomorrow."

It was getting late. He scanned the sidewalks. They were clear so he walked down past her house, double-backed then to her sidewalk. He had to hurry so he wouldn't get caught. That would take the fun out of their game. He looked around one more time and zipped up her porch steps, slid the rose in her mailbox then retreated to his usual hiding place.

Thirty-six

She stepped in the back door and locked it. There was plenty of time to sort through the mail and handle a little paperwork for the office before bed. She opened the electric bill.

"I'm not home enough to pay this much for electricity." The difference in her utility bill from a two-bedroom apartment to a three-bedroom house had put a bite in her fun money. She was due to have her roots touched up but they'd have to wait a couple more weeks. Money hadn't been an issue before the house. She stacked the bills back into a pile and plopped them in the wire basket.

"They're not going away." She snatched them back up and went to her desk drawer to get her checkbook. She hadn't seen a balance this low since she was in college. The electric bill was more than the insurance on her car was this month.

"What in the world?" Why was she getting a bill from Outdoorsman magazine?

"Wrong house."

She picked up all the envelopes and walked to the front of the house. The sun was completely gone with the slightest bit of purple lingering above the trees. Houses had porch lights on and those that didn't had their curtains drawn. Life in a fishbowl.

She unhooked the chain, turned the deadbolt, slid the wedge out from the bottom of the door and opened it. Her mailbox was a long rectangle against the house just outside her door.

Usually she dropped her letters off at the big blue mailbox on the way to work. Too many people were getting things stolen, like their identity, from people invading mailboxes. She figured this should be safe.

She lifted the lid of the mailbox but was sideways and couldn't keep it open and stick the letter out. She stepped down on the porch. The door clapped shut behind her. The breeze was cool this evening. It made her shiver. Twice she looked over her shoulder in the few seconds on the porch. Someone could slink out of the darkness and on to the porch before she knew they were there.

She lifted the lid and saw the rose almost immediately.

Thirty-seven

The lock on her front door clicked. She was coming out. What luck. Both that he was going to watch her and that he made it to his hiding place in time. It would be very disappointing if she ruined the fun by finding out it was him too early.

She came out the door and right to the mailbox. Heat surged through his body. Rachel going directly to his rose could only mean one thing. She was beginning to think like him. Their minds were meshing together as one. Like Adam and Eve, the first two perfect people.

"The symbol of our love." Logan said so quietly he could only feel the vibrations in his throat. He was too close to say it any louder. Only twenty-five feet separated them at this moment. As if on cue Rachel snatched up the rose and flew in to her house.

"Yes, Rachel. It's for you." The branches moved in the breeze and he slid down into them to shield himself from the wind. In another couple of months this would no longer work as a hiding place. The branches would be too bare. He pulled a laminated photo out of his pocket. Much as he had tried to protect it the edges were bent and the plastic wasn't as shiny as when he made it. So many nights of taking it out of his pocket and putting it back in. So they could be together always. Hers was the first face he saw in the morning and the last one at night.

Thirty-eight

She darted her hand in, grabbed the rose, threw the letter in the box and ran in the house

in one lighting motion. Before the screen door could slam behind her this time she had the bolt,

chain and wedge in their place. The rose was on the floor where she had thrown it when she ran

in.

She cried. He had been here. Had he been watching her kissing Curtis on the couch?

Was the rose to taunt her? Was he ever going to leave her alone? She slid down with her back to

the door. The curtains were open, was he watching her now?

She crawled below the window-sill and grabbed the pull strings on the drapes. At least he

wouldn't see her. She continued to the second and third set of curtains then went to the kitchen to

pull those. Outside something scratched across her driveway in the wind. She ran to the window

over her sink closed and latched it. She scanned the room.

The door leading to the basement was cracked open few inches. She flipped on the light

and crept down fear burning her skin and adrenaline pushing her forward. She never used the

sliding door to the basement so she never checked it. She could call Curtis. He couldn't be more

than a mile or two away. She reached down. No cell phone. It was in her purse upstairs. She crept through the near empty basement. The furnace and a few stacks of boxes would be the only

cover for an intruder. She peeked around those and saw nothing. The only other place would be

behind the curtain for the basement's sliding glass door.

She picked up a broken broom handle that she'd remembered was under the steps and

crept forward. Something creaked and she stopped, holding her breath so she could listen for the

slightest sound. Slowly she tiptoed closer to the curtain. It moved slightly and she caught a

scream in her throat.

What she was doing was insanity. She looked back at the steps. It would make more

sense to run upstairs and call the cops. She lifted the bat over her head and in a quick motion

ripped the curtains back and swung the bat. The curtain rod gave way and crashed down on her.

She screamed and ran up the steps never once looking back. She slammed the door shut and

leaned against it.

Not a sound came from the basement. She waited then opened the door a crack. There

was nothing. She bent over and looked in the basement. The curtains were in a pile with the rod

but there was no sign anyone had been in that basement but her. A small bit of relief washed over

her and she ran to the back door to double check its lock. When she was satisfied the kitchen was secure she moved to the second floor and checked every window.

He was close by but he wasn't getting in.

Rachel dialed the police.

A man with a gruff voice answered the phone.

She identified herself, "I've found another rose."

Physiology and Feelings

How do you feel when you're nervous? What does your body do? When you hear a noise that startles you, what is your body's response?

The response from your body is your physiology. We have all read about people having their heartbeat thunder in their ears or their face burn with embarrassment, but what are some other ways we can show a range of emotions based on our body's involuntary response to a situation?

Watch for these things in the story [and note them]. Also, write down on the lines below some ways physiology and biology are tied together. Include these in your own writing.

Thirty-nine

"She's ready to open to me. I should go now. Knock on her door and look at the surprise and love in her eyes." He craned his neck back around to look at her house. How much longer could he stand the build-up of desire? He wanted to have her now. Four weeks had been an arbitrary number; there was no real need to suffer their love in silence.

He dangled the small round charm in front of his eyes. It glimmered in the light of the front porch light. Alpha Mu Epsilon.

"First comes love." He looked at Rachel's photo. Her face was criss-crossed with the shadow of the branches in the street light's glow. So lovely with sweet innocence. But she would surrender to his touch when he revealed who he really was. She would run to him like she had run into her house tonight. Every woman before had surrendered. All of them were shy at first but when the moment of decision came they followed their hearts.

He touched her picture. "Let me tell you all about it. I'll be your fantasy. I will step from the shadow. You will look at me and say 'It was you all along.' Then we'll embrace." He brought the photo to his lips and gently kissed it.

"Next, we will surrender ourselves to the desire burning inside of us." He slid out of his hiding space. "Only four more ribbons are on the shelf." He whispered facing her house. All the curtains were drawn now so he could safely cross the street.

He jogged across and walked straight to Guardian.

"That a good chew treat?" He said using his baby-dog voice. He rubbed Guardian on the head. "You take good care of her until tomorrow." He rubbed Guardian one last time.

When he took Rachel for his own Guardian would come with him. A dog deserved a big yard in the country. Not that nasty little chain in the front yard. He would reward Guardian for his loyalty and his protection of Rachel.

Logan returned to his car and drove off. The next four ribbons were the most important. No more leaving them on the porch or the mailbox. They needed to be personal. Send her a message that would point to him.

"The last one I'll give her personally." He was 2/3 the way to that moment. He glanced in his mirrors side mirror and pulled on to the quiet street. He left his headlights on until he reached the end of the small block. The moon was nearly full in a cloudless sky so with the street lamps he had enough light to pull ahead discreetly.

The patrol car would be around again soon. He flipped on his lights. Almost immediately a car pulled out from behind him. He tried to maintain the calm. The road he was on led out of

the neighborhood and in to the main driveway. He turned right down the side street. The other

car followed.

Had he missed a patrol car? That was impossible unless he'd been spotted with Guardian.

He calmly turned down one street then another. He should have gone to her tonight. Enough on

Romance, it was time for culmination. They should have been together tonight when he was

there with her. His timing was all off. Why had he left? She wanted him tonight. She would have

given in? The lights got closer to him. He needed to keep his head about him. There was no way

anyone saw him or what he'd done.

He slowed down to let the other car pass him. The car stayed on his bumper close enough

for Logan to see past the headlights. There was a man in the front seat. Who was he? Logan

looked back in time to crank the wheel and avoid hitting a parked car. The other car followed

him still.

"Go around." He hissed. No one was going to keep him from his precious Rachel. Logan

reached under the seat of his car and felt around. His fingers latched on the rope and knife right

away but the can of Mace was just beyond his reach. He sat up and slid the rope and knife on his floor mat then leaned down a second time. The little can of Mace rolled back and forth just at the

edge of his grasp. He looked in his mirror and slammed on his breaks. The car behind him

swerved then went around him. Logan bent down and grabbed the can of Mace that had been

thrown forward and stuck it under his thigh.

The car that had pursued him continued on its path down the road before turning in a

parking lot.

Alpha Mu Epsilon would always be rewarded. It was the way of the world.

Forty

She hung up with the police department. What would she do now?

Was he out there when Curtis left?

She began to sob pulling doors closed as she walked down the hall. Did he follow Curtis home and what would he do to him? She wrapped her arms around her body and stood at the top of the steps. She had to move where he wouldn't find her. Telecommuting from a home somewhere far from here wouldn't be too bad with today's technology. She was an owner. What could they say? No?

But Curtis.

She shook with sobs.

She stopped outside her bedroom door. "Leave me alone." She screamed down her steps before she plopped down on the top step to cry. Nothing more could be done. The police had done what they could but they were never here when he left these flowers.

And what if he stopped?

Right now they came every week. Each week they came on a different day. This time they were only forty-eight hours apart. Did that mean he was coming? Did more roses mean she was safer.

Or closer to death.

"I don't want to die." She cried. Visions of her time with Curtis, family, friends and events in her life slid through her memory. Rather than flashing before her eyes her life was giving a goodbye tribute.

And there wasn't much to see.

She had no kids, no husband and nothing other than a business and a few things to be sold.

"Here lies Rachel, she had a business and stuff." She mumbled. It was a pathetic inscription for a tombstone but it was what she had. "Survived by a marketing firm and two parents. Estate auction Friday." She choked out between sniffles. She didn't have a cat, or a plant; she had no living thing to prove she had made a difference in this world at all.

She wiped her nose on the back of her hand but it was no longer sufficient to catch the flow of tears. She lumbered down the steps planting each foot hard. She pulled four or five tissues from the box and wiped her face off.

There was the rose.

It was on the floor by the front door where she had thrown it. Still waiting for her.

She hated that rose. It stole the joy of this evening. She marched over to it. Fear was replaced by rage. She snatched it up from the floor and headed in to the kitchen. The lid to the trashcan popped open when she stomped on the small pedal. She threw it in as hard as she could and spun. The lid plopped closed but it didn't relieve her.

"I hate you." She said and stomped on the trashcan pedal again. She stuck her arm inside. Something slimy and warm covered her fingers. She lifted the rose out its petals and her fingers covered with gravy.

"I…hate…you." She spat as she tore the bloom off and ripped it into as many pieces as possible. Pain shot through her fingers when she tried to break the stem. She looked at the blood and scratches in her palm. A thorn was still lodged in her finger.

The pain felt good. It was a battle scar. Proof she was fighting and not laying down to die.

She wiped the thorns out with a swipe across her jean. The ribbon was undone so she tore it the rest of the way and slammed the stem then the ribbon in the trash.

She was a charging bull.

If she was going to die she would do it fighting.

She'd make her mark. Even if it was by taking her assassin with her.

Show don't tell [and PLEASE don't EXPLAIN]

Every writer who has been writing for long will hear "Show don't Tell!!" chanted at them again and again. A common example is anger. You can say a person is angry or you can show them acting out that anger. Watching someone throw something is far more intense and emotional than hearing that a person was upset.

Whenever possible you need to show the emotions of a character rather than simply saying how they feel. I say, "whenever possible" because sometimes it just doesn't make sense to show and for the sake of pacing you need to just say something.

But when does telling become explaining? That is when a person is TRYING to show but instead of building in emotions, subtle indications and little clues they use adverbs, adjectives, similes and metaphors all together to try to explain what is going on in the scene. Look for examples of that happening as you read then try to rewrite that section to show what is happening.

Forty-one

At twenty minutes to five Friday afternoon Rachel's mom pulled up to the house for the

retreat. She climbed out of her car and adjusted the winter white pantsuit she was wearing.

Rachel looked down at her nice jeans, camisole and jacket. Maybe she should change before she

went.

"Ready to go?" Her mom scanned Rachel's outfit quickly as soon as she came in the

house.

"Yes, but, well I've been thinking that…"

"You're still going aren't you Rachel?"

"Of course, I have my suitcase. I thought I'd come back tomorrow morning. I don't know

if I want to be there for that whole thing."

"Saturday's so much fun. We have a nice breakfast and there are quite a few speakers.

You should stay."

"Mom, I'm really only going to hear Carol Adnaw speak."

"She's giving a talk just before lunch on Saturday too."

"I thought she was talking tonight."

"She is. She's speakin' both days. She couldn't fit everything in she wanted to share on Friday so we rearranged things to give her about forty-five minutes on Saturday morning too."

She'd have to sit through two hours of church talk to hear Carol Adnaw Saturday morning "Let's take two cars and I'll decide when I get there if I want to come back Saturday morning or if I'll stay to the end."

"That'll work out just fine." Her mom reached for the suitcase. Rachel grabbed her other bag. "What's going on with Adam?"

Her mom's face soured. "I'm not sure. I know he's spent a good deal of time with Yvonne on the TDD but he ain't tellin' me bout what they're sayin'."

"So is he going back to California?"

"Now I just told you, don't know. What you gonna go asking me for again." Her mom walked out the back door with Rachel's suitcase. She'd have to talk to Adam directly, when mom wasn't there to watch what they were talking about.

"I can't wait to hear Carol Adnaw speak. Do you think she'll take time after to talk to people. I'd really love to spend some time learning from her." How her mom's church had managed to snag such a well-known speaker still surprised Rachel.

"Oh I hear she is wonderful." Her mom left the suitcase next to Rachel's car.

"Mom, I'm going back in to check the house."

Mom waved her away. Rachel rechecked the front door and windows. "I've got the lights down here on a timer." She scanned the room. "Feels like I'm forgetting something." She stood a few moments. Then since she couldn't think of anything she locked the back door and then stopped by her mother's car, peering in the window. "So, how do I get to this place?"

"Let me look." Her mom reached in the passenger door. She scanned a light blue piece of paper with a photocopied map and scribbled handwriting on it. It should be okay.

Rachel got into her car, and watched as her mother backed out. She started her motor and eased into the street. She wasn't quite sure what to expect at a women's retreat. She had images of either older women with casserole dishes eating or swapping recipes. Or she could see a roomful of women who got as wound up as her mom sometimes hanging from the chandeliers.

Despite some jitters, given her past experience with religion, she was really starting to look forward to the weekend with the ladies. The Fratboy wasn't going to find her this weekend. That was one incentive to be at the retreat. There she was going to be surrounded by other women nestled back in a woods down a hard to find street at the back of a park.

It was a place you only knew how to find if you were there. Even though Carol Adnaw was the invited speaker and even though she was a very famous business woman her mom's church had only done word of mouth advertising. Her mom said it was to keep it focused on God and finding him rather than personalities.

Traffic wasn't bad at all for a Friday afternoon. Most of it was cleared up or heading out of town rather than toward it. There was a bit more traffic as they approached Triangle park. Must have been little league that night. Rachel always thought it was called Triangle park because of the many baseball fields. Her dad had laughed when she told him.

"They're ball diamonds, not triangles." He'd said as he laughed so hard he had tears in his eyes. When he had finally been able to stop laughing he'd told her the park got its name from the two rivers on either side of the park making it look like a triangle.

Most of the downtown area of Woodhaven was run down. People were moving to the edge of town or to the homes near the university. The park had been the exception. It was a remarkably well-kept park being so close to the downtown. The park drew both city-dwellers and suburbanites for the walking trails and ball games.

She turned to follow the jog in the road that led the last stretch to the lodge they were staying in. Her stomach tightened when she saw a sign that pointed to the lodge. It would be fine.

There's no reason to be nervous. She was here to learn from a top executive woman. Church

really couldn't get much easier than that.

Nate had started with a retreat in college. A men's retreat as she recalled. In fact, he went

there a few weeks after their engagement. They had just moved in together and Rachel was

living the dream.

"I hate staying alone in our new house. Can't you go to the retreat next year after our

wedding." She spun the half-carat solitaire back and forth on her finger. "I'll be lonely without

you."

Nate folded a shirt and placed it in his overnight bag. "I'll be home tomorrow night,

Rachel." He pulled her close to him. "You deserve the best husband." He paused to kiss her.

"These men, they are going to show me how to do that."

"But when did you start going to those meetings?" They had attended her parents' church

from time to time but neither of them considered themselves religious. Then he was approached

in the student union by a classmate and three other men. They promised him they could show

him fulfillment the world couldn't offer. She never stayed the living room when they came over, which had now become nearly every night.

Now they were taking Nate with them.

"Rachel, don't worry. It is one night. We have our whole lives to live together." He

zipped his suitcase and kissed her. "I'll make it up to you tomorrow night."

"You'd better."

He lifted his keys off the hook and put his bag down. Rachel followed him to the front

door. "I love you, Rachel."

"I love you too Nate."

He kissed her and walked out the door. She walked to the window and watched him get

in the car with the other three men. She waved down at Nate. He smiled, waved back then

climbed in the back seat. A man climbed in on either side of him in the backseat.

She sat down to look at her bridal magazines. They were only twenty and the wedding

couldn't be extravagant but she'd love Nate since they met in high school. For three years they

were best friends and the first time she…well it was with Nate.

She fell asleep that night on the couch. The next morning she woke to pounding on her

front door. The clock said it was six-thirty. She stumbled to the door. The men were standing there.

"Nate has joined the community."

"What?" She said, still groggy.

"We have come to pick up a few of Nate's things."

"He'll be back tonight."

"No." The larger of the three said, the one she disliked the most. "He has joined the community. He is no longer connected to this world or the lusts of the flesh."

"We're getting married." She looked between the three of them. Their faces like stone.

"No, Nate is married to the church now. He is a part of the community and he's committed his life and worldly possessions to the creator."

Bad memories. Rachel snapped back and followed her mom in to the parking lot adjacent to the lodge. She pulled her car in next to her mom and climbed out.

"Should I bring everything in now or come back for it."

"Go ahead and bring it. I'm getting mine." She hoisted her bag on her shoulder. Rachel nodded and pulled her suitcase out of the trunk of her car and followed her mom up the walk. A woman, likely in her mid-fifties, met them on the sidewalk. Her hair was shoulder length blond and she was dressed more like Rachel in jeans and a nice top. It made Rachel feel a bit less self-conscious about her outfit choices. "Lisa, so good to see you." They hugged. "You are awful dressed up for this aren't you?" The woman leaned to Rachel. "Wouldn't you say so."

"Yep. I think jeans are the way to go." Rachel nodded as she answered.

"No matter. Your mom's always overdressing for these events."

"Well, what else I got to dress up for?"

The two of them began chatting about what Lisa needed to do to help set up. Rachel followed her mom up the sidewalk to the lodge. Inside the front door a young woman who looked to be around Rachel's age sat at a rectangular folding table. There was a white plastic tablecloth on top with sheets of names taped to it. Voices echoed from every direction with people smiling and nodding in various conversations.

Her mom walked around the woman to the table while Rachel tried to figure out where to sign up. "Janice, this is my daughter Rachel."

"So *this* is your daughter Rachel." The woman turned to face her. "I've heard so much about you. You run a business don't you?"

"Yes, a marketing company." Rachel smiled and shifted her bags to her left hand and shook the woman's hand.

"You coming to see our guest speaker?"

"Carol Adnaw? Absolutely. She's top of her game. There's a lot of women who could

learn from her example."

The woman smiled warmly. "I'm sure there is. I hope you get a lot out of her talk."

Rachel returned the smile. Rachel looked back at her name tag to remind herself of the woman's

name. She had been distracted by everything but should have paid better attention.

Next a woman with a clipboard appeared from behind them. "Oh good Lisa. You're here.

We've go the two of you in the room down this hall." The woman took Rachel's mom by the

arm and led her past a couple of plain doors and in to an equally plain room.

The woman with the clipboard crinkled her nose. "Sorry they're pretty bland. Everything

in here is beige but the place offered us a great deal, and everything is clean, so we took it." She

smiled and lowered her voice a touch. "I think next year we'll do it at the hotel we talked about. I

was so embarrassed when we came in to set up this morning." Then raising her voice again "The

common areas are quite nice."

Rachel and her mom set their things down on the beds. "I'm going to go look around."

Rachel called back.

"Fine honey. We'll run into each other I'm sure."

Rachel walked back out to the table with the long list of names.

"Hi my name is Rachel." She scanned down the page and pointed herself out.

"Wonderful. You're in group one." The woman traced over Rachel's name with a yellow

highlighting pen. "Here is your nametag and folder. We're starting at seven-thirty in that room

right over there." The woman pointed to the large living room a few feet away.

"Thank you."

Rachel watched the women. Nearly all of them knew the other. She smiled and nodded at

the few who managed to make eye contact.

"I see you're in group one too." Rachel spun around again and was face to face with

Carol Adnaw.

"Yes, I am." This time she had a genuine smile. "My name's Rachel."

"Carol."

They shook hands.

"I'm so happy to finally meet you." Rachel resisted the urge to gush about everything she'd ever read by or about her.

"Well thank you. God has blessed me."

God. For a moment Rachel had forgotten she was at a church thing. Carol Adnaw was there but this was about church and God stuff too.

Carol continued. "You're the only person I've seen from group one so far besides me. Would you like to sit down with a cup of coffee?"

"Of course. That would be really nice. Wait here and I'll be right back."

Rachel wove back and forth between people and finally found her mom.

"Mom, I've found Carol Adnaw and she wants to have coffee. We'll be right over there." She pointed to the back of the common area.

"Great. I'll find you in just a bit." She turned back to the woman she was talking to then stopped. "Rachel, you're going to need your bag." She slid a canvas bag off of her arm and handed it to Rachel. Inside there was a folder, pen and what looked to be a few cosmetic samples.

A large group of women were milling around the registration table when Rachel got back.

"Was I gone that long?" She motioned to the group.

"No, there were two vans that unloaded and they all walked in together. Do you want to go over to the other room?" Carol motioned. There's a fireplace in there.

Rachel nodded and led the way through a sea of round white tables full of women catching up and swapping stories. Her mom should be able to find her back here. They sat at an empty table.

"Carol, would you like some coffee?"

"Yes, please. Two sugars."

She got the coffees and sat down across form Carol. "How is it you came to be the featured speaker at a church event?"

"My passion is helping women. There are some women who have no financial sense. For those women I love to share financial strategies that will help them be self-sufficient if they ever need to be. Some women need to remember that there is more to this life. That is what women retreats are for. It's when women can reconnect."

"Do you do many of them?"

"I try to do one about every month or every other month."

"Do they pay well?" Rachel looked around at the room of a couple hundred women.

What would cause a woman who filled conference halls to speak to such a small group?

"I think they do." She smiled and blew on her coffee.

Obviously she wasn't going to tell how well they paid. Rachel looked around and quickly

added the number of women then multiplied it by the twenty dollar conference fee. At the most

they'd collected about two thousand dollars. Hardly enough to pay a nationally recognized

speaker.

Carol scooted forward in her chair then leaned her arms on the table. "How long have

you gone to this church?"

"Oh, I've gone off and on for a few years now. My mom is pretty active and she told me

about it." It wasn't a complete lie. She'd been to the church about three or four times a year since

her mom and dad started there.

"You're lucky to have the pastor you do. I've followed his ministry for a while." Carol

paused to blow on her coffee and sip slowly at it. "He's a strong man in the Lord."

"Yes he is." It was all Rachel could think to say back. He was an okay preacher when

she'd attended recently and had told Shannon as much.

"Excuse me, Carol?" A frail older woman broke into their conversation.

"Yes?" Carol smiled at the woman as if thrilled to see her.

"They wanted to have you come back to the green room with the other speakers for tonight."

"Thank you. I'll be right there." The old woman walked away and Carol turned to Rachel.

"Guess I'm on. If you'd be willing after the presentation tonight I'd love to continue our conversation."

"I'd like that. Thank you."

"We'll meet back here." Carol picked up her Styrofoam cup of coffee and walked briskly to join up with the older woman. The two chattered away until they turned a corner and Rachel could no longer see them.

How do you feel about the story?

On the lines below write out your impression of the strengths and weaknesses of the story so far. Go back and read all of the question sections to this point and keep an eye out for those issues as we dig deeper in this story. Evaluate this story and the characters that make it up. Go reread the opening and see if your impressions have shifted or if you now identify issues you

didn't see before.

Forty-two

Rachel set aside the coffee and opted to chew on the small red straw she'd used to stir with. Women of various ages were walking back and forth down rows of folding chairs. Coats, books, and purses were strewn about to hold a person's seat. She wondered how many of them realized the importance of tonight.

It seemed tonight Rachel was in the right place at the right time. Not only would she get to hear an icon of women's business speak, but that same woman wanted to sit down and chat with her after the program. Carol had no way of knowing that Rachel was a business woman and that she had come only to hear Carol speak.

The room held nearly fifteen tables, given Rachel's best guess. Then each table had two to six women. Most of the women looked like they were Rachel's age possibly a bit younger. The people her mom's age were the minority this weekend. More than likely those younger women were all there for the same reason Rachel was.

A woman in crisp black slacks and lavender top stepped up to the microphone on the small platform in one corner of the room.

"Could I have everyone's attention please?" The buzzing chatter lessened but it took the woman saying it a second time before the room got totally quiet.

She went through the regular greetings and welcomes then introduced the speakers.

According to what the woman said there was one woman before Carol then a few

announcements after Carol.

"But first ladies let's stand up and praise the Lord for bringing us here tonight." The

women stood up and began applauding. Rachel looked around and she clapped.

Someone grabbed her shoulders from behind and Rachel spun around.

"Mind if I sit with you?" Rachel's mom smiled and pointed to the chair Carol had been

in.

"Go ahead. You scared the living daylights out of me."

"Sorry." She smiled as she passed then turned to face the stage and clapped with

everyone else until the room got quiet again.

The announcer continued. "We're going to open with a word of prayer then move right

into praise and worship. If you look in our conference folders you'll see the words to the songs

and we'll also have them up here on the overhead projector. Let's prepare to enter worship."

She stepped away and a woman with brown hair, blue jeans and a black sequin top stepped forward. In a booming voice she said, "You ready to praise Jesus?"

The room erupted in applause, whistles and women screaming yes. It was more like being at a college football game than a church conference. Rachel moved her lips to the first song and cut out for a bathroom break during the second. The third song was slowly playing and women were swaying to the rhythm when she got back. The lead vocalist was humming and periodically saying "Thank you Jesus" while the three men who made up the musical accompaniment and back-up singers continued softly.

Rachel wasn't sure what she was supposed to do. Her mom had her hands folded with a Mona Lisa smile on her upturned face. She gently swayed from side to side oblivious to anyone around her.

Rachel fidgeted with her hands and finally crossed her arms and closed her eyes so no one would notice how bored she was. She opened her eyes up after a few moments and glanced down at the lyrics in her folder. This was the last song and it seemed to be that they were going to hold the last note until every woman in the room was in a hypnotic trance. Shouldn't be too long, only Rachel and two other women didn't appear to feel the compulsion to sway.

The music ended and the first speaker stood. The woman talked about church and life as a mother of three preschoolers. Rachel drew pictures of trees and a dog that ended up looking more like a pumpkin while the woman spoke.

"And now ladies join with me in introducing Mrs. Carol Adnaw." The MC stepped back and clapped. Carol approached the lectern and smiled, nodding her head in recognition of the applause. Rachel slapped her hands over and over in the first genuine enthusiasm since the program began.

"Everyone please sit down." Carol paused and women sat down and scooted chairs on the hard floor. "Thank you so much for having me here." She smiled and opened a portfolio pad. "My topic for tonight is minding our business."

Rachel wrote the title on the first page of the tablet she had brought for notes.

Carol continued, "First Thessalonians four verse eleven and twelve in the Amplified Bible says 'Make it your ambition *and* definitely endeavor to live quietly *and* peacefully, to mind your own affairs, and to work with your hands, as we charged you, so that you may bear yourselves becomingly *and* be correct *and* honorable *and* command the respect of the outside world, being dependent on nobody [self-supporting] *and* having need of nothing.' Ladies how many of you are commanding the respect from the outside world?"

Rachel commanded respect in her field. There were many who sought her for advice. She scanned the room and didn't see a single hand go up so she left hers down as well.

Carol leaned forward, "Then ladies, you are disobeying God."

Rachel noted a few nervous laughs and the shuffling of a few bottoms in their seats.

"Paul wrote this letter to the people of Thessalonica and told them that the way the world would respect us would be honorable, live quietly and peacefully and living without lack."

Carol scanned the room. Rachel often tried not to be overly ambitious. To Rachel lack of ambition was laziness, not some great virtue.

Carol smiled and flipped the pages in her Bible. She stepped away and walked from one side of the stage to the other, a distance of a little over eight feet Rachel was guessing, with her floppy Bible laying open. "God's word also tells us that God is able to make all grace (every favor and earthly blessing) come to you in abundance, so that you may always and under all circumstances and whatever the need be self-sufficient [possessing enough to require no aid or support and furnished in abundance for every good work and charitable donation]."

Rachel noted Carol's emphasis on the word abundance. This time about half the room clapped.

"I'm not here tonight to debate whether poverty is a virtue or a curse. I am also not here to debate rich men going through needles and poor people being more spiritual. I am here to talk to you tonight about minding our business. That business is being a representation of Christ to a dying world that needs desperately to feel his love."

The room erupted in applause and cheers with about twelve women standing by Rachel's count. Maybe one or two more. She shuffled a little in her chair. She hoped Carol wasn't upset to have so few respond to her.

Carol walked back to the lectern and set her Bible down. "Ladies, for a long time I was caught between two worlds. I grew up in church with a mom and dad who were good people that took me to Sunday morning service most Sunday mornings. My parents were comfortable, but not rich, when I was a child. My first memories of church were good ones. We learned about Jesus and his miracles, the parables and the Beatitudes. Then later we learned about Daniel and the three boys in the fiery furnace. It was like bedtime stories every week. They were beautiful tales of wonderful characters but they had very little to do with my everyday life."

Rachel's childhood flashed through her mind. Her life had been so much like Carol's. The hair on her arms stood up as if they too understood what a great woman Carol was.

Carol continued. "I do remember the church I grew up in told me that if I aspired for worldly success I was sinning. 'Pride commeth before the fall.' I was told whenever I revealed my desire to be a famous person. So I learned to keep my dreams out of church and to give the right answers to my teachers' questions."

"As I moved into high school my dreams were firmly in place. I knew that Business was the best route to live the affluent lifestyle I craved. I had been taught by society that if I believed in God I was naïve and brainwashed. Since the world was going to give me the future I wanted, rather than the life of lack championed by my Sunday school teacher, I decided that maybe I had outgrown going to church." Rachel leaned back and folded her arms. Hopefully her mom was paying attention. Maybe now she'd understand why Rachel didn't need the church and its rules.

"My parents accepted my decision and ended up joining me at home on Sunday mornings. We decided the time together was more important than going to a church building. After all, God has a piece of himself in each one of us so a group of three was just as much church as a group of three hundred."

"When I moved on to college I pursued my interests and sought to prove to everyone that I had it in me to be famous. I sought to please no one but myself and did what it took to graduate summa cum laude from the business school at my university. When I graduated I stepped immediately in to a job with a six figure salary and every material thing I had thought I wanted. Money was not an issue." She stopped and focused on a woman on the front row. "But it was an empty and lonely life. After eight years of it I was more depressed and surrounded by more stuff then I ever thought I wanted. Worse still, no one was interested in my pain. What does a rich young woman have to be sad about?"

Plenty. The roses, each one, surged in to Rachel's mind. Typical church stuff, bashing people who tried to be and do something bigger. Carol droned on about some of her problems but Rachel saw only the roses and the heartbreak of Nate's betrayal. She looked around at this group of women all pretending their life was in order. She knew none of them were as together as they put on. All of them hid secrets. Rachel wasn't a hypocrite. She lived her life in the open and celebrated the beauty of life without judgment.

Carol lifted the floppy red Bible up over her head and waved it from side to side. "And I read it." She lowered the Bible on to the lectern. "It said God made me with passions and desires to be used to serve him. He gifted me in marketing. I didn't need to feel guilt over my success, but neither should I have self-centered pride."

Carol leaned on her elbows and put her fingers to her lips as if deep in thought. "When I began to work my business as if God owned it, God honored my hard work and rewarded me financially but the difference is now I also honor him in the way I do my work. I pursue honesty, integrity and I always give back."

"This weekend is my tithe. I go out five to seven weekends a year and speak at women's conferences, large and small, at no charge. I honor God with my time and he has rewarded me with joy, peace and even productivity."

"I want to be remembered for more than a woman who had lots of stuff. It is more than being remembered by man. For me life is about being *known* by God." People started standing and clapping. Some even screamed in agreement. Rachel sat there and scribbled doodles on the page. She'd find out the real information when Carol was done with her joy-fest.

"Many people think Christianity is only about what happens after you die but I think the world is more focused on death and the after-life than most believers. God is about the here and now. He talks about money more than prayer. God instructs us to love and to forgive. Those are contemporary messages. There is no need of forgiveness in heaven because there will be no sin. God is interested in the here and now. By contrast many people who don't follow God worry about their legacy or what will be in their obituary. What will people say about them when they are gone."

Carol pointed to her chest. "I'm not worried about what people will think of me when I'm gone. I'm worried about how well I am reflecting Christ here on this earth."

The entire room stood in thunderous applause. Rachel stood and looked around. She had written down a few questions to ask Carol when the two of them got together this evening.

Carol put one hand up and the room quieted down. "I feel impressed to pray over business women right now. Any of you who own, plan on owning, or would like to own a business please come forward. A few women filed to the front.

Rachel's mom nudged her, "Go on up."

"No."

"Why not."

"It's for Christians and I'm not one."

"It's for business women." Her mom pointed. She had a smile on her lips but her eyes were stern. Rachel relented and walked to the front with the other women. The lights were hot around her and she focused on the podium. Everyone had to know who she was, Lisa's daughter, and those who didn't would know before she left. Carol looked down the row at Rachel and smiled. Rachel broke her gaze quickly and focused on the spot where the podium hit the stage.

One by one Carol put her hands on the women's shoulders and prayed with them. Beads of sweat formed under Rachel's top and slid down her shirt. Carol moved down and then stopped in front of Rachel, looking straight into her eyes.

"Hello my new friend." Carol had tenderness, not hard-nosed business sense, in her eyes.

"Hi." Was all Rachel could muster.

"God is going to deliver you. He is always by your side and if you will trust him he will make a way where there seems to be no way."

Rachel's breath caught in her throat. Her body was filled with tingly sensations that defied description. Carol turned her face upward and prayed out loud but Rachel didn't hear any of the words. She was overwhelmed with images. The men she'd slept with, the day she opened the office with Shannon, the day Nate left. Then the roses. She stifled a whimper but in the next instant she felt as if her body were draining of tension and stress. An empty calm started at the top of her head and spread to her toes.

The rose was without thorns. She wasn't afraid of them any longer. She closed her eye and remembered each flower she had found and where she found it. The image was still there but the fear, anger and panic was gone. She turned her face upward. Her body felt as if the sun had peeked out from behind a cloud and was warming them. The searing heat of stage lights was gone and now a gentle warmth enveloped her.

Someone came and touched her shoulders. Rachel opened her eyes and looked to find the whole front empty except for her. Heat burned her cheeks but so did the sense that she wasn't going to die. She turned and looked directly at her mom. Another hole pierced the armor around her heart.

Stereotypes

Although stereotypes are frowned upon in society, they can really add to your writing when used the right way. When you turn a stereotype on its ear [a woman who looks like a supermodel who loves hunting and fixing cars] you can create a new dimension to a character. When you use an actual stereotype [like the backwards small town cop] it doesn't always work. That's because many of us reject the idea of being known based on superficial characteristics.

Identify the subtle and blatant stereotypes in this work that are either traditional stereotypes or a play on the standard expectations. List some of them here and then brainstorm how you could have done them better.

Forty-three

Rachel nibbled at a cheese Danish from the snack table and waited for Carol. Over and over she had played the scenes of the roses and each time marveled that there was no longer any fear there.

"Thank you for waiting." Carol said and sat down.

"No problem." Rachel pushed her Danish to the side and faced Carol.

"What did you think of tonight."

"It wasn't what I expected." Rachel reached into her bag to retrieve her notes. "But it was fine."

Carol tore off a piece of a donut and popped it in her mouth. She chewed slowly for a moment then smiled and faced Rachel head-on. "I think you got exactly what you were looking for tonight."

Rachel paused for a long moment then, realized she was staring and looked away. In a way she had. She felt completely safe for the first time in a long time. But that's not what Carol meant. Carol was just like every other religious person. She was looking for Rachel to get saved.

"I can tell by the look on your face you didn't like my response." Carol pushed aside the donut she'd been munching on and looked right at Rachel. "It's not my place to pry but what did bring you here tonight Rachel?"

Rachel considered the question for a moment. She'd come here to escape the fear and to impress a guy. "I came because I've followed your career and was eager to meet you."

"That could be why you came here but that is not why you're here tonight."

"Then why am I here?" Rachel recoiled, shocked at her own tone.

"I don't believe in coincidence. If I'm wrong and you haven't yet found what you're looking for, you'll find it soon."

Forty-four

At around nine p.m. Rachel walked back to the room with her mom.

"Mom, I'm going home."

"Why?" She spun and looked at Rachel. Her eyes held more concern than

disappointment. Mom was convinced that Rachel had been touched by God. She had told Rachel

as much once she finished her conversation with Carol Adnaw.

"This has been a lot for me to process. I think I need to be alone for a little bit." She

needed to go home and face her fears. The constant fear she lived under now seemed ridiculous

from the outside. A twinge of fear rattled around but she pushed it down with every logical

explanation against what she was feeling.

"I'll try to be back in the morning but there is something I have to do tonight." She

wanted to reassure her mom that she wasn't trying to skip out on their women's retreat. Her mom

raised a skeptical eyebrow at Rachel.

"How 'bout this. I'll grab my toothbrush and deodorant and leave everything else here.

I'll get it when I come back in the morning for the rest of the conference.

Her mom's face softened, "All right. I'll see you in the morning then. They're starting breakfast at eight."

"I'll be here." Rachel hugged her mom, grabbed the cosmetic bag from her suitcase and

headed straight for her car.

The door thudded behind her and threw her into darkness. Only the few security lights in

the parking lot and dim solar lights casting circles of yellow along the sidewalk invaded its

domain. The evening air clung to Rachel's arms. Behind her something scraped and she let out a

small squeal until she saw the leaf skitter past her on the sidewalk.

She paused for a moment and looked back at the door to the lodge. What was she really

trying to prove by going home? She took a step toward the lodge trying to come up with a reason

for her change of heart.

"No." Her voice echoed from the door and briefly stopped the chatter of crickets. She

jammed her hand in her purse to retrieve her keys and walked along, her boots clanking out hard

on the sidewalk.

He could have followed her.

She started walking faster to her car. It would take longer to get back to the lodge then to

get in her drivers seat. She pushed the button to unlock the doors. The dome light flooded the interior. She opened the door, got inside and locked it behind her in one fluid motion. She turned her dome light off and let her eyes adjust again to the darkness.

There were no moving forms, no shadows approaching. She didn't feel any less vulnerable alone in this locked car than she had alone on the dark sidewalk. But now she was committed to going home. She stuck her key in the ignition and let the car idle for a few minutes playing the slide show in her head again. Each rose and where she had found it didn't paralyze her with fear but neither did she feel as invincible as she had inside the lodge.

She drove down the winding tree-lined road that would take her back out to triangle park. Overhead the trees sliced lines across the moon. Carol had assured her that everything was going to be fine. She had said she'd be protected. However, what she said was contingent upon God existing the way they believed. If they were wrong there was no protection.

A tear slid down her cheek. The only way she had a promise that she was going to be safe was if her mom was right about God and Jesus. If Rachel was right she could be driving home to her death. The Fratboy would get her.

She had tried denial, anger and tears and nothing had worked. She wanted Carol to be right. At least this time.

"God if you're out there give me the faith to believe what I've heard is true."

She came to the end of the wooded area and made the jog to Triangle park. Her breathing slowed a bit. The streets were empty most of the way home. Nine o' clock on a Friday night it seemed people were at their destinations.

She turned down her road and drove slowly along. The street was deserted except for a man petting the brown dog a few doors down from her house. Her house was dimly lit with the few lamps she'd left on with the timer. She pulled up her driveway and around to the back of the house.

"I'm going to be fine." She said as she took deliberate strides to her back door. She denied the terror digging its icy fingers in her body.

"I'm going to be *fine*." She repeated with emphasis. The deadbolt clicked as she turned the key and pushed the door open. The clock ticked out the second and she pushed the door shut behind her.

The blinking red light on her answering machine caught her attention. She pushed the play button and removed her shoes.

"Rachel this is Curtis. Welcome home. I wanted to let you know I've been praying for you tonight. I miss you. Call me when you get home." The machine beeped at the end of his

message.

"I thought I left more lights on." Her voice boomed in the silence of the house. She

stepped in the living room and turned on the television eager to hear a voice to silence the one in

her head. It boomed on and made her jump. She fumbled with the volume down on the remote.

Maybe it had been a mistake to come back here. The women at the retreat were wonderful, not

judgmental at all. What did she have to prove by coming back to the house? That she wasn't

scared.

By coming home she had proven that the Frat boy had complete control over her. She

was happy at the retreat and she wanted to leave that to prove that he didn't control her. She

plopped down on the couch.

She was home and it was now almost nine thirty she decided to order a movie on pay-

per-viewher cable, throw on her pajamas and enjoy the rest of her evening. She flipped on the

dining room light on her way to the steps. The candlesticks in the middle of the table were gone

and in its place was her mail and a single white rose.

The icy fingers of terror grabbed her and squeezed. She stood planted with her eyes fixed on the flower. She had been gone for only three hours.

He could be here now.

Her feet gave way and she ran for the kitchen. She dialed Curtis and grabbed a knife out

of the kitchen drawer.

"Hi, I hadn't expected to hear from you tonight."

"He's been here." She blurted out. "Please come."

"Who?" Curtis' voice was firm. "Rachel, who was there."

"Him. He's been here." She paced in a five-foot section of her kitchen and adjusted her

grip on the knife.

"I'm getting in my car now. Rachel, hang up and call the police."

"Curtis, don't hang up please."

"Rachel, if someone is there you need to hang up and call the police now."

"Please. I can't be alone."

"Honey, I'm coming but I won't be there for ten or fifteen minutes. Please hang up and

call the police."

She grabbed her home phone and balanced the cell on her shoulder. "Curtis, don't hang up. I'm calling the police with the land line. She tried to dial but couldn't balance and the knife

fell from her hand. She jumped and dropped the cell. The knife skittered across the floor and hit

the wall blade first.

"Are you still there?" She yelled then grabbed the phone tight against her ear.

"Yes, are you okay?"

"I dropped the phone."

"Call the police Rachel. Set the cell on the counter. I won't hang up but call 9-1-1 now."

She bent down for the knife and took it to the corner of her kitchen then set the phone and

the knife beside her and dialed. She told the dispatcher what had happened.

"We have a patrol in your area, hold the line."

Rachel picked up the cell, "They have someone close by."

"Good, don't talk to me. Talk to them." Curtis said, sounding much calmer.

Rachel's breathing slowed.

"Ma'am?" The dispatcher said.

"Yes. I'm here."

"We have a car less than a mile from your home. I need you to stay on the line until he arrives.”

“Okay.”

Red and blue flashed in her living room when the car pulled in the driveway. “Curtis, the police are here. I’m going to hang up.”

“I’ll be there soon. I love you.”

“I love you too.” Rachel said and flipped the phone shut.

“Ma’am, I’ve had radio contact. That is our patrol car. It is safe for you to hang up with me. They will take care of everything.”

“Thank you.” Rachel pushed the phone off and let the officer in the front door.

She gave him the name of the detective who had been working her case and told him about the evening.

“Rachel.” Curtis burst in the front door.

“Sir.” The officer took a step toward Curtis.

“It’s okay. He’s my boyfriend.”

The officer relaxed. “And you did not come to her house today and do this?” He asked and scratched something on a notepad.

"No I didn't." Curtis said pulling Rachel against him. "She was supposed to be gone until tomorrow."

The officer turned to Rachel, "Who else knew you were going to be out of town?"

"A few people in the office. But I have an alarm." She pointed to the alarm panel on the wall.

"Who has your code?"

"My mom and I but I was with my mom."

He turned to Curtis. "Does he have it?"

"No." Curtis answered.

"Just a moment." The officer took a couple of steps away from the two of them and spoke into the radio clipped to his shoulder.

Curtis walked Rachel into the kitchen away from the officer. "It's going to fine. We'll find out who broke in." He pushed her hair behind her ear as he spoke. "I want you to stay at your parent's house until this blows over. I don't want you to be alone."

"Can't I stay with you?" She didn't want to be alone either but running to mommy and daddy's house meant the Frat Boy was winning.

Curtis hesitated for a moment. "I would love to have you there but I don't think that's best right now. I'll come by the office and follow you to your parent's house every evening. You don't have to be afraid."

"But I don't want my mom to worry."

"Rachel" He tilted her chin up so she was looking straight in his eyes. "I'm not worried about that. I want you safe." His voice was firm. "I love you, Rachel. I can't have anything happen to you."

The words ignited a fire in her chest and made her completely unable to respond. She reached over and wrapped her arms around him. Going to Mom and Dad's house would put her closer to him and would work fine for the time being.

"Curtis, I can't keep running away." She stepped back to face him. "If I do, this will never stop."

"Rachel, this man is crazy, not a genius."

"But he. . ."

"But he never comes when other people are around. He only wants to scare you."

"He came when you were over the other night."

Curtis' mouth dropped open and he took a step back. "Did you see him here?"

"No, when you left I went out to the porch to put a letter in the mailbox and there was a rose."

"How do you know he hadn't left it earlier?"

"Because I got the mail before you came."

His face went ashen and he stared past Rachel.

"Ma'am?" The officer stepped into the kitchen.

"Yes?"

"The detectives will be here shortly. Did you touch anything on the table when you got home?"

"No way." She shook her head for emphasis.

He nodded and stepped back in the other room and she looked over at Curtis.

"Rachel, I still want you with your parents unless you can think of some place else safer. I need to know you're safe."

She looked down.

Curtis touched her arm and she looked back up at him. "How long has this been going

389

on?"

"Since around the time you and I met."

He crinkled his eyebrows and raised his voice slightly. "Why didn't you tell me?"

"At first I thought maybe it was you."

"Breaking in your house?" His voice rose slightly higher.

"No, the first couple of roses were sitting by my car or at the office."

"How many have you gotten?"

"Ten."

"*Ten?*" He lowered his voice a bit. "You've had this happen ten times and this is the first you've told anyone?"

"No, Shannon knew."

"You've had this happen ten times and this is the first you've told me." It sounded like hurt.

"I didn't want to."

"It's…I understand. So then?"

"When I found the one at the office in my desk we let the police know." She looked out at the officer in the other room. He didn't seem to be doing anything but waiting. "They

increased patrols in my neighborhood a few weeks ago."

"Lot of good that did." Curtis shook his head. He ran his fingers through his short blond

hair and turned his face up to the ceiling. "Okay God, now what." He sounded as if her were

talking to someone in the room with him.

"He hasn't tried to contact me or get near me. I think if I stay with my parents like you

said and always have someone with me for a while it will give the police time to try to find him."

Curtis nodded his head and pulled her to his chest. "I am so sorry I didn't protect you."

He squeezed her tight.

"Ma'am? The detectives are here." The officer said.

"You ready to go talk to him?" Curtis pushed a bit of hair back from her face.

She nodded and they walked in to the other room.

Phonetic Dialog

**If you ever read Tom Sawyer or Huck Finn in school you may
remember how Mark Twain wrote his dialogs: Phonetically.**
**You may also remember how difficult it was to decipher what was said.
In fact, many times I had to read a piece of dialog out loud in order to figure**

out what the characters were saying to each other.

While having some phonetic writing early on can add flavor to a story, too much is just distracting.

Find places in this manuscript and in your writing where an attempt to show sounds, animals or even the cadence of speech detracted from the story. Now fix them.

Part III: 3...2...1...Epsilon

Nineteen

"Are you asleep?" Rachel sat up quickly and looked around. Shannon stood in the doorway to her office with a stack of folders and a well-dressed older man. She turned to the man. "Would you excuse me for a moment please?"

He looked at Rachel. "Certainly." Then stepped back for Shannon to close the door.

Rachel pushed a few papers around her desk. "I'm sorry. I was going over the number for-."

"Do you know who that man is?" Shannon said in a low growl

"Uh…Yes, I do…She lifted a folder to find her calendar. She remembered the two of them talking about an appointment today. Where was her calendar? She always kept it next to her keyboard. Her wrist his something hard which was followed by a clank on the desk.

"Rachel!"

The word registered at nearly the same moment Hot coffee began to pour over the edge of the desk and on to her lap. She jumped up when the hot liquid hit her. Shannon grabbed papers off of the desk and started spreading them across the floor.

"I'm sorry, I didn't even see it there."

Shannon didn't say a word. She went out the door and appeared a few moments later with a towel.

"Here."

"Thanks." Rachel said in a near whisper. She sopped up coffee from the papers that remained on the desk. "Found my calendar."

"That's nice." Shannon laid down the few papers left in her hand. "Let's go meet in my office."

Rachel followed without a word.

"Clean yourself up first."

She looked down at the brown splatter that covered the thighs of her khaki pants and the edge of her salmon colored silk blouse. Paper towels in the bathroom were not going to fix this. She pushed the bathroom door open and grabbed a handful of papers towels. The coffee went across her thighs and around to the back of her legs. She spun to look in the full length mirror then walked out. These were beyond salvageable, even for her dry cleaner.

"I'm sorry." Rachel walked in the meeting and sat in a chair next to Shannon. The older man she'd seen before spilling coffee everywhere was seated in a chair across from Shannon. He turned when she entered and offered a nod in greeting.

"It's fine. Shannon here was outlining your plans for the mentorship program with our school." The older man, whose name Rachel still didn't know, said.

"I was telling Mr. Fischer about our mentorship programs with the high school."

"We have one of the best business mentorship programs in the area." Rachel had a passion for working with the high school juniors and seniors. They came ready to learn about the business and having an opportunity to put something positive in their life, even with the additional work, was a highlight of Rachel's year.

"Shannon showed me a bit. It is very impressive."

"Here are some testimonials from other principals and teachers." She handed across a three ring binder. "And these are some letters from student who have gone through our program."

He took the folders and flipped through the pages without reading any of them.

"I have to be honest ladies." He placed the binder in front of him on Shannon's desk.

"You don't have to convince me your program is among the best. I have spoken to a number of my colleagues leading up to this meeting. What concerns me is the reports we've heard that the office may not be fully safe.”

"The students here are never in jeopardy-.” Rachel said.

Mr. Fischer looked at Rachel and the stain on her pants. “The news reports are giving another story and to be quite honest many of the parents have shared with me their reluctance to allow their students to participate in an internship program affiliated with your company until a few of those issues are resolved.”

Shannon stepped in and tried to convince him everything was safe but one look at Rachel would tell anyone that there were problems. Coffee stained, puffy-eyed, scatter-brained Rachel was not a vote of confidence.

They shook hands and he left.

"Well, that went very well.” Rachel said being sarcastic after Shannon had closed the door.

"I’m really glad you can find humor in this.”

"So what else am I going to do>”

"I don’t know Rachel but something’s gotta happen. We don’t have the budget to hire the staff we need to replace the mentorship program.”

"It'll get along fine."

"The work of six part-time students? We can't spread that around to everyone else. We're already running on fumes around here trying to make up for the work you can't do and losing the half-day when the cops were fingerprinting."

"So this is my fault?" Rachel broke in.

"It may not be your fault but you're the cause of all this."

"All of *this*?"

Shannon scooped a spreadsheet off of her desk. "Have you even looked at the numbers this month?"

"I was working on them when you came-."

"Don't bother. I ran the books."

Shannon shoved the sheet of paper in Rachel's hands. She didn't need to look at what it said. She saw the four columns that flashed red.

"We're running this business out of our reserves and there isn't much there." Shannon yelled.

"What do you want me to do about it?" Rachel tossed the paper back to Shannon's desk.

It floated, skitted the top and fell to the floor.

"We think-."

"We? Who is we?"

"The accountant, some of the staff and I think it might be a good idea if you became a silent partner for a little while. Only until this blows over."

"Am I being fired from my own company?"

"No, you can work from home. We need you to not come to the office until these things blow over and this guy gets caught." Shannon reached for Rachel's arm. She jerked back. The whole office wanted her out.

"Fine. I'm out." She jerked the door open, stomped in to her office and slammed the door. Something crunched under her and she looked down. She was standing on some of the wet papers Shannon had spread out when Rachel spilled her coffee. She lifted her foot and the paper clung to her shoe. Enough was enough, she ripped the paper off the bottom of her shoe, jumped over the rest and called Curtis.

Showing Foreign Languages

In the previous section we talked about writing phonetically, but what do you do when you want to integrate foreign language in to your story?

There are a few tips to make the integration of foreign language work:

• Use it periodically and in splashes.

• When someone speaks in a foreign language have the other person respond in English or someone else ask for the translation.

o Example- "Je veux y aller!" Jean-Jacques screamed.

"I know you want to go." Sarah replied. "But we can't."

• Give a bit of foreign language and then shift to English. [The Movie: The Hunt for Red October did this incredibly well in the opening in transitioning from Russian to English.]

It can be difficult to determine how much of a foreign language in the scene is interesting and when it gets distracting. Evaluate its use in this book and in your own writing. Then look at other books that did it skillfully and study their technique.

Finally, go through this manuscript and rewrite sections that don't work in a way that helps the reader understand the language without pausing the action to explain it.

Eighteen

Someone tapped gently on Rachel's office door. She looked up from the papers she was packing up as Curtis stuck his head in the door. He stepped in and closed the door behind him.

"How are you holding up?" He reached for her hand.

"I hate feeling like a burden to everyone."

"You're not a burden. Why would you say something like that?" He touched her cheek with his fingers.

"Because I am. You have to follow me, I live with my parents and everyone in this office-."

"We've talked about this."

"I know." She looked away from him. "I understand your point. I didn't do anything to deserve this."

"And it is not you putting people out. It is this man."

She looked back at him. Even something as vague as *this man* made her stomach do flip-flops. "But it is still my life that is causing this mess."

"What can I do to make you feel better?" He scooted his chair closer to her.

"I don't know. There are so many things on my mind right now."

"Besides the flowers?"

She hesitated. This wasn't the time to discuss their relationship. Curtis had changed his life and schedule to be her daily escort. There was no telling how many appointments he'd not scheduled or canceled to be able to help her. Whenever she asked he told her he'd handled it and not to worry.

"Rachel?"

She looked up at him.

"You faded out there for a second. What's wrong?"

She took a deep breath. "Where do you see us going?"

"In our relationship?"

She nodded her head.

"I don't know yet. What about you?"

"I'm not sure. It feels like things are turning serious but." She stopped. "I know you love me."

"But?" He looked her in the eye and squeezed her hand.

"But there is the religion thing." She'd said it. As much as she worried about having this conversation she couldn't bear to be any more in love with him and then lose him.

"The religion thing." He said as if finding the piece to a puzzle.

"Yes. I know it's a big deal."

"Yes, it is." He nodded.

"So, what about it? I don't know that I am willing to jump on board with your beliefs, although with all that's been happening I wish there was a God who would protect me." Since the retreat she had more than once prayed prayers that started with *if you are real God…*

"And what could make you take the leap from wishing he were real to believing he were real?" He let go of her hand and sat down in the chair next to him.

"I don't know. I've never really thought about it."

"You know the Bible says faith is the proof of things we don't see."

Rachel looked up at the ceiling to gather her thoughts before she answered. "Yes, so if only I had faith then I would have faith."

"It's the best I have for you right now."

"Wait a minute." She stopped packing for a moment and looked square at Curtis. "If you believe the Bible then why are you so freaked out about this guy hurting me?" It was easy to tell people how much they should believe stuff but then walk away and not apply it to your own life.

The room was silent for a long moment. "The best answer I have for you is we live in a fallen world. Evil things happen to wonderful people." His voice cracked as he spoke. "What I can tell you is that the Bible tells me no matter what happens God will make things work out for good for people who love and obey God."

He cleared his throat again before continuing. "That is why I continue to pray that you will allow Him in your heart. It is the best protection I can give you. That is using the power of God to protect you." He smiled. "And until that happens then I will do the next best thing and I will love and protect you in my strength."

That answer made sense. Curtis was doing the best thing he could do in his own estimation. "But can you see this relationship becoming permanent if I don't become a Christian?"

"I try not to think about it."

"Why?"

"Because I love you and I want us to have a future." He cleared his throat. "Or as you put it 'become permanent'."

"And we won't have one if I don't accept your belief system." It was a statement, not a

question.

"All I can tell you is I love you and today I'm going to follow you to your parents house.

Then after we have dinner together I am going to go home. I will pray for you before I go to bed.

In the morning I'll pray for you again." He smiled and took both of her hands in his. "That's

enough for me to think about. Focus on today's problems because tomorrow will have enough of

its own."

While Rachel was mulling over his answer someone knocked on her office door.

"Come in." She said loud enough for them to hear.

The receptionist stepped in the office. "You have a delivery." Then she quickly walked

out. Word must have spread pretty fast that Rachel knew all about the office's little meeting. A

young man stepped around the corner and handed Rachel a clip board with an X on it. Rachel

signed her name and he handed her the long cardboard box.

"Thank you." She said. He nodded and walked out.

"Who is it from?" Curtis asked looking at the address label.

"I'm not sure. There is a typed P.O. box then my work address." She cut through the tape.

"It's light. Probably a poster for one of the marketing campaigns." She turned the tube sideways and a rose slid out with a piece of paper. She dropped the box to the floor and Curtis snatched it up.

"What does it say?" He reached for the slip of paper hooked to the rose.

"Don't touch it." She put her hands up to block him. With her ink pen and letter opener she pulled the folded paper open.

"See you later beautiful." Rachel whispered.

Without a word Curtis bolted out her office door. Rachel followed him as far as the front desk but he was chasing down the delivery boy in the parking lot.

"Call the police. Tell them the Fratboy killer just contacted me again." Rachel said to the woman at the receptionist desk. Outside Curtis was yelling at the man who had delivered the box.

"I've called the police." She said when they walked back in the office.

"He says some guy approached him on campus and gave him $30 and asked him to surprise his girl friend."

"Lady, I had nothing to do with the guy. I was trying to be nice-."

Rachel looked at him shocked. "Do you make it a habit to deliver packages from

strangers on campus? Don't you know there could have been a bomb in there?"

The young man couldn't have been more than nineteen or twenty. He kept his eyes down

and glanced up as he spoke. "He wasn't a total stranger. I pass him a few times a week on my

way to English. We smile and nod at each other."

"Do you know his name?"

"No."

"The police will be here soon."

"The police." He shot his eyes open wide and looked between Curtis and Rachel.

"They're going to want you to give them a description." Curtis said, taking over the

conversation.

"I'm not in trouble am I?"

"I don't think so."

Shannon came out and looked at the group of them. "What happened?"

One of the people leaned over and whispered "The stalker sent a rose to Rachel. This guy delivered it."

Rachel walked over to Shannon to finish. "The note said he'd see me soon."

Shannon threw her arms around Rachel. "If he thinks he's coming then we'll be waiting.

None of us are going to let him hurt you."

Rachel nodded but didn't say a word.

"I mean it Rachel. We're going to beat this guy."

Seventeen

"Here let me help you carry those." Curtis took the books out of Rachel's arms and

followed her up the walk to her parents' house. She unlocked the door, which was always locked

since she came to live with them, and stepped in the house.

The room smelled like onions, garlic and meat. A pot roast was cooking and Rachel's

stomach growled.

"Do you mind taking those on up to my room?" She asked Curtis.

"No, lead the way."

They walked up the steps and put her books down then walked down through the living

room to the kitchen. The crock pot was on the counter but her parents weren't there.

"They must have gone to do some running before I got home." She looked back at Curtis.

"It's fine. I'm not in a rush to get home." He said.

"You're staying for dinner right?" She slid her arm around his waist and leaned in to him.

"Of course."

Curtis' phone vibrated on his hip.

"You need to get that?"

He looked down. "Yes, it's business." He stepped out of the kitchen into the living room.

"Hello Drew."

Rachel took a few steps toward the doorway to listen to the conversation. She didn't realize Drew and Curtis even knew each other.

"No it's not a problem at all. I'm at my girlfriend's parent's house." Curtis said.

There was a short pause.

"No, I didn't get that paperwork. When did you fax it over?"

Another short pause.

"When did they want to close?" Pause. "That soon? I'm not sure if I can get that done in time or not. Let me see what I can get worked out from here and I'll call you." Curtis stopped for a moment. "Wait, let me ask Rachel something."

He walked in kitchen. Rachel jumped away from the door where she was listening and opened the cupboard closest to her.

"Do you have a fax here?" He asked with his finger over the phone mouthpiece.

"No but I have a fax to email. You fax it to the number and it sends to my email. I can print it in .pdf."

"Great thanks." Curtis walked back to the living room then called back. "What's the number?"

She grabbed a business card out and gave it to him. "It's right there on my card."

He nodded his head and she walked back in the other room. What a horrible time to have Drew call. She walked to the cupboard and pulled down four plates. She had no ideas they worked together on anything but her house. Curtis never mentioned Drew. Why would he? He hadn't mentioned other co-workers before either. That meant she had to tell Curtis what happened with Drew.

She snuck back to the doorway.

"You remember the lady we first worked together with? Rachel. That's my girlfriend."

A short pause.

"A couple of months off and on."

Drew don't you dare say anything.

"Yes she is great. She has a fax I can use. Here is the number."

A short pause.

"Oh you do?"

A longer pause.

"When?" Curtis' footsteps in the other room stopped. Rachel tried not to breathe. "No, I *didn't* know that."

A long pause.

"Oh good you're getting everything around." Rachel spun around. Her mom was standing inside the kitchen. "I was going through some boxes in the basement and heard you two come in but you know what it's like when you're almost done with a project."

Rachel heard footsteps behind her and she turned. Curtis was red-faced. "I won't be staying for dinner tonight." He focused on Rachel.

"Why not?" Her mom asked.

He continued to look at Rachel. "I just had a call from one of the real estate agents I work with. They have a last minute deal they need worked up for a closing."

"Curtis." Rachel stepped to him.

"Don't." He held up his hand. "Don't, all right? I need some time to process all this."

"But it's-"

"I'll call you in a couple of days." He turned and walked out of the kitchen, through the living room and out the front door. She heard the door close hard and her feet unstuck from the

floor. She scurried through the house and out the front door after him.

"Curtis please."

"What Rachel? What do you want?" He spun around and faced her.

"I was going to tell you?"

He shook his head and looked away.

"I was but we just got serious and I didn't want to mess anything up."

"Rachel, I've been serious with you all along."

"I'm sorry." She pleaded with him.

"Maybe we *are* too different to make this work."

"No, we really aren't." She reached out and took his hand. "I love you Curtis."

"I love you too but I can't have a relationship based on lies."

"I never lied."

He pulled his hand away. "I can't have one based on half-truths either. I have to be able

to trust you, Rachel."

"You can trust me."

He walked to his car and before climbing in he called back. "I'll get in touch with you in

a few days. Don't call me until then. I need to think."

She looked back at her parents' house. His engine roared as he backed up and sped down the

road. Through the corner of her left eye she saw his tail lights move away from her. Slowly

she made her way back up into the house then straight to her bedroom. She didn't much feel

like eating.

Sixteen

"Mom tell me what happen. I sorry." Adam signed.

"Thank you."

Rachel drew her knees up to her chest and stared off in to space. She had messed things up pretty well by playing her game. For all her talk of living in the moment-."

"I here if need talk." Adam walked over and sat next to Rachel on the edge of her bed.

"I'd rather talk Yvonne." She signed back.

He turned and swiped away a tear with his thumb. "I not want talk about Yvonne."

"Why not?" He didn't have an answer. "Adam, you Yvonne love together. You need bring wife here. Live Ohio again."

"I need know what God want."

"You think God want you here Yvonne there?" She was signing so fast her hands made smacking sounds. "You think God want Yvonne cry alone California and you sad Ohio?"

He stood up and faced her. "You not believe God real. Why you think God talk you about me, Yvonne."

"I don't know God real or no real but I know story Daniel and Lions."

"What you talk about?"

"That king put Daniel with Lions but king know is wrong. He not believe in God but he know Daniel good man. Can see Daniel should not die. He pray, God answer."

"That nothing about my problem."

"Yes, is." Rachel knew what she was trying to say but she didn't have all those Bible verses her brother would listen to. She knew a few stories about Jesus and the one about Daniel. That was her whole arsenal. What she did know is that Adam and Yvonne should be together.

"I not need believe in God know you married, you want Ohio, Yvonne want live Ohio. Maybe God not always tell you do stuff you don't like. Maybe he also tell you do things he know you want do."

"I think about what you say." He turned and walked out. Rachel lifted her cell phone out of her purse and scrolled down to Curtis' cell number. She couldn't call him yet. He didn't want to talk to her but she needed to see his face. She clicked "Ok" on the number and the small photo she snapped of him recently popped up.

Tears rolled down her face. She loved him so bad it hurt. Exactly where she didn't want to be. The phone face dimmed and she opened and closed to reset then scrolled back down and brought up his picture again.

The holes he'd pierced in the armor around her heart were letting feelings she didn't want

to have come in.

Fifteen

"Rachel, it has been four days. Call him." Rachel's mom had moved through sympathy and silence and was at tough love. Rachel had come to predict her mom on things like that. It had been the same when she and Nate broke up. Only then she'd lived in her own apartment and didn't have to talk to her mom about it every night.

"He told me not to call."

"Men never mean that."

Rachel gave her mom a nasty look and went back to the work she had brought home from the office.

"Fine, if you won't call him I'm gonna to him at church on Sunday."

"Do what ya gotta do mom." Rachel said without looking up.

Mercifully her mom gave up and left her alone. She looked at the face of her cell phone to see if there were any missed calls but there was still nothing. He had been upset but she never thought he would take this long to contact her. A day, maybe two, seemed reasonable but she had to prepare her heart for a breakup.

It seemed Christian men were no better than unchristian men. She refused to be sad. No, she was angry at him. What he was doing was far worse than what she did. She didn't intend to

hurt him. In fact, she had not told him so as to spare him hurt. He was trying to hurt her and that

wasn't right.

"Rachel, telephone." Her mom called from the other room.

No one Rachel knew had her parents' number. They all used her cell phone. Rachel stood

up and took the phone from her mom.

"Who is it?" She said after she covered the mouth piece.

"I don't know." She turned and walked away.

"Hello?"

"Hi Rachel. How have you been?" Curtis' voice sounded wonderful.

Her muscles relaxed and she hurried into her room and closed the door. "I've been busy.

How have you been?"

"Busy." There was a long pause. "I miss you."

She closed her eyes and leaned against her headboard. "I miss you too."

"Can I come see you?"

"Now?"

"If you don't mind."

"No, come now."

She hung up the phone and ran to her mirror.

"I look awful." She touched up her makeup and put extra concealer under her eyes to cover the dark circles. Then she took off her sweats and put on jeans and fixed her hair.

She walked across the hall to get her spray gel from the bathroom. "Don't you look nice? Expecting someone special?" Her mom teased.

"Did you call him?"

"I needed to talk to him about Sunday."

Rachel sprayed her hair and went out to the living room. Fifteen minutes later Curtis pulled in the driveway. When she saw him Rachel ran out the front door to meet him. They stood in nearly the same spot they had been at the beginning of the week.

Curtis was the first one to speak. "Adam told me about the theological discussion the two of you had."

"I told him I thought it was ridiculous for two people who love each other not to be together."

"It is-."

"Curtis, I'm really sorry."

He held up his hand. "I overreacted. You we're right. We weren't exclusive."

"But I should have told you."

"I don't know that telling me would have made it any easier to hear."

"Do you forgive me?"

"I love you, Rachel. That means I have to let this go if we have any shot."

"I guess I figured that a couple of dinners with him weren't worth losing you."

"A couple of dinners?" He crinkled his face. "That wasn't what he said."

"What did he say happened?"

"He said you…had a…physical relationship."

"No, we did not."

He took a step toward her.

"This week has been awful." She took the last few steps to him and hugged him. "Why didn't you call?"

"I wasn't sure how you would respond to me after the way I blew up at you."

"I almost called you the first night."

"I wanted to get in touch but…Then your mom called and told me you'd been moping

around the house all week." He smiled at her. "I thought maybe that meant I had a shot of getting

you back."

Using all 5 Senses

We learn about the world around us through our Five Senses. At this very moment you're gathering a huge amount of data. As I'm tying this I realize my arms are a bit cold [I should put on a light sweater]. There is sun coming in through the window [which is very nice] and there is a bird chirping. I also feel an itch in my nose [please don't sneeze] and I'm fighting a smidge of a headache. Oh and I heard my stomach growl and can feel that I'm very hungry.

You don't want to give that much information, it will be distracting, but you do want to be sure you're getting enough information to the reader to let them experience the scene.

Go in to the manuscript and select any five pages at random. Look for the senses. Remember they won't always say "smell" or "sight". Try to identify the subtle senses too.

Fourteen

"I want to come in to the office tomorrow and work for a while." Rachel had already made her peace with the people at the office and their request that she work at home. If she could have a way to escape the roses forever she would do it too. But it had been long enough and Rachel needed to do a few things at the office.

"You want to start coming back every day or you want to come in tomorrow."

"I want to come in tomorrow but I'd like to gradually work my way back in. I'm not the type who can spend weeks at home."

"I know. That's why we work together so well." It was good to hear Shannon laugh again. It was something she had missed hearing.

"So I'll come by tomorrow and work a full day and see how it goes. Maybe I'll come in one day a week and gradually work my way back in to the office."

"It will be nice to have you around the office again.

Thirteen

"Did you hear Yvonne is coming out?" Rachel poured Curtis a cup of coffee.

"So they reconciled?"

"I think so. Adam wouldn't give me many details but he looked much happier than when he got here."

"How could he not?"

"I don't know why he ever left in the first place. They adore each other."

"I hope this means they're moving back to Ohio." He sipped his coffee. "I'll have to remember the story of Daniel next time I talk to a friend with relationship issues."

"I used Daniel another way. It wasn't about his marriage."

"Ah. Still, a useful story." He winked.

She stirred cream in her coffee then spoke without looking up. "I'm going back to my place tonight."

"Do you think that's wise?"

"I've been here for two weeks. I'm tired of hiding. And now with Yvonne coming back I want the two of them to have as much privacy as possible."

Curtis spooned a bit of sugar in his coffee as he spoke. "Do you *want* him to contact you? Going more than a week since he had the rose delivered at work is a good thing."

"Maybe he isn't interested?"

"We're talking about your life, Rachel. There needs to be more than a maybe to put you in harm's way."

"Will you at least listen to my plan?" She took her mug in her hands and leaned forward. Curtis nodded his willingness to at least listen. "Thank you." She sipped her coffee and began.

"I'll change my security code on my alarm today. After work follow me home. I'll set it as soon as you leave, I'll keep my cell by my bedside and I'll even lock my bedroom door." She slid him a piece of paper with her new security code written on it and a key to her house at Curtis. His skepticism was palpable. "I'll be safer at home than I will be here. Mom and dad don't have an alarm or any of it. He'll find me." Her voice cracked and she looked away for a moment.

"Marry me." Curtis said with urgency.

"What?" She felt as if the wind had been knocked out of her.

"Marry me. I'll protect you."

She loosened a bit. He wasn't serious. She loved the words sounded when he said them though and hoped he might say it a third time. It was too soon to get married but each time he said it it sounded a little better. "Curtis we've only been dating for two months."

"I know and I love you. I want to be with you forever. Marry me."

She smiled at him. He said it again. "You're only asking me to marry you so you can be my body guard."

"And because I love you." He smiled. It was hard to tell by his voice if he was serious or not. She knew he was strict about not being alone with a woman over night but getting married so she wouldn't be alone in her house was ridiculous.

"We'll talk about that in a few months."

He smiled and kissed her. "But we will talk about it."

"Yes." Heat surged through Rachel's body. Immediately her childhood fantasies of being a beautiful bride flooded in. "I need to get to work. Let me grab my things while you finish your coffee."

"Rachel." He called behind her. She spun back around to face him. "I'm serious about what I said."

She softened. "I know." She went up to her old bedroom on the second floor for her suitcase and work.

When she came back down the steps he helped her take her things out to the car.

"You're sure about going home tonight?"

"Absolutely."

"Then I'm staying until dark and I want to see you arm your alarm when I walk out the door."

"I figured."

She climbed in the car and drove into work with Curtis behind her. He waited in his car until she was in the office and then waved as he pulled away. She picked up her messages from the front desk and walked back to her office.

"Shannon." She called down the hall while she fiddled with her key. "I need to talk to you when you get a second."

Shannon stood in the doorway. "What's up?"

Rachel smiled. "Come in. Close the door."

Shannon did as she said and Rachel blurted out. "Curtis asked me to marry him."

Shannon's jaw dropped down then she grabbed Rachel's hand. "Let me see the ring."

Rachel pulled her hand away. "We're not engaged." She laughed. "It's only been eight weeks."

"You told him no?" She looked even more surprised than when Rachel said he proposed.

"I don't know if he was entirely serious. We agreed to talk about it in a couple of months."

"That's probably wise but you'd better say yes next time or I'll snag him up." She laughed.

"No you won't. He's not your type."

"He wasn't yours either at first. I think he grows on you." She pointed down at Rachel's hand. "I need to get back over to my office. Don't forget about our conference call at eleven."

"I won't. Did you upload the presentation to the website?"

"Of course."

"As if it was a ridiculous question."

"It worked out last time."

"Uh-huh." Rachel smiled. Shannon turned and went back to her office.

By four the clock hands started dragging. The office was much more constricting now that she had spent a couple weeks away. Rachel looked at the clock only to find it had been less than five minutes since the last time she checked. Tonight she was going to sleep in her own bed for the first time in three weeks. She had gone to the house every few days with Curtis or her mom to check on things, do a little dusting or to get some clothes but she was anxious to sit in her chaise and read a book without mom or dad interrupting.

But would it be the same? Would she be able to relax or would he come back? Fear pricked at her skin.

At four twenty Curtis called.

"Rachel, I just got a last minute appointment for seven. An investment group found a multi-property deal. I have to crunch some numbers for the appointment. Why don't I follow you to your parent's house and then after my appointment I'll take you to your place."

"No, don't do that."

"I don't want you going back alone."

"I won't."

"Who will go with you?"

"I'll have Shannon follow. Come over as soon as your appointment is done."

"I don't like that idea-."

"Curtis, I'll be fine. I want to go home."

He was hesitant, "If you're sure?"

"Positive. I'll see you around eight?"

"It'll be around then. I'll call if I'm going to be much later."

"Good, see you then. Love you."

"Love you too."

They hung up the phone and Rachel turned to the spreadsheet on her computer screen. She'd put up a good front but…No, everything would be fine. There was no sign he'd left anything behind.

"You still balancing those accounts down?" Shannon sat down across from Rachel.

"No, if I were balancing I'd be done. There are seven cents I still can't reconcile."

"Rachel, I'll give you the seven cents. Your time is worth more than that."

Shannon never understood the importance of getting these things to balance, which is why Rachel was in charge of the books. As long as the account was pretty close it was good enough for Shannon. Shannon was the people person, go with the flow. Rachel turned from her

computer.

"On your way out?"

"Got the appointment at five-thirty across town, remember?"

How could she have forgotten? The conference call, the arrangement for Shannon to hash

out the deal and then review for final sign off next week. Rachel had planned the time line.

"Do you need me to go with you and help?"

"No, go home. Have fun with Curtis. I want to see the ring." Shannon smiled. "Will he be

here soon?"

This wasn't working out. Maybe she should reconsider, do it another day? Everyone

would understand her need to be protected. By her mommy and daddy. No. She was going home

and she was going to act like an adult.

"I talked to him right before you came in. He's leaving the office any time." It wasn't a

total lie. He was leaving the office. "There are enough people here for me to stay with."

"Okay then. I'll call you with the results. I'd better get going. Traffic's going to be bad

enough."

"Talk to you then." Rachel turned back to her screen. Everything would be fine. She would drive home and go in the house and set the alarm until Curtis got there.

The alarm.

She had completely forgotten to change the punch code. She dug through her purse and found the card.

"What will your security word be?" The woman on the phone had asked when Rachel finally got through.

"God."

"God?"

"Yes, my security word will be God."

The woman's voice brightened. "He is your deliverer. Good word."

Rachel gathered her things and walked out of the office to her car. *He's your deliverer.* It gave her goose bumps. That was what Carol Adnaw had said at the retreat. It was still eerie for two women to say the exact same thing.

She started home. Carol's words echoed in her head like a bad song that plays over and over until you find yourself singing it. She'd said something about him being at her side and he'd make a way where there seemed to be no way.

"Vague enough for anyone to interpret the way they needed." Rachel was impressed with Carol, and she couldn't deny that feeling of peace at the retreat, but could anyone really know what God was thinking.

Just the same, it would have been nice if it were true. Life would be much easier if there was really a God out there who said "Don't worry" or "Here is who you should marry" or any number of other things people attributed to God.

Showing Faux Pas: She heard the window crash

One common error that I see when editing is people using words like "could" and "heard" and "saw" when we're in the character's point of view. Consider these sentences:

She saw David across the street by the car. Vs. Davis stood on the corner by the car.

In the first sentence, we are being told what "she" saw. In the second, we are actually seeing that through a character's eyes. When we are in a character's point of view then we are to experience everything that they experience. We live thorugh them. You don't look outside and think, "I see a bird on that branch." Instead you think, "What a pretty bird."

These are the kinds of subtle techniques that will take your writing to a

whole new level and no one will know why. The story will just seem better for some reason.

Twelve

Logan pulled into the parking lot of a small city park not far from her house. He opened

the trunk and lifted out the bag of gifts, wedding gifts, for Rachel. They were going to be one

soon. He'd waited patiently each day for her to come home but she never did. It was time to

force the issue. The day was overcast with maybe a small drizzle. Aunt Tulla said it was good

luck if it rained on your wedding day.

He walked out of the parking lot and over to the sidewalk on the other side. Despite the

drizzly day the temperature was warm and he passed a few houses with their windows still open.

Family chatter and noise from television came out. Tonight he was going to be one of them. Not

in this neighborhood but he would start a new life.

He'd be a good daddy. His little boy would grow to love the structure and discipline he

had learned as a boy. He rounded the corner. A police cruiser went up the road. Logan smiled

and waved as the officer drove past. He'd want to have all boys. Rachel would give him

handsome sons. Maybe four or five then a daughter who would be as beautiful and loyal as

Rachel.

He came around the final corner. Rachel's house was down on the left and Guardian's house was closer on the right.

"Guardian. How's my good boy?" He bent over and rubbed the dog's ears. Guardian responded by licking Logan's hand.

"Yes, I have a treat for you today." He pulled a handful of dog biscuits out of his pocket and gave them to the dog one at a time.

"Got a secret for you boy." Logan leaned in closer. "I'm getting married today. Rachel's gonna be mine tonight." The dog sniffed toward Logan, searching for the biscuits. "I know, I've said that every night for the last week but this time it's really going to happen. She's going to come to me."

He handed Guardian another dog biscuit. "And you know what that means? This is the last day of being chained up in this awful place." He rubbed Guardian. It was finally happening. He was going to settle down with the woman of his dreams with his dog on the farm he'd found for them. It was the beginning of his forever.

"Time to go get my bride." He said and stood. "How do I look?"

Logan continued down the street past Rachel's house then around to the street that ran behind her house. He went up the driveway of the couple whose house sat directly behind hers.

The owners of that house were retired and traveled often. If you looked like you belonged

somewhere people never asked you what you were doing. He moved through the trees and into

the back yard.

He looked at his watch. It was Four-fifteen. That gave him a solid hour before Rachel

would get home. She left at the exact same time every day. He followed Rachel to her parent's

house. After dark Logan would watch her through the windows at their home. Seeing her body

through the windows, so close, but being completely unable to touch her made him hunger for

her more.

Alpha Mu Epsilon

That was what sustained him. And tonight he would be rewarded. "Childish." He picked

up the walnut that had fallen out of the door. It was one thing to booby-trap a medicine cabinet

but the back door was too easy to fix. When Rachel tried to act strong was when she was the

most adorable. He unlocked the door and punched in the code. Then he closed the screen door,

leaned the walnut against the screen door and closed the storm door.

He took off his shoes, reset the alarm and went to their bedroom. He slipped off his pants

and shirt and put them in the hamper. Women didn't like it when men left their clothes in a pile on the floor. He was going to be her dream man.

He shaved and put on cologne before he put on his black slacks, crisp white shirt and blue tie that he had bought for this occasion. Exercising self-control was going to be the hardest thing about today.

"Agape Makrothumia Egkrateia" He chanted in the mirror. Love, Patience and Self-Control. Now he had proven all three.

"Against these there is no law." He said chanting the verse that had driven his life.

"You didn't think I could do it. All you good church people with your wooden pews and starched shirts thought you were better than me." Those men like Curtis. He snarled at the thought of the man's name.

He stared at his reflection in the mirror but in his heart he was at home with his Aunt Tulla. "But the fruit of the Spirit is love, joy, peace, longsuffering, gentleness, goodness, faith, Meekness, temperance: against such there is no law." He was too dumb to understand these higher things of God. She'd made sure he knew that. Just the same she thought maybe some of it would stick.

"Alpha Mu Epsilon stuck."

And today was this big pay out. He would have his precious Rachel, the perfect number

twelve. They would live the perfect life of a romance novel. He handsome and romantic and she

beautiful and madly in love with him. He folded the covers back on the bed and walked back

down the steps. The overcast sky made the world like one big shadow. He loved the time of

shadow. He put his tennis shoes in the bag he had brought along then set his wedding gift for

Rachel on the table.

He slipped on the black shoes he'd spit shined and stepped back into the corner of the

living room.

Into the shadow.

Eleven

The entire day had been dreary but the grey clouds that covered the sun started drizzling as Rachel hit the highway. She flipped her wipers on the lowest setting. They scraped across her windshield smearing the small droplets and making an annoying squeak on each pass. She flipped them off and waited until she almost couldn't see. Then she would flip them on and off to clear the windshield.

At ten minutes after five Rachel pulled in her driveway. The curtains were closed in the front just as she had left them when she was over a few days ago. She walked around the outside a bit. Her heart pounded hard in her chest.

"Everything is fine." She said the words but there wasn't a single part of her that believed it. Her ears remained alert to the slightest noise and she looked around quickly, watching for the slightest movement.

She opened the screen door and the walnut she had stuck between the doors dropped on the top step. No one had opened the door since she put it in. She slid the key in the door and pushed it open slowly. She went to the punch pad and put in her new code to disarm the alarm. Everything was as she left it. She exhaled and put her things down on the counter just inside the back door.

Ten

She came.

Logan worked to control his breathing. Epsilon he reminded himself. Let her see the gift first. You have your entire life to live together. Be patient a few moments longer. He needed to bring his body under submission. A man was more animal than human Aunt Tulla told him. That was why they couldn't control their urges. But Logan had. Logan could control them.

Rachel was putting things down. Any moment she would walk through the doorway and their forever would begin.

He focused his eyes on the jewelry box he'd placed on the dining room table. His gift for his new bride.

Nine

The light on the answering machine was blinking. Rachel pushed play and listened to the

messages while she closed and locked the back door. As usual no one of any importance called

her house. Why had she even kept the home line? It would be a few hours until Curtis got here so

she went back to the punch pad and pushed in her new code to arm the alarm system. She'd have

to remember to give him the code.

When was the last time she'd eaten? She rubbed her growling stomach. Everything in the

fridge would be spoiled but there were some canned soups in the cupboard. Should've picked

something up on the way.

"First, let's get out of these clothes." She grabbed a green apple from the fruit bowl as

she walked past and took a bite out of it on her way through the living room. She clicked the

table lamp on and continued to the dining room. She skidded to a stop. In the middle of her

dining room table was a small wooden box, a single white rose, and a silver charm with three

Greek letters.

He had been here again. Once she gathered her composure she stepped back from the

table. Don't touch anything and don't disturb the evidence. Everything was going to be fine. It was only a few feet to the back door and the panic button.

Know the rules before you break them

When I'm editing for a client or I'm teaching a class at a conference I will often hear this phrase, "I read [insert best-selling author] and they broke that rule." My reply is always the same: You must master the rules before you break them. If you went through this entire book listing all of the authors who have done the opposite of what I'm suggesting then you didn't get the full benefit of this book.

The purpose was not to list who can break the rules, the goal of this book is to help you improve your craft. To do that you must identify the things that detract from your story and improve them.

Now that you've read nearly all of the teaching points in the book, go to some of the earlier chapters and see if you identify more issues. Even better, see if you can identify how to correct them.

Then continue reading the final chapters and read the last lessons and start digging in to your own book.

Eight

Logan watched Rachel come through. She turned on the lamp but it's light didn't extend far enough to reach him in the shadow. Off in her own little world like she'd always been. But he was going to interrupt that world.

Then she saw his gift and she stopped. He waited for her to open it but she stared at it. Alpha Mu Epsilon. It was time to claim his reward. He stepped forward, his footsteps muffled by the soft carpet below. Every curve of her body awakened the animal part of him. It was only moments away, their union.

"Hello Beautiful."

Seven

Rachel froze. Her breath caught in her throat and the hair rose on her skin.

"I knew you'd come." He continued. His voice was deep and calm. He was behind her and the sound of his voice was moving closer.

She willed her feet to move. If she ran up the steps and locked the bedroom door she could drop out of the window. Her mind escaped but her body was powerless. She took shallow breaths.

His footsteps came down on the wood floor. He was less than six feet behind her and still she couldn't move.

Why had she lied to Curtis?

"Rachel." He whispered. "Turn around."

She recognized that voice.

"Turn around." He demanded. His sudden yell startled her and she jump. When she turned to face him all chance for escape was gone. In her mind she always imagined she would fight. She wouldn't give in.

Six

He stood just outside of the of the small lamp's light. When she turned to face him it they would finally be ready. Slowly she put her arms down by her side and turned to him. She squinted her eyes at him.

"Are you happy to see me?"

She didn't speak.

She shouldn't make him speak twice. He wanted tonight to be gentle but he was willing to take what was his. "I said are you happy to see me?" He kept his voice low but his tone was firm.

"I can't see you. That lamp is too dim." Her voice cracked. She was afraid. Fear was good. He could work with that.

"Turn on the overhead light."

She obeyed quickly and turned on the dining room light then turned to face him.

"Jeremy?"

"Not who you expected?"

"I…"

"I've known from the first moment you were her." It hadn't come out as eloquently as

he'd hoped. The next thing he said would be better.

"What do you want?"

"The same thing you want. Us."

Five

Rachel stared at Jeremy in her living room. He wasn't the charming man she'd met after

the fender bender. His eyes were large saucers and a toothy smile was plastered to his face. Her

blood turned to ice.

"Us?"

He nodded his head. He never broke his stare it simply slid up and down her body.

"My boyfriend will be here soon."

His eyes flashed anger. He squinted and took two steps closer to her.

"No, he won't. He has a seven o' clock appointment." His smile returned. "I knew we

wouldn't want to be interrupted tonight." He licked his lips.

He walked slowly to her. He stood a few inches taller than her and he was much more

muscular than she had remembered. He was in a starched button up shirt.

He was almost toe to toe with her.

How could she have come in the house and not smell his aftershave. He must have bathed

in it.

"Please don't." She squeaked out.

"Don't what?" He rubbed the end of her hair with his fingers.

Don't give him any ideas. She stood silent.

"Open your present." He motioned with his finger.

She turned and faced the table. The wooden box wasn't more than six inches across. The outside was scuffed like something that has been opened many times. Or something fairly old. She lifted the lid slowly and reached into touch the lock of red hair.

He stepped up, pressed himself up against her and wrapped his arms around her waist.

"There were eleven before you but they were not worthy. You were the one I had been waiting for."

"Eleven?"

He lifted her hair and kissed the back of her neck. When she started to pull away he grabbed her by the throat and pulled her back then slowly began to kiss her again. She closed her eyes. Soon she would wake up from a paranoid nightmare and would be at her parents' house where she should have been this evening.

"The eleven who betrayed me, Rachel. You saw them on the television."

The dead women.

Four

Logan, or as Rachel called him Jeremy, kissed her neck but it did nothing to calm the raging desire inside his body. Never had he been so willing to wait for what he wanted and never had there been such a surge inside. With one of the other eleven the table would have sufficed but he'd be with Rachel forever. They were going to start their life together right.

He was going to give her a husband's love. A husband's love was gentle and tender. A husband protects his wife from anyone who would hurt her. Jeremy was going to protect Rachel from all those people who would seek to lead her astray.

Jeremy would complete her.

"Tell me you love me, Rachel."

Three

"Rachel. Don't make me ask twice."

He turned her around to face him.

"I-I love you."

"And you want to marry me." He squeezed her arm when he said it.

"And I want to marry you." He was going to let her live. Hope surged for a fleeting

moment then died when she considered the life he'd likely have her living.

He reached in his pocket but instead of pulling out a ring as she expected he pulled out a

large knife from his pocket. He unfolded it and lifted the blade to her face.

"Let's move things upstairs." His breath made her recoil. His cologne was powerless

against it. Rachel leaned back against the table. He responded by taking the blade down and

cutting off one button from her blouse. Then a second and third. He stepped back and motioned

to the steps with his head.

God if you really do exist please help me.

She turned and looked back. He lifted the blade and waved it towards the staircase that

led to the upstairs. She went up the steps and at the top turned.

"Our room."

He put his hand on her waist and led her down the hall to her bedroom. The clock on her nightstand only read five-thirty five. Deep sobs rose inside her. This morning had been the last time she'd see her parents, Shannon or Curtis.

I'm so sorry Curtis.

Jeremy led Rachel to the side of the bed and cut the rest of her buttons off before unbuttoning his own shirt.

"I'll be gentle with you beautiful." He untucked his shirt and nodded his head to her blouse. She refused to move. If this was going to happen she wouldn't help.

"Are you a little shy?" His voice was gentle with her again. He leaned down and pressed his lips hard against hers and pushed her back on her bed. She tried to pull away but he grabbed the back of her head and held her still.

"Rachel, are you here."

Jeremy stood up and turned to the voice coming from downstairs. "What is *he* doing here?"

"Rachel?"

Curtis was downstairs. From his voice she could hear him coming toward the steps leading upstairs.

Jeremy leaned in close. His breath was like death. "Don't make me kill him on our special day." He stood back up and put his finger to his lips. If she stayed quiet he would kill Curtis. Jeremy was never going to let her live apart from his sick twisted world.

"Rachel? Is everything okay?" Curtis sounded like he was at the top of the steps.

Jeremy would kill Rachel or Curtis.

God would make a way where there seemed to be no way.

"Curtis!" She screamed. Jeremy lunged for her and she dove from the bed. Curtis burst in the room.

"Run Rachel." Curtis yelled.

She hesitated only an moment then ran out of the bedroom and down the steps. She pressed the panic button on her alarm and dialed 9-1-1.

She held her blouse closed with one hand and went for a knife. Her hands shook and she made her way quickly for the steps. Something shattered overhead and she could hear the struggle.

I think you might be real. If you are, please save Curtis too.

Before she was half way up the stairs someone pounded at the door. She turned and saw the blue and red lights flashing around her curtains. Something overhead crashed again and there were no more sounds of struggle.

She hesitated only a moment longer then ran to the front door and let the officer in.

"He's upstairs. One is my boyfriend and the other is the Fratboy."

The officer paused for a moment and looked at her then went up the steps.

"The bad guy doesn't have his shirt on." She screamed after him. Another officer ran in her front door. She called after him "The bad guy doesn't have his shirt on."

There were muffled yells. Then she heard the gunshot.

Two

Jeremy heard the shot at almost the same moment pain seared through his stomach. A cop stood over him, pistol drawn. A second called for an ambulance in his radio.

Why did they shoot him? It was the other man who didn't belong. Alpha Mu Epsilon. He had earned her. Rachel was his.

The pain was fading. He was sleepy. The men, the two cops and that wife stealer, stood over him. They wouldn't help him. They were watching him die.

He scanned the room. She wasn't there. She had betrayed him too. Just like the others.

He was tired.

Very tired.

One

"No." She screamed when she heard the sharp popping upstairs then slumped at the

bottom of the steps. There was no way she could go up. Even if it was Jeremy she couldn't see…

There was thudding overhead. Rachel looked up the steps and Curtis came around the

corner. There was a red line across one arm and his clothes were disheveled but he was fine.

"He's dead Rachel."

"Oh my God." It was a three word prayer but God knew in her heart God had heard it.

The armor dropped off of her heart and she looked up at Curtis coming down the steps.

God had answered both of their prayers.

Final Thought-Sequels

This book was originally written to be a trilogy. What loose ends were left that could be tied up in a sequel? Even with those few things, did it still feel like the story was complete? Were the characters compelling enough that you wanted to meet them again in another book? Why or Why not?

Epilogue

Rachel stood up to turn off the television.

"No wait. They're going to show you." Curtis brought her back beside him on the couch.

"Aww, they didn't show you." Curtis clicked off the television.

"I looked awful in those reports."

"You looked brave." He reached his arms around her and squeezed. "So, tell me again how you saved me."

"Curtis I've told you this twenty times since yesterday." She threw her arms out dramatically and fell back into the couch.

"I know but I love hearing it."

"I prayed."

He smiled down at her. "And what did you pray?"

"That if God was real that we'd get out alive."

"And?" He turned his ear toward her and leaned toward her.

She leaned down in to his arms and relived the scene again. How she heard the shots, felt as if her heart were burning inside her chest. Then, only an instant later, the sudden calm that replaced it. "I still don't get it."

"Yes you do." He kissed her forehead.

"Okay, I don't entirely understand it, but I think I get it."

Curtis nodded, pleased with her answer. "That's all you need."

She had learned testing God wasn't the best way to start a relationship, and maybe it wasn't, but God had revealed himself to her in the way she needed it. He kept his promise to deliver her. And even though she really didn't understand it somehow she knew He was beside her the whole time.

"Do you have any ideas of what you'd like to do today?" Curtis reached for her hand. She took it in both of her hands.

"I'm open to suggestions."

"Let's Elope." He said with a smile.

"Elope?"

"Yes."

"Don't you think that is a bit fast?" She leaned back on the couch and crossed her legs.

"Not when you know you've found the one God picked for you."

Rachel eyed this man who only a few months ago she'd barely been willing to talk to.

Seemed so ridiculous now that it had taken her so long to see what was right in front of her.

She kissed him then stood up. "Who am I to argue with that logic?" He stayed on the

couch, eyes searching her. "Are you coming or what?"

"You're serious?"

Rachel nodded and reached her hand toward him.

"I'll grab my keys."

He was right. When you found the one God chose for you who was she to doubt God?

The End

Synopsis

In a synopsis you have typically between 1-3 pages to do a bunch of things. You have to:

- Set up the scene
- Introduce the characters
- Tell the main plot points.
- Show the resolution
- And do it in a way that hopefully makes the editor want to read the manuscript.

That can be a daunting task. Thankfully, editors know that and they don't expect the summary to be as exciting as the manuscript itself, but you still need to show you have engaging craft. The example I have here is, again, not an example of everything done right. It is an example of an actual summary. It was done early in my writing career and represents the kind of writing that many editors see. Your goal is to write yours better than mine.

Keeping in mind you only have about 300 words to describe a 60,000 word manuscript, look for ways you'd change this synopsis to better articulate the story and to also get the editors attention.

For added benefit, go through the lessons in this book and find the places where you made changes to the story itself and make those changes to this synopsis. We've included space on the opposing pages so you can edit on the synopsis and then rewrite next to it.

Finally, we included a few exercises at the end of the synopsis for you to consider for this entry and when you're writing your own. Complete the exercises in a separate notebook, on your hard drive or print out your synopsis and do it next to the workbook exercises to craft a great summary of your work.

Overview and Synopsis

Someone is killing young women in Woodhaven. And now he has his eyes on Rachel.

Rachel is a woman wise in the ways of the world and confident in her own abilities. She has a take charge attitude and ambition on overdrive. If only she was as wise in affairs of the heart. Thanks to her mom's matchmaking two men pull her in different directions.

Drew is handsome, charming and successful. He doesn't want to change Rachel but loves her for who she is.

Curtis is down to earth with boyish charm. He is determined to win Rachel and show her love isn't about proving who you are but rather being who you are.

When Rachel begins to receive tokens associated with the Fratboy Killer she starts questioning everything she has believed about life and the hereafter. One Rose at a time the Fratboy is drawing closer to a meeting and the culmination of his fantasies. Will Rachel find out in time who he is?

Or will she too pay the price for Alpha Mu Epsilon?

<u>Main Characters:</u>

Heroine-Rachel, a professional businesswoman in her late twenties. She is not saved and rarely attends church although she believes in God. She is also close to her older deaf brother Jeff. Rachel is a POV character.

Synopsis begins on the next page→

Hero-Curtis is a mortgage broker who eventually wins Rachel's heart. He is active in his church and is introduced to Rachel by her mother. Rachel's mother and Curtis attend the same church.

Drew- He a part of the love triangle and is a love interest of Rachel's when she is trying to decide if Curtis or Drew is the right man for her. He is the real estate agent who sells Rachel her new home.

Logan/Jeremy-Throughout the book the reader is led to believe that either Curtis or Drew is the Fratboy Killer. In the end we learn it is the man Rachel has known as Jeremy and who the reader has known as Logan. This is the other POV character.

A Face in the Shadow is third person POV with Rachel and Logan/Jeremy being the only POV characters except for a brief POV with a minor character [victim] at the beginning of the book.

Our story begins with Logan watching a college girl that he is attracted to walk across campus. Logan is introduced as a worldly man who has been involved with many women, and forceful with a few. He believes this woman to be his rightful possession. This first scene also introduces a phrase that appears throughout the story, Alpha Mu Epsilon.

In the next scene Rachel and her mom are introduced. Rachel is not a believer although her parents and brother are. They have a good relationship but Rachel is not interested in church. This is introduced as a point of tension between Rachel and her mother. During the course of their discussion the subject of the

Fratboy Killer is brought up. He is a man killing young women on campus and leaving white roses and a charm with the Greek letters Alpha Mu Epsilon on them. They also discuss Rachel's deaf brother, Adam, who is having marital problems.

The Fratboy killer is shown to be Logan in this scene when he kills a woman we know only as Jenny who was a long term girlfriend. The reader will always know him as Logan until the final scenes. Logan is shown to be a man who lived a painful past at the hands of Aunt Tulla but he is still a man who has a soft spot for the elderly and dogs.

Rachel's mom finds a possible house for Rachel and this event sets the wheels in motion for the remainder of the story. Rachel meets Drew, the real estate agent, and Curtis, the mortgage broker when looking at this house. Rachel also has the accident that introduced her to Jeremy. The man we will learn at the end of the book is the Fratboy Killer. Shortly after, her brother flies in from his home in California to stay with his family for a few weeks because of his marital woes.

Despite her initial reluctance Rachel decides to move to the town of Woodhaven but not in the house her mom had chosen. Rachel finds a nice house in a middle-class neighborhood that is close to her work as well as her family. Rachel's close friend, and business co-owner, Shannon encourages Rachel to pursue Drew as a romantic interest after she meets him. Rachel visits her parent's new church and notes how different it is from the church she attended growing up. She goes a second time, this time with Shannon for "moral support" Where her mom introduces her to Curtis. When she leaves the church she finds a rose on her car.

Rachel rationalizes away the rose on her car. She doesn't fit the stalker's MO. When she goes to Drew's office to make an offer on a house He asks her out. She agrees. The date goes fairly well but when he asks her out on a second date she

refuses. Despite one success her mom's matchmaking days aren't quite over. Rachel's mom invites her over for a meal with Curtis. Curtis, Rachel and her brother Adam have a wonderful time and the three become friends. The story of Logan and his obsession continues to weave in and out of the scenes with him seemingly able to locate Rachel wherever she is. This will often lead the reader to believe that it is Curtis or Drew who is the Fratboy but it is the fairly harmless conversations Rachel has with Logan that usually gives him the information he needs to find her.

Moving day at the new house both men are there. After Drew leaves Curtis stays behind to eat with Rachel. Their friendship is growing. Curtis says he thinks loyalty is a huge thing. It is hard to trust people. She agrees and says that's why she prefers to live in the moment and not get all hung up on dos and don'ts. Things are smooth until religion is brought up. Rachel doesn't reject God completely but she doesn't believe anyone can know if God is like the Christian god or some other.

Logan continues to appear as he talks about his love for Rachel and why the other eleven women didn't measure up. He decides God has given him Rachel to be "perfect number twelve". He also decides at this time that he must give her one rose a week for twelve weeks to round out the perfection. This sets the scene for increasing tension.

Rachel agrees to a second date with Curtis but his time they talk a bit more about their beliefs which leads to a tense meal. The next day Drew calls and she agrees to another date. However on the date she begins to feel with Drew. She's interested in Drew because he is handsome but she feels more comfortable with Curtis. She is indecisive and ends up going with Drew back to his home but leaves shortly after arriving. Drew is shown to have a nasty temper. She goes home and calls Shannon. While talking there is a knock at the door. It is after dark, nearly 9pm. Opens front door and on the ledge of her porch is a white rose and black

ribbon. He is standing a distance off but is watching from the shadow. He knows there is another man.

We are now back with Rachel and her mom at coffee shop. Rachel is convinced Drew is the stalker and he is taunting her. She cannot sleep and agrees to spend a day at mom's to get much needed rest. After coffee remembers dent needs repaired from the accident and goes out with Curtis while it is being fixed. They have a nice dinner and decide when they will get together again. Rachel finds another rose. While Rachel is out of town with Shannon, Logan is watching Rachel's house after dark. He comes out of his hiding place and lets himself in her house.

Drew calls out of the clear blue and wants to know how Rachel is. He wants another date. Rachel is very hesitant but he says he'd just like one more chance to get together. Rachel reluctantly agrees. The next day at work Shannon accuses Rachel of self-destructing by dating both men. While they continue to argue Rachel opens her desk drawer and finds a rose. Despite the rose and the fear it arouses Rachel and Drew go out. She realizes the spark just isn't there. His anger flares again.

This is when Rachel and Curtis finally become a solid couple, despite their differences. Shortly after there is Rose #8. The reader knows there are only four left but to Rachel it is the stalker continuing to taunt her. She takes the flower inside and tosses it in kitchen trash can. Rachel wants to at least try to make the relationship work so she goes to a women's retreat with her mom. On her way we learn she is negative about church because her fiancé ten years ago went on a religious retreat and was sucked in to a cult. The heartbreak of that turned her off to God and church. She goes to see a businesswoman who is keynote speaker but while there she does have an experience with God. She is confused by it and not sure if it was God. She feels emboldened though and returns home.

Her mail is in a pile on her table and there is a rose on top. For the first time Rachel tells Curtis about the roses and the stalker.

Rachel goes to stay with her parents after that rose for protection. Curtis checks on Rachel often at the office and is there when the Fratboy sends a rose to the office that says "See you soon beautiful." Curtis storms out of the office and to campus. He is mad and irrational. He finds nothing out so he follows Rachel home. That is when Drew calls and Curtis finds out she had been dating the two of them at the same time. Curtis arranges for Rachel's brother to follow her to and from work to keep her safe then tells Rachel he needs space.

With the help of her mother Rachel and Curtis reconcile after a few days. Also her brother Adam is reconciling with his wife, Yvonne. Rachel decides that would make it a good time to go back home. They make arrangements for her to be with someone at all times but a last minute appointment detains both Curtis and Shannon. Rachel decides to go home alone.

Logan is waiting for her. It is his wedding day and Logan is prepared to give Rachel what he perceives to be every woman's dream wedding. When Rachel drives home she is a bit nervous but remembers the lady at the retreat telling her "God is going to deliver you. He is always by your side and if you will trust him he will make a way where there seems to be no way." That makes her feel better.

The final scenes alternate between Rachel and Logan's POV. We see him expecting Rachel to be overwhelmed with joy. We see Rachel confident that the stalker is no longer able to get in to her house. Until she sees his gift on the table. He speaks and at this point the Fratboy is revealed to be Jeremy. He says Alpha Mu Epsilon, Agape Makrothumia Egkrateia, which is Greek for love, patience and longsuffering. The tension is maintained in these scenes as the reader alternates back and forth between Rachel and Jeremy/Logan to see how each perceives the same scene.

The Fratboy had made the false appointment for Curtis so both Rachel and Logan/Jeremy know Curtis isn't coming.

Then Curtis does arrive and there is a struggle. Rachel breaks free and runs down the steps to call 9-1-1. She remembers the promise God had given her at the retreat and is in awe that he had saved her from the danger. Police were patrolling in her area because they were aware of the contact the stalker had had with her so they arrive quickly. The cops run upstairs and there is gun fire. We see through Logan's eyes. He is abandoned, alone and confused. Why wasn't Rachel, his bride, there to save him? Why weren't the police arresting the man who stole his wife? He is very sleepy and closes his eyes.

Our story ends with Rachel and Curtis watching the news reports of the Fratboy's arrest. The reports recount the eleven other victims but it is background noise to Rachel and Curtis' conversation. Rachel has accepted that God is real and that he loves her. She has also accepted that Curtis loves her. They decide to Elope.

Exercises:

You need to introduce the main characters right at the start. Keeping in mind the character arc, how can you best describe the way the characters start in this book?

What are the key plot points during the course of the story? What is the primary plot? How do all of these things play out in the character arc?

Are there any specific requirements for the publishing house? How can you show that your book meets those requirements?

About the Author

Tiffany Colter is the author of dozens of books, CDs, DVDs, seminars and webinars on topics ranging from writing great novels to business marketing and systems. She also includes personal development books focused on parenting special needs children, reaching your goals during times of trial, and even time management.

As the owner of Writing Career Coach, Tiffany has spent more than 5 years committed to teaching writers "How to make a living at this writing thing." She also teaches businesses, personal developers and trainers how to use words to connect with their target demographic.

Tiffany is the proud mom of 4 girls and is married to her best friend, Chris. They share an old farm house on their hobby farm with 3 large dogs, 8 outside cats, chickens, ducks, and two sheep.

Tiffany is available to speak to groups or to coach individuals. Details are available by contacting Writing Career Coach. www.WritingCareerCoach.com